SECRET CAMELOT

The Lost Legends of King Arthur

SECRET CAMELOT

The Lost Legends of King Arthur

John Matthews

Illustrated by Gary Andrews

BLANDFORD

A BLANDFORD BOOK

First published in the UK 1997 by Blandford
A Cassell Imprint
Cassell plc, Wellington House
125 Strand, London WC2R 0BB

Distributed in the United States by
Sterling Publishing Co., Inc.
387 Park Avenue South,
New York, NY 10016-8810

A Cataloguing-in-Publication Data entry for this title
is available from the British Library

ISBN 0-7137-2646-6

Typeset by AccComputing, Castle Cary, Somerset
Printed and bound in Great Britain by Bath Press

To the memory of John Masefield (1878–1967)
A great poet and a fine Arthurian

Contents

Introduction

FROM the moment when an obscure Celtic hero named Arthur stepped upon the stage of history some time in the sixth century, he gave birth to a literary phenomenon which has not ceased to astonish all those who encounter it. From a few scarce oral tales and traditions concerning the life and deeds of this man, circulating throughout Europe, sprang a vast edifice of medieval tales concerning 'King' Arthur and his noble knights.

Today there can be few people who have not heard how the boy Arthur drew the Sword from the Stone, or of the love of Lancelot and Guinevere, or how the knights rode out in search of the Holy Grail. Yet the reality behind these legends, though less well known, is no less fascinating.

After the Romans left Britain in *c.* AD 410 the country fell into a period of confusion, with petty kings and chieftains vying for power, and the Saxons beginning to encroach further and further into Britain, while the warlike Picts and Scots from beyond Hadrian's Wall raided deep and deeper into British lands. Out of this dark period of our history arose the story of a man who single-handedly united the warring Celtic tribes and, at their head, drove the invaders back to the shores of the sea. In all the accounts which have survived – and there are few of these which can be truly regarded as historical – this man was called Arthur, and though little real evidence survives for his true identity, what can be said is that *someone* acted as a rallying point for the beleaguered Britons and their warring tribes, and

that the result was a resounding victory over their enemies.

From here on the stories of Arthur grew and developed at an astonishing rate. Oral tales, circulating throughout Britain, were carried across the sea to Brittany, where refugees from the Saxons had fled. These stories became the currency of wandering storytellers and bards, and in time they filtered down into what is now France. From there they returned, with the Norman invaders in 1066, but in a changed form. The old Celtic tales of Arthur and his heroes had been given fashionable courtly dress. From here on they were medieval stories, in which knights, rather than rough warriors, fought more symbolic evils than that of invaders from across the seas. The development of Arthurian romances became almost an industry, with literally hundreds of manuscripts appearing in the years between the beginning of the eleventh to the middle of the fifteenth century. These stories embodied the ideas and traditions of their time, the notion of chivalry and the belief in magic. To Arthur's small band of heroes many more were added – Lancelot, Galahad, Gawain, and others. The saga of Merlin, originally separate from the Arthurian tales, became drawn into their sphere of influence, and the mighty story of the Grail added a spiritual dimension.

When I started work on the book which became *The Unknown Arthur: Forgotten Tales of the Round Table* (London, Blandford, 1995) it was my intention to retell, for a contemporary audience, some of the less familiar tales from this great literary heritage. I wanted to retell them for an adult audience, but also for the younger readers who had become its chief readers since the nineteenth century. It soon became obvious that there were enough unfamiliar stories of Arthur and his heroes to fill several volumes, and I am very happy to be given the opportunity of telling more of these in the present collection. Despite the popularity of Sir Thomas Malory's *Le Morte d'Arthur* – undimmed today as when it first appeared in the fifteenth century – and of the Arthurian stories generally, there remain a surprisingly large number of texts either untranslated or in often clumsy nineteenth-century editions. Thanks to the work of a new generation of scholars, this situation is slowly improving. The last three years have seen the publication in English, for the first time in its entirety, of the mighty *Vulgate Cycle*, a thirteenth-century compilation of Arthurian literature which became the central source for Malory's own version of the stories. (See *The Lancelot-Grail: The Old French Arthurian Vulgate and Post Vulgate in Translation*, General Editor Norris J. Lacy, London and New York, Garland Publishing, 1993–6.) For the first time the general reader can compare the two texts, and see just how well Malory reduced this vast and unwieldy original to create his great book. Several other texts have also found their way into modern English translations in recent years. These independent stories, such as *The Lay of Tyolet* (pages 92–8) or *The Story of Caradoc* (pages 13–29), which did not make it into Malory's sprawling saga, remain little known, either because of their length, or more often because they are preserved in obscure manuscripts which remain largely the territory of scholars and students of medieval literature.

The selection of stories which go to make up this volume vary from those such as *The Story of Lanzalet* (pages 147–73), which offers a very different portrait of the great knight Sir Lancelot, to *The Story of Perceval* (pages 30–47), which focuses on the quest for the Grail and brings out some profoundly different meanings from the story as we find it in Malory. Once again, as in the previous collection, I have also included three

stories from the loosely knit cycle of poems and romances relating to the figure of Gawain. Once recognized as one of the key figures among the Round Table fellowship, Gawain underwent a steady and consistent demotion, until by the time we get to Malory's account he is little better than a murderer and a womanizer. The early versions of his story, represented here in *Gorlagros and Gawain* (pages 114–27), *Gawain and the Earl of Carlisle* (pages 84–91) and *The Rise of Gawain* (pages 99–113), tell a very different tale, in which Gawain is the hero *par excellence* and gets into some truly astonishing adventures.

The most unusual – and certainly the strangest – story in the book is *The Story of the Crop-Eared Dog* (pages 57–70), a medieval Irish text which deserves to be better known. It is full of extraordinary flights of fancy, proving that the Celtic imagination was far from dead by this date – several hundred years after the epics of the great heroes Cuchulainn and Fionn were written down. Of the rest, *Jaufre* (pages 128–46) is something of a parody of the romance genre; while *The Story of Caradoc* (pages 13–29) introduces us to an unusual story of love and family jealousy as full of twists and turns as any contemporary novel.

As before, I have tried to let each of the stories speak for itself, and resisted an occasional urge to 'improve' on the original for a modern audience. In fact there is very little that cannot be appreciated by readers today, with the possible exception of the occasional concept which seems foreign to our current sensibilities. Where these appear – for example in *The Crop-Eared Dog*, where the concept of *gaesa* (magical prohibition) is introduced – I have tried to explain these as fully as possible in the introduction to each story. As before, these are not translations in any real sense of the word, though they do reflect the language and content of the original works as closely as possible.

Arthurian literature as a whole has been a life-long passion of mine, and when, a number of years ago, I first came across the Arthurian poetry of John Masefield, I was so impressed by what I read that I wrote to the author, only to receive the news that he had died a few days earlier. Now, while working on this current book, I received a copy of the newly edited collection of Masefield's Arthurian poetry and plays (*Arthurian Poets: John Masefield*, edited by David Llewellyn Dodds, Cambridge, Boydell & Brewer, 1995) in which I found the following paragraph:

Has not the time come for a re-making and re-issue of the epic by a body of good scholars and writers? Is not the time ripe for an Authorised Version using old poems and fables little used by or unknown to Malory...? It is our English epic; we ought to make more use of it than we do.

These words seemed so appropriate that I immediately wanted to place them at the beginning of the book, and I felt prompted to dedicate the collection to the memory of this great English poet. If I have, in any way, succeeded in retrieving some of the forgotten stories of the Arthurian tradition for a new generation, I am more than content. I like to think Masefield would have approved of what I have done, though he would doubtless have done it with more poetry.

Finally, I hope that those who read this book may find as much pleasure in reading it as I have in its writing, and that they may feel encouraged to go and seek out the original versions of the texts (a full list of which will be found in the introduction to each story), bearing in mind that there is no substitute for the real thing.

And, who knows, there may yet be a third volume of these tales to come. There are still enough 'forgotten' tales of Arthur to fill several more!

John Matthews
Oxford, England

1
The Story of Caradoc

THE *Livre du Caradoc* is part of a much longer romance, or series of romances, grouped under the general heading of *The Continuations of the Old French Perceval of Chrétien de Troyes* (edited by William Roach and Robert H. Ivy, Philadelphia, University of Pennsylvania Press, 1950). Despite this it is clearly intended to form a complete tale on its own, narrating the history of its hero from birth to his establishment as a successful Round Table knight. The poem forms part of the *First Continuation*, which exists in three different versions, generally called the Short, the Long, and the Mixed. These versions vary in length between 3,300 and 5,000 lines, suggesting that each was copied by a different hand from a single source. Each author sought to add or expand the details of the story. Thus the longer version contains a version of *The Story of the Horn*, a similar tale to that told here in *The Boy and the Mantle* (see pages 76–83), as well as the episode of the beheading game, better known from its most famous retelling in the fourteenth-century poem *Sir Gawain and the Green Knight*.

Caradoc himself is, as his name would suggest, of Welsh origin, and is almost certainly the same character who appears in Celtic literature as Caradoc *Vreichvras* (Strong Arm), the son of Llyr Marini and Tegau Eufron. It is probable that the episode of the poem which includes the hero's acquisition of the serpent attached to his body, causing him to have a 'shrunken' arm (*Briefbras*), derives from a misunderstanding of this epithet. In Welsh tradition Caradoc is a legendary or semi-legendary ancestor of the house of Morganwg,

while history claims him as the founder of the kingdom of Gwent some time around the fifth century. This makes him slightly earlier than Arthur, and may well be another example of the way in which the heroic war-leader subsumed many earlier heroes as part of his fabled warband. I have omitted the final episode of the poem, which repeats the story of the magical testing horn, already retold in *The Unknown Arthur*, because it seems like an unnecessary addition to the tale, which really ends with Caradoc's healing. I have added one suggestion to the end, which is not in the original text – that Guinier's title was 'Golden Breast'. This idea derives from the fact that Caradoc's mother is called this in the Welsh tradition and seems a reasonable supposition.

The story itself is one of the finest of its kind I have ever come across, and it is astonishing that it has remained so little known until now. The psychological motivation of the characters is far more developed than usual in these romances, and the whole story of Caradoc's strange birth and the subsequent treatment of his mother ranks among the finest pieces of storytelling in the entire Arthurian corpus. Even the often-repeated theme of the beheading game is more clearly explained here, and the general drive of the story keeps one guessing throughout, with far less of the stock situation than in general; where such episodes do enter they are skilfully used. Over all, the story seems to me to echo many themes from Celtic tradition, expertly woven into a medieval romance by the anonymous author.

The poem has only recently been translated

in its entirety by Ross G. Arthur in his book *Three Arthurian Romances* (London, J. M. Dent: Everyman Editions, 1996) and I have made extensive use of this in preparing my own version. The episode of the beheading test was translated by Elizabeth Brewer and can be found in her excellent collection of Gawain material, *Sir Gawain and the Green Knight: Sources and Analogues* (Cambridge, D. S. Brewer, 1992). The notes to the edition of the *Continuations* by Roach and Ivy are of great value when it comes to understanding the background of the work. The only critical study which has appeared to date is by Margurite Rossi: 'Sur l'episode de Cradoc de la Continuation Gauvain' in *Mélanges de langue et litterature françaises du Moyen Age et de Rennaissance offerts à Charles Foulon*, vol. 2, Rennes, Marche Romane, 1980.

NE DAY WHEN KING ARTHUR was holding court at Quinilli, there came to him a strong young knight named Caradoc, who was lord, in his own right, of the country of Vannes and related to the king by marriage. The young lord was in search of a wife and, as was the custom in these times, he wanted the king to find one for him. And soon after, Arthur did just that, marrying him to the beautiful Ysave of Carahes. The wedding was a very splendid affair, and noble men and women came from all over the country to attend. Among them was a man skilled in enchantment whose name was Eliavres, and when he saw Ysave he fell deeply in love with her and desired her so much that he devised a terrible scheme to obtain his ends.

On their wedding night the couple thought they lay together, but in fact Eliavres cast about them both such spells and confusion that they had no idea of the truth – which was that Caradoc lay with a greyhound bitch, while the enchanter enjoyed the delights of love with Ysave, who believed that she was with Caradoc. The same thing occurred on the second night, when Caradoc thought he enjoyed his wife but in fact lay all night with a pig. And on the third night it was a mare that he held in his arms and whose favours he enjoyed! Eliavres, meanwhile, spent the nights with Ysave, and on the third night engendered a child upon her.

Soon after, the court disbanded, and King Caradoc and his new queen returned to their own lands where, in due course, Ysave gave birth to a beautiful son. King Caradoc was well pleased and gave the child his own name.

The child grew tall and strong and handsome, and soon began to outstrip his tutors in all things. When he was only ten he asked his father if he might go and visit his uncle's court and learn what he could of the ways of chivalry at the Round Table. King Caradoc was glad to agree, for his pride in his son knew no bounds. And so the young Caradoc set forth, accompanied by a party of his father's knights and several of his own young friends, and they took ship together, arriving in Britain and making their way to Cardeuil, where King Arthur was holding court.

The king was very glad to see the noble youth, and made a great fuss of him, taking him hunting and instructing him personally in the arts of coursing and hawking, as well as telling him much concerning the arts of war and chivalry, the proper way to behave around ladies, and such noble pursuits as the games of chess and checkers.

Thus Caradoc remained at the royal court and learned everything that he could. He was often in the company of the king and queen, and became firm friends with Sir Gawain and Sir Yvain, as well as many other knights and ladies who were resident at the court. By the time he was fifteen he was as strong and well favoured as any of the knights and, though yet untried, he was prepared for his first adventure whenever it came his way.

Now King Arthur was much enamoured of hunting and, since the land was at peace, he remained at Cardeuil for several years, enjoying the plentiful game to be found in the woods and meadows around the city. But one day he decided that it was too long since he had worn his crown and held a great court and that he wished to do so soon. And, he declared, at the same time he wished to make his young nephew a knight. All agreed that this was an excellent idea, and plans were set in motion at once for a great celebration, with a tournament and feasting and general celebration.

That was a court to remember for long years. Knights and nobles came from all over the lands of Arthur to celebrate with him. Not only Caradoc, but fifty other young men were destined for knighthood, and the king saw to it that they were royally clad. Queen Guinevere herself sent embroidered shirts to all the would-be knights, and when the day came the king himself gave his nephew the accolade, while Sir Gawain fastened on his right spur and Sir Yvain his left. Then, when the ceremony was over, they all went to the cathedral to hear mass, and after that to the great hall, where the feast was prepared. Yet as Sir Kay the seneschal was about to have the trumpet sounded to summon everyone to dine, King Arthur reminded him that it was ever his custom, on such occasions, that they should forebear to eat until they had seen or heard a wonder.

At this moment, a knight came riding towards the court and entered there in great haste. He fell on his knee before the king and asked him for a gift. 'If I may I shall grant it to you,' replied Arthur. 'Tell me what you desire.'

'Sire,' replied the knight, 'I ask but one thing, and that is a blow on the neck in exchange for another.'

'What can you mean?' replied Arthur.

'Sire, all I ask is that I should give my sword to one of your knights. If he can strike off my head, then so be it; but, if I survive, I shall have the right to return the blow one year from now in your sight.'

'By St John!' exclaimed Sir Kay. 'A man would have to be simple to accept such an offer.'

'I have asked for this gift,' said the knight. 'If you refuse me it will soon be known everywhere that King Arthur's word is worth nothing.' And so saying he drew his sword and held it up for all to see.

At that Caradoc, who was standing near, rushed forward and seized the weapon.

'Are you the best of these knights?' demanded the challenger.

'No, only the greatest fool,' answered Caradoc. Then he raised the sword and the knight laid his head on the table, stretching his neck for the blow.

After a moment's hesitation Caradoc delivered his stroke. The blow was so hard that it cut through the knight's neck and buried the blade in the table. The challenger's head flew from his body, but to everyone's horror he followed it and, picking it up, set it once more on his shoulders. Then he spoke, calmly, as if nothing had happened.

'Now that I have received a blow I am satisfied – but remember, I shall return in a year to return the favour.' He looked at Caradoc. 'Do not forget!' So saying he departed from the hall before anyone could say or do anything to stop him.

Everyone looked sorrowfully at Caradoc, who was quite cheerful, if a little pale. 'Do not fear, uncle,' he said to Arthur. 'My fate is in God's hands now.'

Then Arthur commanded everyone who was present to attend the court exactly one year from then, and all promised to do so. Then they went to dine, though few were in any mood to eat or enjoy themselves that day.

Thus the year turned, and Caradoc went forth in search of adventure as any newly made knight would do. Great were the deeds he performed, and his name was spoken of in many places. As the time drew near for the dawning of Pentecost, when the court would assemble again, everyone began to think of the terrible fate that awaited the young hero, and people came from all over the land to witness it, not only those who had been present the year before, but others, whose curiosity to see what would happen brought them to Cardeuil. Yet though they had heard, along with everyone else, what had occurred the year before, King Caradoc and Queen Ysave did not come, being too saddened by the news to bring themselves to witness the death of their son.

Pentecost came, and a great feast was prepared. Mass was heard, and all went into the hall to dine. Then came the one who had survived Caradoc's blow. He called to the young knight to come forth. Caradoc leapt forward without hesitating, but the king himself spoke up.

'Wait, sir knight. If you will spare my nephew's head I will give you a great ransom.'

'What do you offer?' demanded the challenger thoughtfully, leaning on his sword.

'All the gold and silver plate you see in this court,' answered the king.

'Not enough,' said the knight, and raised his sword.

'Wait! All the treasure that is in my coffers shall be yours if you spare him.'

'Not enough. I would rather have his head,' said the other.

Then the queen came forward with all her ladies.

'Sir,' she said, 'I beg you for this boy's life. I offer you these ladies, the most beautiful in all the land, if you will agree.'

'They are fair indeed,' replied the knight politely. 'But I have no need of them.' Then, when he saw that the queen and many of the other ladies were distressed, he added, 'If you do not want to watch I suggest you return to your quarters.'

Then he turned again to Caradoc, who cried aloud, 'Do what you must, sir knight. Let us delay no longer.' And he laid his head on the table just as the other had done a year before.

The knight raised his sword and brought it down – but he only struck Caradoc's neck with the flat of the blade. Then, as the youth leapt up, he said, 'Come, it would be a great shame if I were to kill you.' Then he looked to the king. 'With your leave, my lord, I wish to speak to the young man privately.'

In astonishment the king nodded, and the two men went to one side. There the knight spoke quietly to Caradoc. 'I will tell you why I spared you. I am your father and you are my son.'

'That is not possible,' answered Caradoc fiercely. 'I will defend my mother's honour with my last breath. She is not and never was your lover.'

But the knight bade him be silent; then he recounted everything that had occurred all those years before, how he had deceived King Caradoc and had lain with Ysave and begotten the young man upon her.

Caradoc listened with mounting anger and disbelief. When the knight fell silent at last he cried, 'I do not believe any of this. It never happened! If you repeat this to anyone else I will seek you out and kill you!'

The knight said nothing more, but simply turned on his heel and left the court as swiftly and mysteriously as he had come.

Then there was great rejoicing in the court, and many came forward to praise Caradoc and to give thanks that his life had been spared. None noticed how withdrawn and silent he had become, yet as soon as he could he excused himself and, for the first time in many years, went home to Vannes.

There, in the city of Nantres, he found King Caradoc and Queen Ysave. When he heard that the young man was there, the king went forth to welcome him and embraced him warmly. 'Welcome home, my son,' he said.

'Why do you greet me so,' answered Caradoc, 'since I am not your son?'

'Not my son!' cried the king. 'What foolishness is this?'

Then Caradoc took him to one side and repeated everything that the challenger had told him. 'I tell you these things not to hurt you,' he said, 'for of all men I honour you as my true father – whatever the truth.'

At this moment the queen arrived and rushed forward to embrace her son. But Caradoc thrust her away, saying coldly, 'I can no longer bear to see you, my lady. You have done too much to hurt my lord the king.'

'What can you mean?' cried Ysave.

Then the king turned upon her and ordered her to go from his sight. 'For you have done so much evil to me that I no longer wish to see you.' And so saying both men turned away from her and waited, unspeaking, until she had left the room. You may be sure that the queen was distraught, for she knew nothing of what Caradoc had told her husband, any more than she knew what had happened at the time of her wedding.

When she was gone the king brokenly asked Caradoc what he should do with her. 'For you are just as much harmed by these terrible deeds as I.'

'I wish her no harm,' said Caradoc, 'since she is, in truth, my mother. If you will be guided by me, you will build a strong tower and shut her away with only women for company. That way the enchanter can never have her again, and no one may boast that he had what was rightly yours.'

This the king did, and the tower was soon built and Ysave enclosed within it. She had only her women for company, just as Caradoc had suggested, and no one spoke to her or saw her save those who attended her. And if the people of Vannes wondered at this strange act of their king they were none the wiser, for he remained silent and withdrawn, and the young Caradoc, as soon as the tower was complete and his mother shut away, left at once for Arthur's court.

He arrived in the month of May, when the roses were all in bloom. It was nearing the time for the royal court to assemble again, and Caradoc remained there as lords and ladies came from every part of the land.

Now among the nobles who set out at that time was a young lord from Cornwall named Cador, who brought with him his sister Guinier, a very beautiful maiden who was as gentle and loyal as she was fair. Their father, the King of Cornwall, had died that summer, and his son came to swear fealty to King Arthur. However, on the way, an adventure befell them which was to have far-reaching consequences.

Now you must know that before the old king died, a certain knight named Aalardin du Lac had sought the hand of Guinier in marriage. She, however, had spurned him, and both her father and brother had defended her right to choose a man she liked. And so matters stood, and the king died, and Cador and his sister set out for Arthur's court. But, as they rode, Aalardin came after them and overtook them.

Cador was only lightly armed, but when he saw the other knight coming, he turned to face him and to defend Guinier. Alas for them both, Aalardin knocked Cador from his horse with the first blow of his spear, and the young lord lay upon the earth with a broken leg. Aalardin stood over him and said: 'If only you and your father had granted my suit when you could. Now I shall take what I asked for, but not for myself! I want you to know that I shall give your sister to my men for their sport. Think of that as you lie there!' Then he seized the reins of Guinier's horse and rode away with her.

You may imagine how the maiden cried out against the cruel blow that fate had dealt her. And, even as Aalardin spurred his mount to carry her away, there came in sight another rider. It was Caradoc, on his way to Arthur's court after carrying out an errand. When he saw the wounded man lying in the road and heard the piteous cries of the maiden he swiftly gave pursuit, crying upon Aalardin to stop.

He, when he saw the fully armed knight approaching, turned and drew his sword. 'Get away, sir,' he shouted, 'this is none of your business!'

'I think it is, when I hear a lady call out in such distress. Let her go or prove yourself against me.'

Cursing, Aalardin swung his sword, cutting off Caradoc's lance near where he held it. Caradoc responded by striking him over the head with the butt of the spear, felling him from his horse. Then Caradoc dismounted and battle commenced.

That was a mighty battle indeed! The two knights were well matched and for a long while neither could gain the advantage. Indeed there is no telling how long they might have continued, if Aalardin's sword had not broken. At this he gave ground and surrendered, placing himself at the mercy of Caradoc. He, breathing hard from his long fight, ordered the knight to surrender to the lady he had tried to carry off. This Sir Aalardin did, but Guinier refused him. 'I can no more accept your surrender than I can find it in my heart to forgive you. I must know how my brother fares. If he is dead from the wounds you gave him, you shall pay for it!'

'My lady,' replied the knight, 'I am more than willing to do as you ask. By all means let us go back to where he fell.'

So all three rode to where Cador had fallen. He lay still upon the way, scarcely breathing. The two knights, who were themselves weak and weary from their battle, lifted him together onto Caradoc's horse, then the young knight mounted behind and supported the wounded man on the saddle before him.

'We must find shelter,' said Caradoc, 'and soon, or I fear this good man will not see the light of day again.'

They rode on slowly until they saw, off to one side of the road, a large and splendid tent. From within they could all hear the voices of many lords and ladies raised in song. Caradoc and Guinier stared in astonishment and wondered aloud who the owner of this remarkable tent could be. Then Aalardin confessed that it was his, and that those within were his own people.

Then he said: 'Do you see in front of the entrance to the tent are two golden statues? Let me tell you about them. They are automata, which move and do many marvellous things. The one on the right opens the door to the tent; the one on the left closes it again. But this is not all they do. The right-hand statue plays the harp most beautifully and, if a woman enters there who claims to be a virgin when she is not, then the harp will go out of tune, and a string break. The left-hand statue holds a spear and, if any false or churlish fellow enters there, he will find that the spear is thrown at him!'

Then Aalardin dismounted painfully from his horse and called out to those within. And when they came out they gathered around and helped the wounded Cador down and carried him inside. Then came forward a most beautiful maiden, whom Aalardin introduced as his sister, and he asked that she care for the badly wounded knight, and also for Caradoc and himself. But for Guinier he bade her care as if she were her sister.

To all this the Maiden of the Pavilion (for this is the only name I have heard her called) agreed readily. You may be sure that all four people were cared for as well as ever they could be. And so they all began to mend their hurts, and in the weeks that followed the three knights became firm friends, and Aalardin begged forgiveness of Guinier and it was given. And she, the beautiful sister of Cador, began to fall in love with Caradoc, while the Maiden of the Pavilion looked with longing at Cador.

Thus the weeks passed, until the three knights were well enough to ride again, and Caradoc declared his intention of returning to King Arthur's court, for he was sure to have been missed by now and longed to be home. Cador also wanted to continue his journey, and Aalardin wished to accompany them. Thus the whole party set forth, in merry mood, on the road to Caerleon, where the court was newly assembled.

As they neared the city they began to meet other people on the road, and learned from them of a great tournament which was to be held there. Organized by two kings, Cadoalent of Ireland and Ris of Valen, it was rumoured to have been arranged to impress a certain lady. All three knights wished to take part, and by chance it fell to Aalardin to go first. He put on his finest armour and, mounted upon his favourite steed, rode in the direction of the lists. On the way he passed a tower from which a maiden looked out upon the passing throng. When she saw the bold knight passing she leaned out and called to him. Aalardin reined in and greeted her gently.

'Sir,' she said, 'forgive me for speaking thus boldly to you, but my heart tells me you are the best of all those I have seen pass this way! My name is Guigenor and I am the daughter of Sir Guiromelant and the Lady Clarrisant, Sir Gawain's sister. I am pursued by both King Cadoalent and King Ris, and this tournament to which you are even now doubtless headed is intended to prove to me which of the two is the better man and therefore the one I should take. Sir, I hate them both, and never will I marry either one. If you will be so good as to look with kindness upon my plight, I shall evermore think of you as my knight.'

When Aalardin heard these words, and looked upon the lady Guigenor his heart was moved, both by her plight and by her beauty. Forthwith he swore to uphold her honour in the tournament. Whereupon the lady tossed down her sleeve to him, to wear as a favour in the fighting to come. Then Aalardin rode on, his heart high with expectation.

I will not take much time to tell of the tournament and all the great deeds that were done there. Suffice it that there were many brave and bold knights present, including some of the finest of King Arthur's Round Table fellowship. The knights who fought for the two kings were particularly outstanding in their prowess, none more so than Aalardin and Cador who soon joined with his companion and fought as bravely as ever a man could. You may be sure that the maiden of the tower, Guigenor, watched every move that Aalardin made, and when she saw what an excellent fighter he was her heart warmed to him even more. He was brave as well as comely! Another maiden, Ydain, who was the niece of Sir Yvain and a cousin of Caradoc's, could not help but notice the brave display made by Cador, and she sought among her companions to know who he was. When she heard that he was the son of the King of Cornwall she was glad indeed, and sent him a favour to wear in her honour.

Extraordinary feats of courage were achieved that day. Knights were unhorsed, spears and swords broken, armour dinted and shields shattered. Many a brave man sent prisoners to the lady of his choice, and among them Cador sent the champion Guingambresil to the lady Ydain, whose favour he now wore, and whose bright eyes and fair form had charmed him utterly.

Soon after Caradoc himself joined the fray, displaying all his great skill and power and overcoming everyone who stood in his way. On that day both Sir Gawain and Sir Yvain chose to fight, and both encountered Caradoc. Both were defeated by him. Never had such a mighty fighter appeared in that land; everywhere people spoke of him with wonder. He was truly the most outstanding knight to enter the lists. Because of him King Ris and his men, on whose side Caradoc fought, began to win the day – despite the efforts of Cador and Aalardin, who fought against him for King Cadoalent.

In the end the three heroes won the day and attained the greatest honours in the tournament. When the time came for them to reveal their names – for as was the custom they had fought in disguise, or under a plain shield – there was much rejoicing. Gawain, especially, was glad to greet his cousin Caradoc. Even the two kings agreed to shake hands and pledge friendship to each other, the more so once they saw that the lady Guigenor, over whom they had fought, loved Aalardin.

Thus at the end, amid general rejoicing, Guigenor married her knight, while the beautiful Ydain chose to marry Cador, to whom he had utterly lost his heart. As for Caradoc, he was well pleased, for he had his own love Guinier by his side. Even the Maiden of the Pavilion, Aalardin's sister, was made happy. For though she had felt drawn to Cador while nursing him back to health, her eye had been caught by another young knight, Sir Perceval of Wales, who had deported himself so well in the tournament that everyone said that he would soon be as great a knight as any at the Round Table. And thus three weddings were celebrated, those of Guigenor, Ydain and the Maiden of the Pavilion, and the tournament broke up amid great rejoicing. Caradoc, Cador and Aalardin all returned home with King Arthur, who demanded that they remain at court for the time being and grace his table with their presence.

Now we must return to Caradoc's mother, Lady Ysave, who all this time had remained enclosed in the tower built for her by King Caradoc. And there the enchanter, Eliavres, who had caused all the trouble in the first place, found her. He took to visiting her often, using his knowledge of magic to penetrate the locked doors and high windows of the tower. At first I believe the lady was far from happy to see him, for it was through his magic that she came to be imprisoned in so ignominious a way. But in time he won her round, reminding her of the way her husband and son had behaved towards her, and pledging his own love to her in terms she could not long refuse.

Things might have continued thus for a great deal longer, had it not been for a mistake which the enchanter made. In order to please the lady whom he loved so much, he brought ghostly musicians into the tower to play for her. But they could be heard outside as well, and soon the king's followers could no longer keep silent. They sent messengers to King Caradoc, who seldom came to Nantres these days, telling him of the sounds of revelry which issued nightly from the tower.

The king sighed deeply, and sent men to watch for Eliavres. In vain, for with his magic he was able to move invisibly, and to enter the tower unseen. Thus in the end the king despaired, and sent for his son.

When Caradoc received the news he was greatly troubled. He begged leave of King Arthur and set out at once for Vannes, having entrusted Guinier to the care of her brother Cador. He was afraid that if he took her with him, she would learn the secret of his mother's disgrace and turn against him. As it happened he was not to see his love for a long time, and much hardship was to encompass them before they were reunited.

Arrived in Brittany, Caradoc went at once to his father, who told him all that had occurred. Caradoc was angry beyond measure at this, and set a trap to capture Eliavres. Despite the enchanter's skills, Caradoc succeeded in capturing him while he was with the lady Ysave. Thus the son was reunited with both his parents, but unhappily, as you may imagine! Caradoc handed over Eliavres to the King, since he could scarcely take revenge on his own father. King Caradoc devised a terrible punishment. He forced the enchanter to do just what he had tricked the king into doing years before. Eliavres was forced to lie with a greyhound, a sow and a mare.

Now hear what happened, though it grieves me to speak of it. From this carnality emerged three offspring: a huge greyhound which was named Guinloc, a boar called Tortain, and a stallion which they named Loriagort. These were Caradoc's 'brothers' in their way. As to the enchanter himself, once this dreadful deed was accomplished he was set free, though Caradoc longed to see him dead and would have flayed him alive if he had not been his father.

As for Eliavres himself, he suffered greatly. At the earliest opportunity he stole back to the tower and there visited the queen, who had now so completely transferred her feeling to him that she wept and bemoaned his fate with as much vehemence as if he had been her lover from the start. Then her sorrow turned to cold anger and she urged him to be avenged on Caradoc.

'I cannot kill him, he is my son after all,' said the enchanter.

'Waste no pity on him, for he wasted none upon you,' cried Ysave.

'I cannot kill him,' said Eliavres. 'But I can cause him to live only half a life, if you will help me.'

'Gladly,' replied the queen, who seemed to have forgotten that Caradoc was her son.

The enchanter went away and returned with a terrible poisonous snake which he hid in a closet in the Queen's room. Then he instructed her what to do and departed.

Soon Caradoc came, wanting to see how his mother fared. To him she seemed nothing but kindness, and even begged his forgiveness for the betrayal of the king. Caradoc, though inwardly sorrowful, felt some measure of peace at this. He stayed with his mother for much of the day, until as dusk began to fall she complained of a headache and declared that she must let down her hair and comb it out. 'Do you fetch me the comb from within that cupboard,' she asked, and Caradoc went willingly to do so. Alas! when he reached inside the serpent sank its fangs into his flesh and curled itself around his arm.

In dreadful agony Caradoc strove to free himself from its bite. But the harder he struggled to free himself the tighter grew its hold, until he almost fainted with the pain. The queen meanwhile made a great show of horror and anguish, screaming for help for her poor son. The king and his servants came running, to find Caradoc lying on the ground while his mother sobbed over him. The king was so enraged that he was ready to kill Ysave at once, for he believed her responsible despite her protestations of innocence. Her women took her into another room before he could do her harm, and the king turned his attention to helping his son.

Caradoc was carried forth and laid in a great bed in another part of the castle. There he lay scarcely conscious, while the king sent far and wide for doctors and for anyone with knowledge of healing to save his son. Many came, but none of them could effect a change in the young man, who grew paler and thinner with each day that passed. He could scarcely sleep from the pain, and ate but little. The doctors gave him two years to live at best, some even less than that. King Caradoc despaired.

The queen, meanwhile, was triumphant that the plot she had hatched with Eliavres had succeeded so well. She gloated over her son's sickness, the terrible pains he felt, for these she saw as a fitting punishment for all the suffering she had experienced since his discovery of the trick played upon her and King Caradoc.

Others were less happy. When King Arthur received the news he was smitten with a deep sorrow. He declared at once that he would not rest until he found a cure for the young man's suffering, and set out as soon as he might in a ship bound for Brittany. Delayed by storms and finally blown off course, the king arrived in Normandy instead and proceeded towards Nantres.

Word soon reached Cornwall, where Cador groaned aloud at the news. As for Guinier, she almost fainted from the shock and cursed heaven for inflicting such torment upon her lover and forcing her own heart to break. 'Alas!' she cried to Cador. 'Fair sweet brother, I implore you to take me at once to where he lies. If I may see him but once more before he dies then I, too, shall die happy.'

Rumour soon reached Caradoc that King Arthur of Britain himself was coming to see him, and that Cador had left Cornwall and was on his way by sea with his beloved Guinier. But instead of comforting him, this only made him feel worse, for he could not bear them to see him so changed and wasted from the deadly bite of the serpent. Thus he devised a desperate plan. There was a messenger who had come from Britain with word of King Arthur, and that night Caradoc begged the man to stay with him, pleading that he wanted no one present who had known him as he was before. Then, when they were alone, he spoke of a certain very holy hermit who lived close by in the forest. 'I am certain this good man can bring me relief,' he said. 'If you would but help me to go to him you would earn my undying gratitude.'

The messenger willingly agreed after Caradoc assured him that it was for the best and that he sought to save his family from any further sorrow. As darkness fell and the castle grew silent, the two men stole outside, escaping unseen through a narrow postern gate. Then they set off on foot through the forest, the messenger supporting Caradoc, who was almost too enfeebled to walk.

They soon reached the hermit's cell and there Caradoc made his confession, telling the wise man everything that had happened and bemoaning his own guilt concerning both his mother and his true father. 'I see now that I was unjust to blame the queen for the sorrow that has come upon us all; even Eliavres acted out of love, albeit misguided. I have acted wrongly to them and now I suffer the consequences. I pray that the good God will have mercy on me and upon them.'

The hermit felt nothing but pity for the young man who suffered so greatly both in body and soul, and he saw that he was genuinely contrite. Therefore he gave him absolution and invited him to remain there for as long as he wanted. Caradoc gladly accepted and asked the hermit not to reveal his presence no matter who came looking for him. And he swore the messenger to secrecy also, and then sent him away.

Thus he led a simple life in the forest, eating only one day a week and fasting for the rest. And in this way he found solace, and even a measure of healing, for though the serpent was still fastened just as tightly around his arm, yet the pain seemed to abate a little, so that Caradoc was able to live in peace for a time.

Meanwhile King Arthur had arrived in Brittany with all his followers, and shortly after that came Cador and Guinier. They were met with news from King Caradoc that his son was fled, none knew where. Then was there great sorrow amongst all those who had come to see the young man. Guinier, above all, was heartbroken. She knew why Caradoc had run off, and she longed to be with him – even though it meant her own death. A great search was mounted, though in truth he was close at hand, just a short distance from the city in the hermit's cell. But when the seekers came there they saw only the old man himself, and a young neophyte clad in a simple robe with a hood that concealed his face. So gaunt and marked by suffering was Caradoc that it was doubtful if anyone would have known him, save perhaps Guinier, who after long months of waiting, herself set out upon the road in search of her beloved. She and Cador together journeyed through the lands of Arthur until they returned at last to Cornwall, and there Guinier remained, praying daily for the safe return of her beloved, while Cador went on alone, always searching for his friend.

Two years passed, and at the end of that time Cador returned to Brittany, worn out with fruitless searching. Caradoc, meanwhile, left the hermitage, driven by who knew what terrible longing to find a new place. He found his way to a sheltered valley where stood a lonely chapel seldom visited by anyone. There he took up residence in a deep thicket of trees, living on roots and berries and water from a stream that ran close by. Every week he went to the little chapel to pray and hear mass, and the good brothers who lived there treated him and gave him what little food they could spare. And here at last, by chance, came Cador. He sought shelter with the brothers and asked, as he did in every place that he found people living, if they had seen a tall, dark-haired man who had a terrible snake fastened to his right arm.

'Indeed, we have,' answered the monks. 'He comes her often and we treat him as best we might. You will see him tomorrow if you remain here.'

Overjoyed to hear this, Cador lay down on the rough bed provided, though in truth he slept but little that night, and in the morning was up early awaiting the coming of the one he had sought for so long. In case Caradoc should take flight when he saw him, Cador stood at the back of the chapel with his cloak pulled around him, and there he saw the emaciated figure of his friend enter and kneel down and begin to pray. He was bearded and unkempt, wrapped in an assortment of ragged garments, with big shoes on his feet. Cador would not have recognized him, but when he heard his voice he ran forward and gently embraced his friend.

'Before God, how long have I searched for you!' he cried. 'And all the while you were here. Why did you run off like that? You knew that I would care for you, and as for Guinier, had you no thought for her?'

When he heard the name of his love, Caradoc began to weep. He found no words to answer Cador, but instead fell down upon the earth and lay there unspeaking. Cador, much moved by the terrible suffering of his friend, tried to raise him, all the while pleading to him to return to Nantres and place himself in the hands of those best able to care for him.

But no matter how he begged, Caradoc only shook his head and pulled away from Cador's touch. Then the Cornish knight knew that he wasted his breath, and turning to the brothers begged them to care for his friend for a while longer, promising them great reward. The he rode in haste to Nantres and sought out Caradoc's mother, who lived now in almost total seclusion.

'Madame,' he said, 'I am come to tell you that your son is still alive. I have thought about the matter all the time I have been searching for him, and I truly believe that you are the only person who can offer a cure for him, if you will. Many, including myself, have thought ill of you for betraying your son to such a terrible fate, but I know that if you can help him now you will regain favour in the eyes of all people.'

The queen turned pale. 'Is my son truly living?' she asked.

'He is indeed,' replied Cador. 'Will you help him?'

'Return to me on the morrow,' said Ysave. 'I will see what I can accomplish.'

That night the enchanter Eliavres came to visit the queen, as he still did with remarkable faithfulness. Unseen as ever by any of the guards, he entered her bed and together they knew great joy. But Queen Ysave was uneasy and could find no rest until she had unburdened herself.

'I know that it was at my behest that you found the means to cause my son suffering,' she said. 'Yet now I regret what we did. I fear for my immortal soul if what was done is not undone. My love, I have learned that Caradoc still lives. Is there anything that can be done to free him?'

'If this is your true desire,' said the enchanter, 'I will tell you.'

Then Ysave wept and begged him to tell her, and Eliavres answered that there was indeed a way in which Caradoc might be cured. 'If a maiden can be found who is his match in goodness of heart and spirit, she might save him. If two barrels are brought, one filled with milk and the other with vinegar, and if they are placed no more than three feet apart, on the full moon; and if the maiden gets into one and Caradoc into the other, and if the maiden places her right breast on the rim of her barrel and calls out to the snake, it will surely leave Caradoc's wasted body in search of richer fare. While it passes between them, if a man is ready with a sword he could cut the vile creature in twain. This is the only way that I know of to save our son.'

Then Ysave wept and thanked him and on the morrow she sent for Cador and told him all that Eliavres had said. Thus was a spark of hope ignited in Cador's heart, and he thought deeply upon all that had been said. And he knew at once that there was but one being in all the world who might do what was needful, and that was his sister. Therefore he left at once for Cornwall, taking the next available ship, and soon after he was with Guinier. You may imagine her joy when she heard that Caradoc was found! Then Cador told her everything that Queen Ysave had said to him, and Guinier declared that nothing on earth would prevent her from going to him and offering her body to the snake.

Thus they took ship and returned to Brittany, where they made their way to the little chapel. When Caradoc laid eyes upon his love he tried to hide himself, so great was the shame he felt at his appearance, all wasted and with shrunken flesh and beard and hair all bedraggled and unwashed. But Guinier took him gently in her arms and kissed him with such joy that all who saw it could not help but weep. Then Cador told his old friend how he might indeed be cured.

Caradoc, his face streaked with tears, spoke more forcibly than he had in a long while.

'This may not be. I will not suffer my love to risk so much.'

'You shall not deny me,' Guinier said. 'This much may I do for you. I have no wish to live without you.'

At first Caradoc would not be persuaded, but neither Cador nor the maiden would be denied. They sent for two tubs to be brought and filled, one with vinegar and the other with milk, just as the queen had told them. Then Caradoc climbed into the tub filled with vinegar and immersed himself to the neck, while Guinier climbed naked into the tub of milk and laid her soft white breast upon the edge. The she called out to the snake, reminding it that there was little sustenance left in Caradoc any longer, but in her there was much goodness and plenty. And the snake, which hated vinegar as much as it longed for a tastier meal, leapt from Caradoc's arm and arced across the distance between the two tubs. Cador, who had hidden behind a curtain, leapt forth and cut off its head with a single blow. In doing so he also sliced off Guinier's right nipple; then he fell upon the evil beast and cut it into many parts so that it was quite dead.

Then there was great rejoicing and Guinier and Caradoc, helped from their tubs, embraced and wept and consoled each other for their wounds and, laughing as well as weeping, were taken into the care of the brothers. The hermit with whom Caradoc had long stayed was summoned and took over the care of the young man, who began to recover with remarkable speed. Guinier too was treated, her breast bound up and salves applied to the wound caused by her brother's sword. In a surprisingly short time Caradoc was restored to his former strength, though it was to be some time before he felt able to undertake adventures such as the kind he had once lived for. The arm which had borne the snake curled around it for so long, though it recovered its former strength, was ever after larger than its fellow, and for this reason Caradoc later received the epithet *Briefbras*, meaning 'great arm'.

Soon after, word of his recovery reached the ears of King Caradoc, who at once rushed to the little chapel and there greeted his son with great joy. Caradoc too was glad to see the man whom he still called father, and they embraced and wept and were filled with joy for the youth's recovery.

Thereafter they returned to Nantres, where Caradoc spoke with his mother. And there at last their old anger towards one another was laid to rest and they made their peace. Caradoc intervened with the king to have his mother set free of her long imprisonment, and it is said that in time the king and queen remembered the great love they had once felt for one another and were reconciled.

As for young Caradoc, he journeyed to King Arthur's court and there was well received. Many honours were heaped upon him, and in due course, with the blessing of King Arthur and her brother Cador, himself now crowned King of Cornwall, Caradoc married his dear Guinier. After this he lived a long life and had many adventures – too many to tell of here. It is said that Guinier was the most faithful wife of any man living in those times, and that when the old enchanter Eliavres sent a beautiful horn to test the fidelity of the women of Arthur's court, she alone was proved to be true. And it is said of her that in time Caradoc's old friend Aalardin du Lac provided her with a miraculous golden nipple, to replace that which Cador had cut off, and that because of this she was known far and wide as 'Golden Breast'. Whether this is true or not I cannot say, but of one thing I am certain: Caradoc and Guinier lived a long and happy life together, and when in time the old king died, Caradoc became King of Vannes and reigned well and happily for many years.

2

The Story of Perceval

ACCOUNTS of the Grail are numerous and vary considerably in quality and intent. *The Story of the Grail* by the twelfth-century French poet Chrétien de Troyes is a bare-bones retelling of an earlier Celtic source. The multi-volume *Vulgate Cycle* sets the entire Arthurian story against the background of the Grail, interpreting it in a wholly theological way. Other versions vary from the highly charged and symbolically overweighted *Parzifal* of Wolfram von Eschenbach to the elliptical *Diu Crone* of Heinrich von dem Tülin.

Falling somewhere between all of these is the text upon which the following story is based. *The Prose Perceval*, more generally known as *The Didot Perceval* after one of the manuscript's early owners, is a masterly abridgement of a vast tale into a brief but telling story, full of mystery and magic. It describes the coming of the Grail and the effect this had on the Arthurian world, tells some of Perceval's adventures, and ends with a brief rendition of the *Mort Artu* or Death of Arthur. I have chosen to extract parts from all of these sections, except the last, though I have further abridged them in places in order to tell the story both economically and clearly.

In essence the story is about contrasts, and tells the story of a simple youth (Perceval) discovering the ways of the world and the spirit. His many failures are balanced by his final success – though, uniquely within this corpus of

material, he is helped somewhat by Merlin, who is very much a behind-the-scenes operator in this tale. The text is also unusual in that it describes the Grail as emitting music, and refers to the mysterious 'enchantments' which lie over Britain until the Grail is found. The mention of Merlin's retirement to his *esplumoire* is also interesting. This word has no exact meaning, but seems to relate to the word for a 'moulting cage' for birds of prey. This suggests that the old wise man retires to 'moult' or leave behind the ways of the world, and to watch from within all that takes place outside. This concept, though hinted at in other texts, is nowhere more clearly stated than here.

The text dates from some time between 1190 and 1215 and exists in two dissimilar versions, which none the less tell more or less the same story. The version used here is that of the E manuscript which was translated by Dell Skeels as *The Romance of Perceval in Prose* (Seattle and London, Washington University Press, 1966). Professor Skeels's introduction and notes have been very useful in preparing this version, as has the commentary of Albert Pauphilet, 'Le Roman en Prose de Perceval' contained in *Melanges d'histoire du Moyen Age offerts a M. Ferdinand Lot* (Paris, Champion, 1925). The best edition to date is that of William Roach, *The Didot Perceval* (Philadelphia, University of Pennsylvania Press, 1941) which includes both versions of the text.

OT LONG AFTER KING ARTHUR won the test of the Sword in the Stone, and had been crowned, Merlin the Wise came to him and said: 'Sire, I cannot stay here any longer, for I am bidden to journey to another place from where I may observe what passes within the world. But before I depart there are certain things that you must know.' Then, as King Arthur listened, Merlin spoke to him of the Holy Grail, that had been used by Our Lord himself to celebrate the Last Supper, and how after the events of the Crucifixion, the risen Lord had entrusted the Grail to the keeping of Joseph of Arimathea. He in turn gave it into the hands of his brother-in-law, Brons, who brought the sacred relic to Britain, where it lay still, on a mysterious and beautiful island, guarded by this same Brons, who had suffered a terrible wound that would not heal. 'And you may be certain,' said Merlin, 'that this good man cannot find rest and recovery until a knight of this court comes to this hidden place and asks a certain question. When he does so the wounded king, who is called the Fisher King because he once fed his followers from a single fish as Our Lord fed the five thousand, will be healed and the enchantment which has lain upon the Land of Britain since before the time of your father will be lifted. All these things I tell you so that you may be prepared for what is to happen when I am no longer here to advise you. And this also will I tell you. When he was given the Holy Grail, Joseph of Arimathea had made a table in the likeness of that at which Our Lord celebrated the Last Supper. Twelve places there were at this table, and one that was always empty in token of the betrayer Judas. In our own time I had made a table that is in likeness of the one made by Joseph – it is the Round Table at which you and your knights will sit. There will a place empty there also, until a destined one comes to fill it. When that knight comes you will know that the mysteries of the Grail are beginning.'

And when he had said these things, which much puzzled the young king, Merlin departed, and none might stay him. And he went into Northumberland, to his old master Blaise, to whom he told all that had happened since the beginning of time, and all that was to come in the time of King Arthur.

Now King Arthur ruled well and justly for many years, and knights came from far and wide to fill a seat at the great Round Table. It was said, and justly so, that no knight was worth his salt until he had served at least a year at Arthur's court. Word of this reached Alain le Gros, who was a son of the Fisher King, and he declared that when his son, who was named Perceval, came of age, he should go to King Arthur. Many times he spoke of this openly to the youth, and each time the boy's mother spoke against it. But Perceval heard only his father's words, and when the time came for Alain to die, his son waited only until he was buried before he set out for Arthur's court. And he went so quietly and without speaking to anyone, that no one knew he was gone until the end of the day. Then his mother wept and prayed that he should not be eaten by wild animals, and when no word came from her son she became sick, and in a little while she died.

But Perceval knew nothing of this, and continued on his way until he reached the court of King Arthur, where he found a good greeting and soon proved himself both gentle in manners and skilled in the use of arms. For though he knew next to nothing of such matters when he arrived at the court, yet he learned quickly, and was soon accepted among the other knights until finally he came to sit at the Round Table itself along with Lancelot of the Lake, Sir Gawain of Orkney and his brothers, Sir Ywain Blanchmains, Sir Sagramor, and many more.

Thus all was well within the land of Logres, until it befell that one year King Arthur desired to hold court at Pentecost. And this he determined, that it should be the greatest court in all the world, and that every good knight and all their ladies should attend. And there he would seat the twelve peers from amongst his knights at the Round Table, for he wished to exalt the order that he had founded, and the work of Merlin who had made the table in the time of his father.

When the time came for this gathering to take place it was the greatest that had ever been seen in that land. Men said that King Arthur was the finest and most regal lord ever to wear a crown, and that never in all the history of the world had such an illustrious and noble gathering assembled. Over a hundred knights and their ladies sat down at the table in the great hall to celebrate the festival of Pentecost and that was the greatest assembly and most joyful and splendid affair that anyone living could remember. And afterwards they repaired to the lists and there held a great tournament at which King Arthur himself rode upon the field with a baton of ivory to see that there was peace and accord between the combatants. With him rode the young knight Perceval, who had taken the name li Galois. And he was much troubled that he could not himself fight in the tournament because of a wound in his hand which made it difficult to hold a spear or sword. But despite the fact that he made no brave show of arms, yet he caught the attention of Elaine of Orkney, who was sister to Sir Gawain and the daughter of King Lot and who was reckoned the fairest maiden in all the lands at that time.

When she saw Sir Perceval riding pale and proud beside the king she fell deeply in love with him, and that night, when everyone was turning towards their beds, she sent word that Elaine the daughter of King Lot asked him to joust in her name the next day. And to this end she sent a messenger bearing a suit of red armour and asking that he accept it as a gift from one who admired him deeply.

The Story of Caradoc

The Story of Perceval

Perceval was much flattered that so lovely and noble a lady should show him favour, and sent word that he would indeed fight for her on the morrow. And you may be sure that he slept but little that night, but fell to exercising his hand that it might better serve him in the jousts.

Next day the king and all his court heard mass in the cathedral, and then the twelve peers of the Round Table assembled and ate together. And the king honoured them greatly and spoke highly of their courage and bravery and of their goodness. Then once again they repaired to the jousting.

Now came Perceval clad in the scarlet mail sent to him by Elaine, and on that day he performed such feats of arms that no one might withstand him, not even Sir Lancelot or Sir Gawain. And many people who saw these feats began to say aloud that the knight in red should be asked to sit at the Round Table. Thus at the end of the day King Arthur called the knight to come before him, and asked him his name.

Then Perceval took off his helmet and all were astonished. And Perceval explained that the armour was a gift from one who loved him, at which everyone smiled, and Lancelot remarked that such deeds, when done in the name of love, were less astonishing, though they ought still to be rewarded. To this King Arthur agreed, and said to Perceval that, if he desired it, as soon as a place became vacant at the Round Table he should have it. But Perceval looked and saw that there was already an empty seat, and he asked who might sit there.

'That seat is a great wonder,' replied the king, and told him what Merlin had said, that this was an empty place in token of the betrayer. 'And he told me furthermore,' said Arthur, 'that once a proud disciple of Joseph's attempted to sit in that place and was swallowed up. Only the best knight in the world may sit there.'

Then Perceval looked at the seat and in his heart he longed to sit there. But when he spoke of this to Arthur the king shook his head. 'By no means,' said he. 'You are a good knight indeed, too good to be lost to us – but I doubt that you are the best in the world.'

Now when they heard this many of the knights, including Sir Gawain and Sir Lancelot, spoke up and begged the king to let Perceval try the test of the perilous seat. And at first Arthur would not agree, but in a while with a sigh he said that if Perceval was of a mind to try this then try it he might. And Perceval said that he did this in humility, and because his heart bade him, not because he deemed himself the best knight in the world. Then he crossed himself and uttered a prayer, and seated himself in the chair.

At once there was a terrible sound, as though the earth itself groaned aloud, and the chair split, emitting a cloud of black smoke such that no one present could see more than a space around them. Then a great voice spoke which said: 'King Arthur, know that you have done a deed which will cause suffering to all your land; and know further that this knight Sir Perceval shall suffer great pains because of his rashness, and that only because of the goodness of his father Alain le Gros and his grandfather Brons, that is known as the Fisher King, is his life spared. And know too that the object known as the Grail, that was given into the keeping of Joseph of Arimathea by Christ himself, is in this land; and only when one of the knights of this fellowship has done great deeds and achieved many perilous adventures will he come at last to the castle of the Fisher King. There, he must ask a question concerning the Grail and, if it be the right question, then shall the king be healed and the stone which has broken this day be reunited. And then and only then will the enchantments be lifted from the land of Britain.'

Then the voice fell silent, and all there marvelled. Then as one man all the knights swore that they would go forth in search of the Grail; and Perceval, who was greatly ashamed at his rash act and the sorrow which it had brought upon everyone there, swore that he would never remain in any place for longer than one night until he found the castle of the Fisher King and undid the enchantments.

King Arthur was sorrowful when he heard this, for he believed in his heart that he would never more see his great fellowship. Yet he could not fail to give them leave to depart, though he did so with a heavy heart.

Thus next day the fellowship set forth, and rode for a time together until they reached a place where several roads met at a stone cross. Then Perceval said: 'We shall meet with no adventure while we ride thus together. Let us therefore go our own ways, and hope that God will bring us together again one day.' And to this they all assented, and each one chose a path to follow and went forth upon it. And many adventures they had, you may be certain, but I will not speak of these but turn me to the deeds of Sir Perceval.

In the days that followed the young knight met with many singular adventures, and in each one he conducted himself with grace and nobility, always dealing with his adversaries as a knight should, and causing more than one fair lady to weep for longing when he continued upon his way. For Perceval would stop in no place more than a night, just as he had sworn, but rode upon the quest of the Grail with single-minded intent.

And thus he came one day to a castle amid a dark forest, and saw that the drawbridge was down and the gates open, and he entered thereby with caution and saw no one. Dismounting at the horse-block he tethered his steed and went inside. The castle seemed empty on every side, despite the fact that fresh rushes were strewn upon the floors. And Perceval wondered greatly at this, and where the people of the castle might be.

When he had looked around he returned to the great hall and there espied a chessboard set up before the window as though in readiness for play. And the chessboard was of silver and the pieces of black and white ivory. Perceval stood in contemplation for a time, looking at the fine chess set. Then he moved one of the pieces, and to his astonishment an opposing piece moved of its own volition against him. In wonder Perceval moved a second piece and lo! another piece moved against him. Then the knight sat down at the table and began to play. He played three games, and each time he was beaten. Then he was angry and said aloud: 'By my faith, I am no beginner at this game, yet I am beaten every time. This is an evil magic I think, and no one else should have to suffer it.'

Then he took up the pieces and placed them in the skirt of his hauberk and went to the window. But as he was about to throw them into the moat a voice came to him. 'If you throw the chess pieces away you will bring great harm upon you!'

Perceval looked up and saw a damsel in a window above the one where he stood.

'I will forebear if you will come down and speak with me.'

'I do not care to do so,' she replied.

'Then I shall cast them away,' said Perceval.

'No!' exclaimed the lady. 'I would rather come down.'

So Perceval took the pieces back to the silver board and placed them upon it, whereat they arranged themselves as neatly as they had been before play.

Then the damsel entered, with as many as five other ladies and servants who hastened to disarm the knight and to care for his horse. And the damsel welcomed the knight sweetly and bade him sit with her. Then was Perceval filled with love for her, and right there and then he asked for her love. The maiden, who was indeed very fair, smiled at him and answered: 'Sir, I well believe that I could love you, even though I know nothing of you at all. But I will need assurance that you are as valiant in deeds as you are ardent in your wooing.'

'Damsel,' said Sir Perceval, 'you may ask anything of me, so long as it be not against my vows.'

'Very well,' said the damsel, 'I shall tell you what I most desire. In the wood near here is a white stag. I bid you capture it and bring me its head. And to help you in this I will give you a bratchet which is most skilful in the chase.'

To this Perceval agreed, then, as dusk was already falling, they ate a fine supper and retired to bed. Perceval lay awake for much of the night, thinking of the damsel and how greatly he loved her. Then in the morning he prepared to set forth in search of the stag. And the maiden brought her dog to him and commanded that he care for it with his life. To this he gave his word, and with the dog perched on his horse's neck, he went forth into the wood.

Soon the dog gave tongue and Perceval set it down on the road, whereat it hastened to lead him to where the stag hid in a thicket. And Perceval gave chase to the beast, which was as white as snow and heavily antlered. And in a while he caught up with it and slew it and took its head. But as he was hanging it by his saddle-bow there came an old woman riding on a palfrey, and she snatched up the little bratchet and rode off at full speed.

Then Perceval angrily mounted his steed and gave chase. And when he overtook her he seized the bridle of her steed and cried out to her to stop and to give back the dog. But she only looked at him evilly and said: 'A curse be upon you if you say this dog is yours. I know that you have stolen it, and I will take it back to him that owns it.'

'That is untrue,' said Perceval. 'For the dog belongs to my lady, and you shall not have it.'

'Now you may use force against me if you wish, though you know it is false to do so,' said the old woman. 'But if you will do one service for me I shall deliver it you willingly.'

'What service is that?' asked Perceval.

'A little further along this road you will see a stone tomb, and on it is painted a picture of a knight. If you will go there and say aloud that he who painted the image is false, then I promise you shall have back this bratchet without further delay.'

And Perceval said that he would, and rode on his way until he saw the tomb with the painting upon it. Then he looked all around him and said, out loud as he was bidden: 'False was the one who painted this image.' And when he said this he turned to go back the way he came, but then he heard a great noise behind and when he looked over his shoulder saw a huge knight coming toward him at great pace. He was clad from head to foot in black armour, and his horse was of the same hue, and when he saw him Perceval was sore afraid. Then he recalled that he was a knight of the Round Table, and so he crossed himself and set his spear in rest and charged toward the Black Knight.

They met with a huge and fearsome crash and both fell from their horses and lay stunned on the earth for a while. Then they recovered and fell to battling against each other with tremendous force, until at last Perceval struck his opponent such a blow on the helm that it felled him. But at once the knight jumped up and continued his assault. And thus it ever was, that as fast as Perceval struck down his adversary, the other arose again with renewed strength.

Then as they fought there came another knight, all clad in armour, and he rode right up to where the two men were battling, and took up the stag's head from where it hung at Perceval's saddle, and snatched the bratchet from the old woman and so rode off. When he saw this Perceval was so angered that he redoubled his efforts and gave the Black Knight such a buffet that he fell back. Perceval followed up with such a rain of blows that his opponent retreated before him and then, to Perceval's astonishment, ran to the tomb and opened it and jumped inside, pulling the lid to after him.

Perceval, wondering greatly, cried out three times to him to come out, but the tomb remained firmly closed. Then the knight knew that he would get no further there, and turned to where the old woman still sat upon her palfrey.

'Who was that knight who took the stag's head and my lady's bratchet?' he demanded, but the old woman merely shrugged and said: 'Evil curse the one who asks me about that, since I know nothing of it. If you have lost the dog, you should look for it.'

When he heard this Perceval knew that he wasted his breath, and he turned away and mounted his steed and rode in the direction which the knight had taken as fast as he might. But though he searched for a long while, and always asked after the knight with the bratchet and the stag's head, he found no trace of him.

So Perceval rode for many days until he came at length into a forest that seemed dead. Thick entanglements of dead undergrowth fouled the way, yet the knight pressed on until he came at length to a great castle. And as he came near to the walls a damsel came forth and greeted him and told him that he was welcome to stay there that night. This Perceval willingly accepted, for he was tired from stuggling with the forest. And so the maiden led him inside and helped him to unarm, and other women came forward and took away his horse to feed it. Then they all went inside and the maiden directed Perceval to a chair and sat down opposite him. She looked upon him for a long while and then suddenly began to weep, whereat Perceval asked what it was that grieved her.

'Sir,' answered the damsel, 'I have a brother and we are both the children of a brave knight and his lady. When my brother was still young our father died, and soon after my brother departed for King Arthur's court, whence he had always longed to go. And after he departed our mother took sick and died, since when I have heard no word from my brother. It seemed for a moment that you reminded me of him.'

Then Perceval looked at the damsel and he looked around him at the hall and it was as as if scales fell from his eyes. And he rose and took the maiden in his arms and said, 'Sister, I am Perceval, your brother.' And the two fell to weeping and kissing each other.

Then the damsel's folk entered there and were amazed, until she broke away from her brother's embrace long enough to tell them who he was. And there was great rejoicing, and food and wine were brought, and brother and sister sat for long hours talking of the events that had passed. And the maiden asked if he had yet found the castle of his grandfather the Fisher King. 'Not yet,' replied Perceval, 'but assuredly I will not rest until I have done so.'

'Surely you should give up this search,' said his sister. 'For you have laboured long and found nothing. Remain here I beg you, for you are still young, and I fear for your life if you continue through this dangerous land.'

'Nothing would please me greater, if I had completed my quest,' said Perceval. 'But until I have done so I may not stay.'

Then Perceval's sister wept, and when she could speak again she begged him to do one thing for her before he set forth again, and that was to visit a certain wise hermit who lived close by in the forest. 'For he is our uncle and was brother to our father Alain le Gros. And he has told me much of our grandfather Brons, who is called the Fisher King. And he has said that he has the Grail with him, and that it shall pass to you, if you can only find it.'

Perceval said that he would most willingly go to see the hermit, and next day they set forth to his house. And when they arrived the hermit himself came forth to meet them, leaning upon a crutch, for he was very old. And when he saw that it was his niece who was come there, he wondered aloud who the knight was that accompanied her.

'Dear uncle, this is my own brother, Perceval, who left to go to King Arthur's court. Now he is returned a great knight and is engaged upon the quest for the Grail.'

The old hermit greeted Perceval warmly and embraced him. Then he asked if he had yet been to the castle of the Fisher King, that was his own brother and the knight's grandfather. Perceval shook his head and answered that he sought it, but in vain. Then the hermit responded: 'Let me tell you that my brother and I were both present when the Holy Spirit commanded Brons to carry the Grail to this land in the far West. And also it said that an heir would be born to Alain le Gros that would one day become the keeper of the Grail himself, and the Fisher King would be unable to die until that heir should come to his castle and achieve the mystery of the Grail. I believe that heir may well be you, Perceval. But you must take care to follow the path of the Grail faithfully, for you are of a lineage that God has greatly honoured, and if you pursue the path of honour you will find that an exalted destiny awaits you.'

'Sir,' said Perceval, much moved, 'I shall do all that I may to honour this trust.'

And with that the hermit blessed him, and wept for sight of him, and that night all three remained a long while in prayer before retiring. Then, when the sun rose, Perceval begged leave of the hermit to follow the Grail, and the wise man blessed him again and said that he would continue to pray for him. And Perceval and his sister departed together for her castle.

They had not gone far when a fully armed knight came galloping towards them at great speed, crying out to Perceval to defend himself or give up the maiden who rode with him. But Perceval was so deeply sunk in thought for his task and, if the truth be known, of the lady of the bratchet to whom he had failed to return with the stag's head that he failed even to notice the knight until his sister cried out loud to him. Then he saw the knight coming and without even thinking he set his spear in rest and met the other head on. The stranger's lance shattered, but Perceval's drove right through shield and hauberk and into his breast, killing him outright.

Then Perceval mourned the death of his opponent. 'For,' he said, 'I wish that I had defeated you rather than killed you. I do not even know your name.'

Perceval dragged the dead knight across his horse's saddle and they rode on to the castle, where they were received by his sister's people and made comfortable. But next morning, Perceval called for his horse and armour. And when she saw that his sister grew sorrowful.

'Are you going to leave, when you have only recently returned home?'

'I must follow the path of the Grail as my uncle told me,' replied the knight. 'But you may be sure I shall return as soon as ever I can, so long as my life is spared.'

Then despite all his sister's pleading Perceval set forth again on his road, and followed it wherever fate led. And the way was long, and took the knight through lands both rich and barren. Perceval slept by turns on the earth and in castles where hospitality was readily granted. Then one day he came to a place where there was a very fair meadow, and a stream running beside it, and a fording place. Beside the ford was a tent, and a knight awaited all who came there and forbade them passage unless they jousted with him. This Perceval did, and quickly overthrew the fellow. Then he demanded wherefore he prevented travellers from passing that way or from getting water.

'Sir, I will tell you,' said the knight, whose name was Urban of the Black Pine. 'I am a knight of Arthur's court, and after I received the accolade from the king I set forth in search of adventure. And, if I may say so, I found few who could withstand me. Thus one night I was on the road, and a storm overtook me. Lightning flashed from the sky, and by its light I saw a maiden riding swiftly ahead of me. I followed her and soon arrived at the fairest castle in the world. The gates stood open and I followed the maiden within. She greeted me warmly and made me welcome. Within few days I had fallen in love with her and made bold to woo her. She said that she would be my love so long as I never went beyond sight of the castle. I answered that I would do so willingly, but that I would be sad to give up errantry. Then the maiden said that I should wait beside this tent and offer battle to all who came this way. That way I could be with her and still enjoy the life of a knight. Since then I have been here almost a year, and have not been beaten until now. And furthermore, if I had remained undefeated just a few more days I would have been named the best knight in the world.'

Perceval looked around him. 'Where then is this castle of which you speak?'

'Only I can see it,' replied the knight. Then he looked at Perceval and said, 'Now that you have defeated me you must remain here for a year and defend the Ford Perilous.'

'Not for nothing will I remain here,' answered Perceval. 'I am on a quest that will not wait. But I bid you cease lying in wait for those who come here and return to King Arthur.'

To this the knight agreed, but scarcely had he spoken when a great noise broke out on all sides, from an unseen source, that sounded like the crumbling and crashing of stones, and a black cloud enveloped them both. Then a great voice spoke, that said: 'Perceval li Galois, you have done a terrible deed this day, and all of womanhood shall curse you for it!' And to the knight it said: 'Urban, you too have failed me. Hurry now or you will lose me.'

When the knight of the ford heard this he fell on his knees before Perceval. 'Sir, you have beaten me fairly and I owe you my life. But I beg you not to send me away from this place! Let me go to my lady.'

'By no means!' cried Perceval. 'You shall go to King Arthur!'

At this Urban tried to run away, but Perceval seized him and held him back. And as they struggled the voice came again, urging Urban to make haste. And when he heard this the knight drew his sword and would have attacked Perceval again, though he had given his word when he was overcome.

Angrily Perceval fought back, but as they were engaged a cloud of great black birds appeared and began to attack Perceval furiously. He was so angered that he struck the knight to the ground with a single blow and then, turning upon the birds, ran one of them through with his sword. As it fell to the earth its form shivered and it became the body of a maiden of surpassing beauty. Perceval was astonished and stared in wonder as the rest of the birds broke off the attack and, seizing the fallen body, carried it into the air and away from sight.

Urban, meanwhile, lay groaning where he had fallen. As Perceval stood over him, the knight opened his eyes and begged for mercy. 'I may spare you,' said Perceval, 'but first you must tell me the meaning of what took place just now.'

'I will, gladly,' replied Urban. 'The great noise which you heard was the breaking of the walls of my lady's castle. For when I was overcome and promised to return to King Arthur, her magic failed her. Then it was her voice that you heard, cursing both of us. Lastly it was my lady herself and her women who became birds and attacked you. She whom you wounded was the sister of my lady. But she is not harmed at all, for even now she is in Avalon, where my lady and her women may go in an instant by ways known only to them.'

Then Perceval marvelled greatly, and Urban begged him again to release him so that he might return to his love. Perceval bent his head and gave him permission, and Urban was so glad that he ran off up the road, forgetting his horse and all his equipment. Perceval watched him go, and laughed to see him. Then as he watched he saw a damsel appear on a black horse and carry him up before her. In moments they were gone from sight, far more swiftly than mortal riders could go. And Perceval shook his head and rode upon his way, for he knew it would be folly to pursue them.

Now Perceval entered a part of the land which seemed deserted. Night after night he was forced to sleep on the ground, and it became harder and harder to find anything to eat. Then he was sorrowful, and thought much upon the nature of his quest and of his worthiness to achieve the Grail. And by and by he came to a meeting of four ways, and there the most beautiful tree he had ever seen grew by the roadside. Next to it stood an intricately carved cross. As Perceval reined in his mount he heard a sound in the tree, and looking up saw two naked children, a boy and a girl, as it seemed about six years of age, clambering about from branch to branch. Perceval called out to them and asked them to speak to him.

'Perceval li Galois,' said one of the children, 'we are come here to help you, if you will let us. Yonder lies your road. Do but follow it and you will see things that will aid you in the completion of your endeavour – if it right for you to do so.' And so saying both children pointed towards the right-hand path.

Perceval was filled with wonder and looked to where they pointed. And when he looked again towards the tree it was no longer there, and the children also were not to be seen. Whereat he deemed this to have been a true vision – if the children were not demons. But as he wondered whether he should take the road indicated, there came a shadow that passed before him, causing his horse to snort and rear. And a voice came to him, that said: 'Perceval, you have heard of Merlin. He wishes you to know that the two children were indeed messengers of God, and that if you follow this path, if you are worthy of it you shall succeed in your quest.' Then the voice was silent, and though Perceval called out three times to it, it answered him not.

Thus the knight set forth on the way that was indicated. He liked it not for it was open country, and he could not rid himself of a feeling that he was being watched. And so he came to a rich land through which a broad river coursed. And there in the midst of the water he saw a small boat, and in the boat lay an old man, richly clad, fishing from the side. Two servants were with him, and he called out to Perceval, inviting him to stay that night in his castle, which lay upstream a short way. And Perceval was glad, for it seemed a long while since he had slept in a bed. So he took his way, but as he rode on he saw no sign of a castle, and began to misdoubt the words of the old man in the boat.

And so he wandered for a while until dusk began to fall, and then he came upon a castle that lay in a sheltered valley. Never had he seen so fine and splendid a place, and his spirits lifted at once. He rode up to the gate and was admitted by the porter, who took his mount and gave him into the care of several squires who escorted him into the hall and made him comfortable. When he had been there a short time, there came in four servants, who between them carried an old man – the same, Perceval realized, that he had seen fishing earlier that day. He seemed so frail that he could not stand unaided, but must be borne about in the arms of his servants.

When he saw the old man, who indeed seemed like a king, Perceval jumped to his feet and said, 'Sir, you should not have troubled yourself to greet me.'

But the old man smiled and said, 'I wish to honour you, sir knight.' Then he called to his servants and bade them bring food and drink for his guest. They brought tables swiftly and set them up, and laid them with white cloths and placed dishes of gold and silver upon them. Then, as Perceval and the old man were about to begin eating, there came into the hall the most curious procession that the knight had ever seen.

First there came a damsel, very richly dressed, who bore in either hand two silver platters. After her came a youth carrying a lance; and three drops of blood came from its head. And last of all there came another youth, who bore between his hands the vessel with which Our Lord celebrated the first Eucharist. And when they saw it the king and all his people bowed their heads in prayer while Perceval looked upon it and wondered greatly at its beauty and richness. But though he was much moved to ask concerning the procession, he remembered how his mother had often told him not to ask too many questions, and therefore he kept silent while it passed before him and went out of the hall by another door. And Perceval was so tired from the nights spent out in the open, when he had slept little, that he almost fell asleep at the table. Then was the old king very sad indeed, for in truth he was the very Fisher King whom Perceval sought, his own grandfather who had brought the Grail to the land of Britain. And it had been prophesied that when the best knight in the world came to the castle where he lived and asked concerning the strange procession, then and only then would the old king be permitted to die. And he had been alive these many hundred years, and longed greatly to depart. But he could not, and Perceval failed to ask the question that he should.

Then the old king begged leave to be excused and went to bed, and

Perceval follow soon after, being put to bed in a splendid room with a soft mattress and pillows. But he still wondered greatly about the procession, and thought that he would ask of the youths who carried the spear and the vessel in the morning.

Next day Perceval rose and went in search of his host. But though he walked all through the castle he could find no one, and when he went outside it was the same. Then he saw that his arms were cleaned and laid out for him, and in the stable he found his horse all saddled and bridled and well fed. So he mounted and rode forth, expecting at any moment to see someone from the castle, whom he deemed must have gone forth to gather fresh rushes or herbs for the old fisherman.

All morning Perceval rode through the forest and saw no one. Then he spied a maiden wandering in the wood, and she wept bitterly. And when he came up to her she said: 'Ah, Perceval, Perceval, what a wretch you are. For last night you lay in the castle of the Fisher King, and you saw the procession of the Grail, and yet you said nothing. Know then that if you had asked concerning the wonders you saw, that your grandfather would have been healed and the enchantments which lie upon this land of Britain would have been lifted. But you are too foolish, and you have not done sufficient deeds to warrant such a reward. For you might indeed have become the new guardian of the most holy Grail!'

When he heard these words Perceval himself began to weep. And he cried aloud that he would never rest until he had undone the evil of that day, and he promised to return at once to his grandfather's house and ask the question which he should have asked. But the damsel only wept and shook her head. And so Perceval commended her to God and turned back the way he had come.

But now he found that, although he tried to retrace his steps, the way went differently, and though he rode for the next two days without stopping for sleep and scarcely for rest, he could in no wise find the Fisher King's castle. At the end of that time he saw ahead of him a maiden, sitting by the side of the road, and on a tree by her side hung the white stag's head which Perceval himself had cut off. And when he saw it he was very glad and rode right up to the tree and snatched it down without a word to the damsel. And she, angered by his impetuous act, cried out for him to put back the head. But Perceval merely laughed and said that he would not do so, for it belonged to another and to her he would return it.

While they spoke thus Perceval heard a noise of barking, and there came first a doe, running, and in pursuit of it the very bratchet which he had lost previously. And when it saw Perceval it leapt up into his arms and was very glad. But the maiden cried out in anger, and with that there came in sight the knight who had taken the dog. He too called out to

Perceval to give back the bratchet, but Perceval said, 'By no means, sir. You must be mad to ask this, since you stole this dog from me but a moon ago.'

'Then defend yourself!' shouted the knight, and the two rode at each other with great fury. But Perceval was quickly the victor, and the knight grovelled in the earth before him. 'I will spare you on one condition, that you tell me why you stole the bratchet, and if you know the identity of the knight of the tomb and the old woman who cursed me so roundly.'

'That I will, and willingly,' replied the knight, 'though I am ashamed to tell you everything. For you must know that the knight of the tomb was my brother, and he was at one time the finest knight in the world – until he met a faery woman who claimed his love and enchanted him. And she rode with him to a fair meadow, where they stopped to eat and there my brother fell asleep. When he awoke he found himself in the most magnificent castle he had ever seen, and the faery woman told him that here he would be able to prove himself the best knight against anyone who came that way. And she showed him a tomb that stood by the castle – though none could see it save those whom she allowed – and bade him remain there and challenge all comers. As to the old woman whom you saw there, she is in truth the very same faery, who can seem like the most beautiful maiden when she chooses.'

Perceval expressed his wonder at this, then he asked if he knew anything about the damsel of the Chessboard Castle who had given him the bratchet and asked for the stag's head.

'Indeed I can,' said the knight. 'She is also an otherworldly woman, the sister of she who enchanted my brother. I am sure that she sent you on the quest of the white stag because she knew that it would lead you to the tomb and thus to a battle with my brother. She hoped that you would kill him, I believe, for she is in deadly rivalry with her sister for his love, and therefore I believe that she seeks his death rather than that her sister should have him.'

Then Perceval began to feel anger at the deception to which he had been submitted. And he asked if he were far from the Chessboard Castle, for by now he was wholly lost. The knight replied that he need only follow the road he was on and that he should arrive before nightfall. Then Perceval made him promise to go to King Arthur and to surrender himself, and he set off as quickly as he might for the Chessboard Castle.

He soon reached his destination, and was met by the damsel of the castle who, when she saw him coming, opened the gates and came forth herself to greet him. And she told him how much she had wondered at his long absence and that she had been somewhat angry with him because of it.

Then Perceval told her all that had occurred from the moment he had departed from her in quest of the white stag, and how he had learned at last the identity of the knight of the tomb and the reason for the theft of the bratchet and the stag's head. And when she heard all of this the damsel was very glad and praised him greatly. Then she said that she hoped he would remain with her and be her lover. But at this Perceval could only shake his head. 'For though in truth I love you, yet I have taken a vow not to remain in any one place for longer than a single night until I have succeeded in my quest.' And he told her of his search for the Grail.

Then the maiden said that he must do what he must, but that she hoped he would return to her as soon as he might. To this Perceval gave his word, for he loved her as much as she him, and then he set forth again at once, for he would not remain there even one night, having already slept under that roof before.

So Perceval continued upon his way, and many adventures he had; but never once did he find his way back to the castle of his grandfather. And thus seven years passed and Perceval continued to wander. And so long was he upon the way, and in such poor conditions, that in the end his wits left him and he forgot who he was and even the reason for his quest.

And so it befell that upon the morning of Easter he came upon a group of pilgrims making their way to church to hear mass. And they wondered greatly how he rode in full armour and with weapons at the ready on such a day. At first Perceval only looked at them madly, but then suddenly his mind cleared, and he remembered his quest and all that had happened to him since he left King Arthur's court. And then he fell from his horse and knelt at the roadside and prayed aloud for forgiveness. And the pilgrims gently helped him to stand and took him with them to the chapel where they were to hear mass. And lo! it was the very same chapel at which Perceval's uncle, the hermit, lived his holy life. When he saw Perceval he was overjoyed, and the knight fell at his feet and begged absolution and confessed to him all that had happened since he left there. And the hermit blessed and forgave him, so that his soul was eased. Thereafter Perceval remained with him in the hermitage for three months, for he was absolved for that time of his vow. But when he would have gone to visit his sister he learned that she had died a year or more before that, and that she was buried close by. Then he wept most bitterly and asked to see her grave, and when he saw it he wept again and offered prayers for her soul.

Then nothing would prevent him from going forth again in quest of his grandfather's castle. 'For I have waited over long already, and nothing more must prevent me from the testing of my true path.'

Then the hermit blessed him and gave him leave to go, for he saw that nothing else would do for him. And so Perceval set forth again, and rode day and night in search of the Fisher King. His way led him through many more adventures, and with each one his fame increased, but still he did not find what he sought.

Then on a day he saw coming toward him an old man carrying a scythe as though he were a reaper. And when he saw Perceval he went up to him and seized his bridle. 'Why are you idling here when you should be at the castle of the Grail?' he demanded. Perceval was astonished at this and asked the old man how he knew so much about him.

'I knew your name even before you were born,' replied the reaper.

'How may this be?' asked Perceval in wonder.

'I am Merlin,' answered the old man. 'I have come from Northumberland to help you.'

'Sir,' said Perceval, 'I have heard much of you and of your wisdom from my lord King Arthur. If it be that you can tell me how to reach my grandfather's house I shall be forever in your debt.'

'I know that you seek the castle of the Fisher King,' said Merlin. 'If you follow the path I shall indicate you will be there within the year.'

'Is there no quicker way?' asked Perceval.

'You are overly impatient. Go where I send you and trust that all shall be well. And, when once you find your goal, do not forget to ask about what you see.'

'I will,' said Perceval. And with that Merlin showed him the way that he should follow, and then vanished away he wist not where.

So Perceval followed the road as he had been shown, and within the same day he saw his grandfather's castle. Then his heart was high and he rode to the gates and was well received. Servants took his horse and arms and clad him in fine raiment and then lead him into the hall where his grandfather sat. The old king was much cheered to see him and rose as well he might to greet him. He seemed little changed, save that he was perhaps more gaunt and fragile than before. And he and Perceval sat and talked of many things until it was time for supper. Tables were brought in and set before the old king and the knight.

Then, just as it had been before, so it was again. There came a procession through the hall of the bleeding lance, the Grail and the two small platters. And when he had looked upon them Perceval asked concerning them. And at this there was a great noise and a bright light, and when they were gone Perceval saw that the Fisher King was as strong as ever he had been, and he leapt up like a young man and knelt before Perceval, who raised him up and said, 'Sire, know that I am the son of Alain le Gros, and your grandson.'

Then the Fisher King was very glad, and he embraced Perceval and led him before the holy objects. And he said: 'Son, know that this is the spear with which Longinus struck Our Lord in the side as he hung upon the cross, and this vessel, that is called the Grail, is the same with which the

Last Supper was celebrated, and in which Joseph of Arimathea caught some of the blood of the Saviour.'

Then Brons, who was also called the Fisher King, knelt before the Grail and requested that he should be released from his long service of the sacred vessel. And there came forth a music from the Grail and a scent as of paradise, and a voice spoke telling Brons that he should teach the secret words that Christ told to Joseph to his grandson, who should be the new guardian of the vessel. 'Do this, and in three days you shall walk in the fields of heaven,' said the voice.

And so it was that Brons told the secret words to Perceval, and much more besides, and on the third day he died as the voice had foretold. And on that same day, where King Arthur was in his court there came a noise of such magnitude that all were afraid, and the stone which had split when Perceval sat upon it was reunited, at which all were astonished.

But soon after there came Merlin, who had not been seen at court for many a year, and he told King Arthur all that had occurred. 'And know this: the greatest miracle that could occur in this time has happened, for the Fisher King is healed and Perceval, your knight, is now lord of the Grail. And thus the enchantments are lifted from these lands, and all shall be well.'

Then Merlin vanished away, and returned to his master Blaise and told him all that had taken place so that he might write it down in a great book. And I have heard it said that afterwards Blaise went to the castle of the Grail to be with Perceval, while Merlin went into his *esplumoire*, where no living soul might see him again. And thus was the Quest for the Grail achieved by Sir Perceval, and the enchantments that were upon the land of Britain lifted in that time.

3

The Knight with the Sword

THE Story of Knight with the Sword, or *Le Chevalier à L'Epée*, is one of several shorter romances featuring Gawain. Most of these, including the example included here, establish the hero as someone with a particular devotion to women – or, as some would have it, as a 'ladies' man'. The fact that this hides a deeper theme, whereby Gawain serves a more archetypal representation of the feminine – the Goddess – is demonstrated in a number of texts in which Gawain features as the hero. In *Le Chevalier à L'Epée* the story seems weighted somewhat towards the masculine view, but this is really no more than an expression of the medieval attitude towards women, who were seen as little more than chattels to be passed from hand to hand according to the requirements of their male relatives. As the poem's most recent translator, Ross G. Arthur, has wisely remarked: 'we need only imagine what the heroine's life was like before she met Gawain, and what happened to her after they parted...and what would have happened to Gawain if it were not for the help she gave him', to understand the real drift of the story.

Much of what happens in this story may seem odd to us today, but is mostly dictated by the manners and customs of the day. It was quite common for knights to dispute over a woman and for her to be handed from one to the other after they had fought to see who was the strongest. The episode of the Perilous Bed that features largely in this romance is a widespread motif which is found in several other surviving romances, including the *Perceval* of Chrétien de Troyes and the famous *Vulgate Cycle* of romances. The same episode occurs in another story included here, based on the *Lanzalet* of Ulrich von Zatzikhoven (see pages 147–73). There the outcome is somewhat different, and I have included both versions for the reader's interest. In most instances the hero involved is Gawain, which leads one to suppose that this was a well-established tradition possibly pre-dating the medieval texts in which it appears.

The poem dates from the early thirteenth century, and is attributed to an author who signs himself Paien de Maisières and who may also be the writer of another short Gawain romance, *The Mule without a Bridle* (see John Matthews, *The Unknown Arthur*, London, Blandford, 1995). It has been edited several times, most notably by Edward C. Armstrong in *Le Chevalier à L'Epée* (Baltimore, Murphy, 1990) and by R.C. Johnson and D.D.R. Owen in *Two Old French Gauvain Romances* (Edinburgh and London, Scottish Academic Press, 1972). To date, two translations have appeared: one in *From Cuchulainn to Gawain* by Elizabeth Brewer (Cambridge, D.S. Brewer, 1973), and the most recent by Ross G. Arthur in *Three Arthurian Romances* (London, J.M. Dent, 1996) both of which I have made use of in my own version.

HE TIME HAS COME TO TELL A STORY of that great knight Sir Gawain. Wherever tales are told of the knights of the Round Table his name is sure to be mentioned, and praise duly given to him. For of all the knights of Arthur he was the best – better some say than Lancelot, or Tristan – justly famed for his courtesy to all, and for his gentleness towards all women.

This tale tells of a time, one summer, when King Arthur was at Cardeuil. Many of the knights were away on adventures of their own, but Gawain, Kay and Yvain were all present, as was the queen. Gawain, as was his wont, became bored of the life at court, and began to hanker after a new adventure. To this end he dressed himself in his finest clothes, saddled Gringolet and rode out alone, following the road which led into the great forest to the north of the city. As he rode he fell to thinking of another adventure which had happened some time before, the outcome of which still puzzled him somewhat. So engrossed in this was he that he let his mount choose the way forward, and it was not until much later that he awoke to the fact that dusk was falling, and that he had no idea where he was. Deciding to turn back, Gawain followed a narrow track which led in what he hoped was the direction of Cardeuil.

He had not gone far when he saw the glow of a fire off to one side of the track, and made his way there in the hope of finding a woodcutter or charcoal burner who would put him on the right road. When he came within sight of the fire, however, he saw a charger tethered to a tree and a knight seated by the fire enjoying his supper. Gawain greeted him courteously, and the knight replied in kind, asking where he was going at that time of day. Gawain replied that he had lost his way and asked how best he might find his way back to Cardeuil.

'You are far from there,' answered the knight cheerfully. 'I can put you on the right road tomorrow – on condition that you stay and keep me company this night.'

'That I will be glad to do,' replied Gawain, and the two men settled down by the fire, to share food and conversation. The knight asked Gawain to tell him of his adventures, which the great hero did without hesitation. But I will tell you now that the other was not so truthful, and made up much of what he told his new-found companion. As to the reason for this – well, you shall discover all if you read on!

Next morning Gawain awoke first, followed shortly after by the knight, who smilingly told him that since his house was closer than Cardeuil Gawain might like to accompany him there, where he could be sure of the finest hospitality. To this Gawain agreed, and the two men rode on in companionable fashion until they left the forest behind and came into open land. Then the knight excused himself, declaring that he must ride ahead and make sure that all was prepared as befitted an honoured guest. Then he rode off in haste, leaving Gawain to follow more slowly and enjoy the bright splendour of the day.

Nor far along the road Gawain passed a group of shepherds. He greeted them courteously and rode on, but as he did so, he heard one of them say to the others: 'What a shame that so fine and gentle a knight will soon be dead.'

When he heard this Gawain was puzzled. At once he turned back and spoke to the shepherds, asking them what they meant by this remark.

'It is simple enough, my lord,' answered the one who had spoken before. 'We have seen many men follow that knight on the grey horse who passed this way a little while ago – but we have never seen a single one of them come back.'

'Why do you think this should be so?' asked Gawain. 'Have you heard anything of what happened to these men?'

'They do say,' answered the shepherd, 'that if anyone contradicts the knight he kills them at once. Such is the story we have heard; but since no one has ever seen anyone return from there we cannot say if it is true or not.'

'Well, I thank you for your words,' said Gawain, 'though I fear I cannot turn aside for a mere child's tale.'

'Then fare well, sir knight,' said the shepherd. 'We trust you will come to no harm.'

Gawain rode on until he sighted the castle. It lay in a sheltered valley and seemed like the finest he had ever seen that did not belong to a king or a prince. The moat was wide and deep, crossed by a stone bridge, and within the walls were many fine outbuildings. The keep itself was richly decorated with carvings and its roof shone as though it was made of gold. Gawain rode right up to the gates, which stood open in welcome, and entered without fear. Crossing the large tournament field he reached the courtyard and was met by the knight himself and three squires who took his horse and armour and weapons. Then his host led him inside.

The hall was as fine as anything Gawain had ever seen. A huge fire burned in the hearth, and couches covered with purple silk were arranged before it.

'You are most welcome, fair sir,' said the lord of the castle. 'Even now your dinner is being prepared. Meanwhile I bid you relax and be at ease. If there is anything at all which causes you displeasure be sure to tell me at once.' He smiled. 'Now I must go in search of my daughter, for I want you to meet her, and I am sure she will be delighted to converse with so great and courteous a knight.'

The lord returned in a matter of moments, bringing with him by the hand the girl of whom he had spoken. When Gawain saw her he jumped up and bowed low to her. He could not ever remember seeing a more beautiful creature; her eyes, her lips, her hair and above all her lovely form, were graceful and fine as that of any woman living. She, in her turn, saw in Gawain the finest and most handsome knight ever to cross her path, and she blushed at once at the mere thought of being in his presence.

Her father, smiling, led her to the couch on which Gawain had been sitting and bade her be seated at his side. 'Sir,' he said, 'I present my daughter to you. It is my hope that she should provide you with pleasant company for as long as you are in my house. Be certain to tell me if she displeases you in any way.'

'I am sure that so fair a maiden could never cause displeasure,' replied Gawain. His host smiled even more widely at this, and took himself off to enquire after the meal.

Gawain seated himself next to the girl and engaged her in polite conversation. Despite his dismissal of the shepherd's warning he could not silence some measure of disquiet, for there was something about his host's demeanour which did not seem to him natural. Therefore he was careful to say nothing that might be understood as too forward or uncivil, though at the same time he made it clear – by look and gesture only – that he was greatly attracted to the maiden. His naturally courteous nature stood him in good stead here, and it was not long before the maiden read his intent and answered him directly.

'Sir,' she said, 'I well understand your feelings – you honour me greatly, and your courtesy is such as any woman would wish to respond to at once. Yet I must warn you that my father is a dangerous man, and would have you killed for less than you have said to me this day. At all costs be careful what you say, and be sure not to gainsay him in anything he may ask of you, for to do so would bring only disaster.'

Before Gawain could answer, his host returned and announced that the meal was ready. Tables were brought and set up before them with knives and plates and cups of gold and silver, and water with towels of the finest linen to wash their hands. A splendid range of dishes were then brought in and placed before them. And all the while the host urged Gawain to engage his daughter in conversation, and subtly implied that if he were to fall in love with her he would raise no objection to it.

When they had dined, the lord declared his intention of going out to inspect the woodlands around the castle. He insisted that Gawain should remain where he was, and to his daughter he gave instructions to do everything she could to make their guest comfortable.

Once the knight had departed Gawain and the maiden sat down together in a quiet corner and began to discuss the matter of her father's strange behaviour.

'Had I known what he was planning I would have tried to warn you,' she said. 'As it is I do not know how best to help you escape. I am sure that my father has instructed his servants to keep watch and to see that you do not leave here before he returns.'

'Do not fear, maiden,' said Sir Gawain. 'In truth your father has shown me nothing but kindness and courtesy, and I can scarcely blame him for that. I would be churlish if I thought ill of him for any reason that I have been shown.'

'I hope you are right,' said the maiden. 'There is a saying I have heard which is: "Never praise the day until it is over, and never thank your host until morning." God grant that you may leave here tomorrow with nothing but good words for your host of this night.'

Shortly after, the knight returned. He seemed glad to see Gawain, and that he was apparently getting along so well with his daughter. He asked if Gawain was hungry again, and required anything for supper, but the hero declined with polite words, asking only for fruit and a little wine before bed. His host seemed well pleased with this, and called to his servants to make up a bed. 'For tonight, Sir Gawain, I wish you to lie in my own bed,' he declared. 'I would have you be as comfortable as possible.' He smiled. 'Indeed, nothing pleases me more than that any guest should have everything he wants. The only thing that distresses me is to offer hospitality to those who fail to ask for anything that gives them joy.'

Gawain assured him that he was well pleased, and that there was nothing more that he required. The host nodded sagely and clapped his hands. At once servants appeared with tapers to light them to bed. The knight himself ushered Gawain into his room. And very fine it was too, decorated with rich hangings and illuminated with tall candles in golden sconces. The bed itself was large and bedecked with silk and samite and with the softest pillows imaginable.

'Rest well, sir knight,' said the host, 'and be sure to leave the candles burning. That would please me greatly.' With these words he withdrew, but as the door to the chamber closed Gawain saw that the maiden had entered, and was standing quietly by the bed. Before he could say anything, she removed her shift and slipped naked between the sheets. Then she laid a finger to her lips and whispered, 'Sir, it is my father's wish.'

Full of wonder Gawain undressed and got into bed. He lay beside the maiden for a time, then took her in his arms. For a while they lay thus, until Gawain's ardour began to get the better of him and he clasped her closer and began to kiss her face and breasts. Then, when he would have had his way with her, she said, 'Forebear, sir, I am not unguarded.'

Gawain looked around. By the light of the candles he could see nothing untoward in the room.

'Tell me the truth,' he said. 'Is there someone present whom I cannot see?'

'Do you see that sword that hangs on the wall?' the maiden asked. Gawain looked and saw a great weapon in a richly embroidered sheath hanging on the wall opposite the bed. 'It is an enchanted sword,' the maiden told him. 'If anyone does anything in this room which is not absolutely honest and true to the highest moral code, it leaps forth of its own volition and runs him through. If you do what you want with me you will die. Many have tried in the past,' she added sadly. 'I have seen many dead men lie beside me in the morning, their blood rather than mine staining the sheets.'

Gawain was aghast. Never had he heard of such a thing. Then he began to wonder if the girl was not simply saying this in order to save herself, and he reflected that if ever it came out that he had lain all night next to a woman, and the two of them naked, but had done nothing, he would never be able to hold his head up again.

'I do not fear this enchantment,' he said boldly, 'half as much as I long to hold you and love you.' And he clasped the maiden so tightly that she cried out. At once the sword leapt out of its sheath and drove point down into the bed. It shaved a piece of skin from Gawain's flank and stuck through the sheets and covers into the frame of the bed itself. Then just as swiftly it withdrew and returned to its scabbard.

Gawain lay stunned with shock, all desire quite gone from him. Gently the maiden staunched the trickle of blood from his side. 'Now lie still, my lord,' she said. 'I do believe that you thought my words nothing more than an excuse. Yet I promise you I have never warned any other man as I did you. You are lucky to escape with no more than a scratch! Be still now and forebear to touch me in that way again and you may survive the night.'

Now Gawain felt both anger and shame. Anger that he had been brought to this place, and shame that his prowess as a lover of women was frustrated. He looked at the sword and then at the maiden, wishing that the candles did not burn so bright, for they showed all the beauty of the maiden, and awoke in him again all his former desire. Despite himself he could not help reaching out to caress her.

At once the sword flashed forth again, this time causing a slight wound in Gawain's neck. It sliced through the sheet by his ear and returned to its sheath. Then Gawain realized there was nothing he could do, and lay still and silent. After a moment the maiden asked him if he were still alive.

'Aye,' he said. 'But you will get no more trouble from me this night.'

Thus they both lay until the morning, neither speaking nor sleeping. With the dawn the host came knocking at the door of the chamber. When he entered and saw that Gawain was still alive he could not conceal his wonder. 'What! Are you still living?'

'That I am, my lord,' replied Gawain, 'though it is no thanks to you.'

Coming closer the knight saw the blood on the sheets. 'So!' he cried. 'You have tried to dishonour my daughter. How is it you are not dead?'

Then Gawain saw that there was no point in trying to hide the events of the night. 'That sword did the damage to me that you see. Yet I am not much hurt. I can assure you that your daughter is just the same now as she was last night.'

The host stared at Gawain in astonishment. 'So, it has happened at last,' he said. 'I have waited long for this moment, sir knight. That sword has great and powerful spells set round it, that it should kill every unworthy man who lay beside my daughter. Only when one came who was the best would it spare him. I see that it has chosen you. I am glad that this long enchantment is finally over. Sir, you may have my daughter. Besides which, everything else in my castle is yours to do with as you will.'

'Sir,' said Gawain, 'this maiden is enough of a reward for any man. I have no need of anything else.'

Then came a time of rejoicing. For word soon spread that a knight had come who had lain beside the maiden and not been killed by the sword. The lord's people began to arrive from every part of his lands, and a feast was prepared at which everyone had enough to eat and more. Entertainers sang and played and merry sports were enjoyed by all. At the end of the day the knight himself married his daughter to Gawain, and then led them back to the room where the enchanted sword hung. The he left them alone, and this time there was no barrier between them. You may be sure it was no sword that was unsheathed that night! For Gawain and the maiden desired each other greatly, and passed the night in joyful disports.

Thus Gawain remained at the knight's castle for several weeks, until it was borne in upon him that he had set out from Cardeuil in search of a day's adventure and stayed away for far longer than that. Then his thoughts turned towards the court and his friends and his king. He spoke to the host, asking leave to return home and to take the maiden with him. To this the host gladly gave his ascent, for he knew that his child would be honoured at Arthur's court. Therefore next day Gawain and his lady set forth, but they had not gone far before the maiden wanted to turn back, for she sorely missed her greyhounds which she had raised from a litter, and had spent long months training. Willingly Gawain returned and fetched them for her; then they rode on companionably together until they espied a fully armed knight riding towards them. Without a word of greeting, or challenge, he galloped up and seized hold of the maiden's reins and made to ride off with her.

Now Gawain had no armour or weapons with him save for his sword, having deemed that he would simply return to the court with his lady. Yet he spurred his mount fiercely and came abreast with the stranger.

'Sir,' he cried, 'you can see that I am not armed. Yet you have behaved very churlishly by attempting to take my lady from me in this fashion. I bid you unarm and then let us fight on equal terms. Or if you will not, then wait here while I return to the castle which lies close by and I will bring armour of my own. Then we shall have a proper contest, and if you win this lady fairly you may have her!'

The knight glared back at Gawain haughtily. 'You are in no position to command me to do anything,' he said. 'But since you are unarmed, let us have a contest of another kind. You say this lady is your love and expect me to believe that simply because she rides with you. I say let us place the maiden in the road here and you and I shall withdraw to either side. Then she can choose between us. If she wants to go with you I will not contest it; if she chooses me you will allow it.'

'Very well,' said Gawain, for in his heart he was certain that the maiden loved him so well that she would choose him without hesitation. Thus the two knights withdrew a little and both called out to the maiden to choose between them.

Now hear what the maiden did. She sat on her horse and looked from one to the other. She was thinking that Gawain would indeed protect her if she went to him, but she also wondered if he were truly strong enough to overcome the stranger. Gawain wondered only why she was taking so long to come to him. Then he saw with astonishment that she turned her horse and rode towards the stranger. You may be sure that Gawain felt nothing but grief at this, and that this grief turned swiftly to anger. Yet he said nothing, for his courtly training would not permit him to speak unkindly to any lady.

'Now sir,' said the knight, 'are you in agreement that the lady has chosen to ride with me?'

'Believe me when I say that you will get no trouble from me,' said Gawain grimly. 'I shall never fight over anything that does not care for me!'

And so the stranger knight and the maiden rode off together, but when they had gone only a little way the maiden began to cry piteously for her greyhounds, which were left behind with Gawain.

'Weep not, maiden,' said the knight. 'You shall have your dogs.' Then he rode back the way they had come until he overtook Gawain and called upon him to stop.

'Those dogs belong to my lady!' he roared. 'Give them up at once.'

Gawain looked at him scornfully. 'Shall we make the same arrangement?' he said. 'Let us have the dogs decide.'

He untethered the dogs and went apart a little way. Then both knights called and whistled. The greyhounds at once went to Gawain, whom they knew from the maiden's home. 'It seems they have chosen,' he said.

Then the maiden, who had ridden up, cried that she would not go another step until the dogs were returned to her. Gawain shook his head. 'You shall not have them,' he said. 'They chose to remain with me just as you chose to go with this knight. They at least are faithful,' he added with a touch of bitterness.

'Sir, will you give up the dogs?' cried the knight.

Gawain shook his head.

'Then we must fight after all,' said the knight.

'As you will,' said Gawain, and drew his sword.

Thus they fell to hacking and hewing, and even though Gawain wore no body armour he soon defeated the stranger and dispatched him with a single blow.

Then the maiden, weeping, threw herself at his feet. 'Ah, sir,' she said, 'now am I glad that you are the victor, and if I behaved foolishly towards you I beg for your forgiveness. I was afraid that you would be hurt since you had no armour. I only wanted to save you from harm.'

'It seems to me that you care for me less than for your dogs,' said Gawain bluntly. 'Indeed, I see that this is so, and that you never really loved me at all. It is well said that women are faithless, and so I have found to be the case.'

Then Gawain recovered his horse and rode away, ignoring the cries of the maiden; nor did he ever see her again after that, and nor can I say what happened to her. As for Gawain he returned to Cardeuil a sadder and wiser man, and told his adventure to King Arthur and the knights, how at the beginning it was fine and dangerous, but how it ended badly because of the faithless woman.

4

The Story of the Crop-Eared Dog

EACHTRA an Mhadra Mhaoil or *The Story of the Crop-Eared Dog* is one of two or three remarkable Arthurian stories written in medieval Irish and dating from the fifteenth century. They are virtually unique for a number of reasons, the most important being that they encapsulate an entire world of Celtic storytelling in an Arthurian form. It seems unlikely that there was ever a large-scale Irish tradition of Arthurian stories – Arthur was first and foremost a British hero. However, he was also a Celt, and this meant that in a Celtic-speaking culture such as Ireland it was inevitable that his deeds should be celebrated. But what deeds! Nowhere else, in all the vast architecture of the Arthurian mythos, was there ever a court, or characters, quite like these. Right from the start, where Arthur is invoked as 'King Arthur, the son of Iubhar (Uther), the son of Ambrosius, the son of Constantine' who convenes a hunting expedition 'in the Dangerous Forest, on the Plain of Wonders', we can see coming together two great storytelling styles: the ornate, magical work of the Celtic bards, and the rich imaginative world of the medieval romancers. Nor is one disappointed by what follows, a sensational, wild, extraordinary tale of magic and adventure which few – if any – of the Norman and Anglo-Norman writers was ever to achieve.

Though the texts are late in composition, dating from the fifteenth to the sixteenth centuries, they may well reflect a much earlier strand of Celtic storytelling. So far no precise analogies have come to light for either *The Story of the Crop-Eared Dog* or its companion piece *The Story of the Eagle-Boy*. A third Irish text, *Ceilidhe Iosgaide Leithe*, or *The Visit of the Grey Hammed Lady*, seems to owe more to ancient Faery tradition in Ireland than to Arthurian literature, and may well, as has been suggested by several other scholars, have had its Arthurian content grafted onto an older tale. A fourth story, *Eachtra an Amadain Mor*, or *The Story of the Great Fool*, may be a direct echo of the Perceval story (see pages 30–47). Certainly, in the present story, the fantastic islands, each with its own guardian or champion, seem to derive from the form of Celtic tale known as *Immrama* or Voyages. Here it has been superimposed over the typical knightly exploit where the hero meets with a different adventure at every turn of the road or clearing in the forest. Whatever the truth, these stories make for fascinating reading, and open a window onto a whole new dimension of Arthurian tales.

For this reason, I am especially glad to include this story here, and would encourage any interested reader to seek out the original text, which includes *The Story of the Eagle-Boy*, an equally wondrous tale, in the edition and translation by R.A.S. MacAlister (Dublin, Early Irish Text Society, 1910). I have retained MacAlister's numbered sections throughout.

I

ING ARTHUR, THE SON OF UTHER, the son of Ambrosius, the son of Constantine, convened a great hunt in the Dangerous Forest on the Plain of Wonders. Never in all the world was such a gathering brought together. More warriors and women, singers and poets, musicians and servants were there than there are joints in the human body, or days in the year, or plants on the earth. There were the twelve knights of the Round Table, the twelve knights of council, the twelve knight of activity, the two hundred and two score knights of the Great Table, and the seven thousand knights of the royal household.

And all this great company began to spread out through the Dangerous Forest and across the Plain of Wonders, following the trail of the hunt through glen and valley and thicket. But for that first day the king of the world sat in his own tent and listened to the voices and whistles of the huntsmen, the barking of the dogs, the shouts of the nobles and the songs of the bards and said nothing. And at the end of the day the hunt returned with word that they had caught nothing. And so, as they all foregathered for the evening feast, they petitioned the great king to ask what they should do. And King Arthur replied in a loud clear voice: 'My people, there are many *gaesa* upon me' (by which he meant that commands were laid upon him that he could not refuse) 'and one of them is that I must convene this great hunt once every seventeen years, and if the first day is unsuccessful, then I must remain for the second, and the third and so on until the hunt has brought back the spoils.'

And when he had said this the king looked around upon every side and saw coming toward him a young champion dressed in a tunic of fine silk and armour of the utmost splendour, and with a mantle of gold around him. And at his side he had a beautiful sword with a hilt of gold, and about his brows a thin diadem of gold, and in his right hand two white ash spears, and in the other he carried a lantern. He was as handsome as the dawn, with fair white skin and clear grey eyes, and shapely mouth, and there was not a single thing with which you could have found fault.

And this stranger came right up and stood before King Arthur, who asked who he was and what he wanted there.

'I have come to seek combat with three of your best warriors, for I have heard that there is not a king in all the world with a better or more glorious band of heroes, and I would find out for myself if this is true.'

When they heard this the entire court changed in a moment from a mood of welcome to one of hostility, and they rose up against the Knight of the Lantern as though he was their bitterest foe. He, on seeing this, thrust the edge of his shield into the earth, and his two spears beside it, and drew his gold-hilted sword, and stood ready for combat. And King

Arthur looked about him and asked who among his household would accept this challenge.

The White Knight, who was the son of the King of France, stepped forward, and the two of them drew apart and engaged in combat. The very ground quaked at their meeting, and both fought with all their strength. But the White Knight was no match for the stranger, and in a little while he stood beaten and bound as a prisoner to the Knight of the Lantern.

Then the Black Knight, who was the son of the King of Caolachs, came forward in his turn, and engaged in mighty battle against the stranger. But the Knight of the Lantern defeated him just as easily as he had the other, and bound him. Then he took on several more of Arthur's heroes, and none might stand against him save a youth named Galahad, who managed to hold his own, until the Knight of the Lantern suddenly departed, pouring a dark druid mist around him so that none might see where he went. And after he was gone the king and all those whom the knight had beaten could in no wise leave that place, but stood still and frozen, save that they could speak and move their eyes.

Then Arthur looked around at his defeated warriors and said: 'Evil betide this day! If the women of the Red Hall ever hear of this we shall be mocked until we enter the grave! There is only one thing to do; we must stay here until we find someone to help us defeat the Knight of the Lantern.'

'That is sound advice,' said Galahad.

And so the whole court waited, as though in a spell, and the sun rode high in the sky and all began to feel a great thirst. And King Arthur spoke to Galahad: 'I wish you might fetch me some water.'

'Sire,' replied the youth, 'if you will lend me your arms and tell me where I may find a well, I shall be glad to go.'

'Alas,' said Arthur, 'the only spring near here lies in a valley full of monsters and evil creatures. I would not order anyone to go there, even if I was dying of thirst.'

'Say not so!' cried Galahad. 'I shall go at once, for it would be improper for anyone less than a knight to go on your behalf.'

'My thanks to you, Sir Galahad,' said the king. 'Be sure to take the Quartered Cup which holds enough for fifty men, and go to the Fountain of Virtues, which lies to the West in the Plain of Wonders.'

So Galahad set out at once, wearing the king's own armour, and he took the best route that he knew to the Fountain of Virtues, which was a very fair and marvellous place, and beside which grew a mighty tree. Then Galahad filled the great horn to the brim, and at once he heard a great roaring noise coming from the roots of the tree. And as he looked he saw a strange grey dog come forth. It had neither ears nor tail, and so thick and shaggy was its pelt that one could have stuck apples on the spikes of it, and around its neck it wore a heavy iron collar.

The Crop-Eared Dog came bounding up to Galahad, and to his aston-ishment it spoke to him, asking him why he came there.

'In truth I did not come here to tell stories,' answered the knight. 'I am more used to give gold and silver to listen to stories rather than tell them to others.'

'I ask in the hope that you will tell me your news willingly,' said the dog, 'for if you do I shall be your friend; but if you do not I will surely destroy you.'

'I am come in search of water for the King of the World, whom I serve,' said Galahad. 'My name is Galahad of Cordibus and there, now you have all my news.'

When he heard this the dog welcomed the knight most heartily, and asked him why the great King Arthur should send one so young alone across the Plain of Wonders.

So Galahad told him all about the Knight of the Lantern and how he had defeated so many of Arthur's heroes, and how they dared not leave in case the women of the Red Hall found out and made them all the subject of ridicule.

'Now I perceive,' said the Crop-Eared Dog, 'that the Knight of the Lantern has laid a binding spell upon your king and his men. And believe me that there is no one else in all this land who can release them except me. Therefore take me back with you, and I will help. For I fear that the Knight of the Lantern will return tonight to cut off the heads of all those whom he has bespelled. And I assure you that there is not a man in all the kingdom who could beat him in a fight unaided.'

And so Galahad took the Crop-Eared Dog back to the Dangerous Forest, and there he gave the king and his warriors a drink from the great horn. And scarcely had he done so when they saw the Knight of the Lantern approaching with his drawn sword in one hand and his lantern held high in the other.

When the Crop-Eared Dog saw his enemy approaching, he pulled away from Sir Galahad and ran full-tilt at him. And when the Knight of the Lantern saw him coming he at once turned around and departed as swiftly as he had come, leaving such a dark mist of druidry behind him that no one could follow him even if they tried. Then Galahad and the dog returned to King Arthur, and the dog said that they would go to the top of a certain hill in the morning and there they would be sure to pick up the track of the knight. Then he released the spell of holding which had bound the king and his men, and there was much rejoicing because of this, as well as much wonder at the Crop-Eared Dog.

And so early next morning Galahad and the dog arose and prepared to depart; and King Arthur and his warriors and the women of the court all wished them health and long life and a safe journey, for though there were those who would have prevented the youth from setting forth, he would not be gainsaid. And so they went to the hill that the dog had indicated and there the beast cast about until he caught the scent of his enemy's going, and declared that the Knight of the Lantern had in fact gone over the sea, where they must follow if they wished to capture him. And so Galahad returned to King Arthur and asked for a ship, and the king granted it gladly and sent word to the harbour that a craft should be prepared, and that it should be well victualled, and provided with gold for giving and arms for expelling. And so Galahad and the Crop-Eared Dog set out and went aboard the ship. The knight raised the great sails and they sailed out of the harbour and onto the tumultuous sea.

II

THEY WERE ON THE OCEAN FOR FIVE DAYS and five nights, and at the end of that time they sighted an island.

'Steer for that place,' said the Crop-Eared Dog.

So Galahad brought the ship safely to shore and dropped the anchor. And they went ashore and wandered through that place, finding it the fairest they had ever seen, with lush vegetation, tall trees and streams of pure water that fed the green earth. And they came at last to a beautiful house and went within. There was a great fire burning on the hearth, and tables spread with cloths of pure flax, and golden plates thereon, laden with fine food. But there was not a soul to be seen except for one old man, of whom Galahad asked to know who was the owner of the house and what the name of the island.

The old man stared at him rudely and said, 'Were you brought up in a cave that you have not heard of this place?'

This made Galahad so angry that he drew his sword and would have beheaded the old man, had he not cried peace and praised the young knight's strength. Then he told them that the name of the place was the Dark Island, and that a great champion lived there. Galahad asked about the Knight of the Lantern, and the old man replied that he had been there lately but that now he was gone.

'Tell me where he has gone, if you know,' demanded Galahad fiercely.

'That is no hard thing,' said the old man, 'for he has gone to a place of his in a land not far from here. On the shore of that land there is a great cave, and beside it a tower which is called the Tower of the Dark Cave. There the Knight of the Lantern always stays when he comes to that land. It has two doors, one issuing on the land, the other on the sea, and at the sea-door he keeps a ship always ready, with which to defend his stronghold. But let me tell you now that he is most likely to flee before you to the Island of Warrior Women. For there is his greatest friend and ally the Druidess Abhlach, who is the daughter of Fergus the White, the King of Scythia. You will never encounter one more strong in magic than she, and she guards certain treasures which belong to the Knight of the Lantern, for as long as these are protected he cannot be hurt, much less killed.'

'Tell me more of this,' demanded Galahad.

'I will tell you everything I know, for I have no love for the Knight of the Lantern,' said the old man. 'Regarding these treasures I can tell you that there are three: the cup of the King of Iorruaidh, which Deilbhghrein, the king's daughter, gave him as a wooing gift. While he has this his strength will not abate, even though he fights for a day and a night. The second treasure is the cauldron of the King of France, which the Knight of the Lantern took after he slew the king. While he has this, if he washes himself in it once every year no age will fall upon him. And the third treasure is the ring of the King of India, who is in truth the knight's own father. And its virtue is that whoever looks at the jewel which is set therein, any wound he has will at once be healed. And now I have told you everything I know.'

Then Galahad thanked the old man, and he made them welcome and invited them to share his master's table. Which they did, with pleasure, and afterwards slept that night in the house. But on the morrow they rose early and Galahad asked how they might find their way to the cave and the tower that were the Knight of the Lantern's stronghold. The old man gave them directions willingly, and they went aboard the ship and set sail as they were directed. And when they came close to the land where the knight lived the dog said: 'Let us devise a scheme to defeat our enemy. Take the collar and chain that is about my neck and go onto the land. Then, when you are close to the tower, shake the chain so that the knight will think it is I who am coming. Then he will flee from the seaward door into his ship; but I shall be hidden there and will fight with him. If by chance he ventures forth from the other door, you will be there to stop him.'

'That is well said,' answered Galahad.

But, while the two comrades were laying their trap, Abhlach the Druidess was aware of them and all they planned to do. And she put on her magical green cloak and made a great leap which took her from the Island of the Warrior Women to the Tower of the Dark Cave. And there she found the Knight of the Lantern and told him what was afoot. At which he became greatly afraid, until Abhlach said to him that she had brought a magical *curragh* with her, and that in this they could escape without being seen, even by the Crop-Eared Dog.

And so it was. The druidess and the knight got into the magical boat and sped across the surface of the sea unseen. And only when they were almost from sight did the dog know that they were there, by which time it was too late to capture them. So the dog swam to the shore and found Sir Galahad and told him what had happened. 'But be not cast down,' said the dog, 'for I promise you we shall discover the knight if we have to search the whole world.'

III

SO THEN THE CROP-EARED DOG and King Arthur's knight set forth again on the ship and did not stop until they reached the Island of the Warrior Women and went ashore there. But Abhlach and the Knight of the Lantern were already gone, and there waiting to meet them were the queen of the island and all her women, armed to the teeth, and ready to defend themselves against all comers.

And so there began a long and furious battle there on the shore of the island, and the outcome of it was that Sir Galahad, with the help of the Crop-Eared Dog, won a great victory, and when they left the island they had with them the three treasures which belonged to the Knight of the Lantern, which had been left behind in the speed of their flight. And when they sailed away they left the hall that had been the home of Abhlach in flames. Then they set sail again on the ocean, in pursuit of their enemies.

IV

THEREAFTER THEY WERE THREE DAYS and three nights on the sea, until Sir Galahad saw land to the West and told it to the dog.
'Go in to that place,' said the dog, 'for it is the home of the King of Little-Isle, who is the father-in-law of the Knight of the Lantern, and I am certain that he is close by.'

So they sailed in close to the shore and dropped anchor, and the dog gave Galahad a silver whistle and told him to go ahead to the king's hall and to pretend to be a bard. 'For if you play the whistle it will be as though you were the best musician in the world. But if you see the Knight of the Lantern blow it once, sharply, and I shall hear it and come swiftly to where you are. Meanwhile I shall remain outside, and will wrap myself in a druid mist so that no one can see me.'

So Galahad did as he was bidden and went straight to the house and knocked. And he said that he brought a poem for the king, at which he was admitted, and went inside. There he saw the Knight of the Lantern, and at once he blew the whistle. Then the Crop-Eared Dog burst into the hall and began battling with the warriors who were gathered there. But the Knight of the Lantern had recognized the whistle, and he fled swiftly away.

Then Galahad and the Crop-Eared Dog fought side by side until they had defeated all the warriors of the place and killed the king who was the knight's father-in-law. Then the dog said that they must wait for nine days and nine nights, and that at the end of this time the knight would be sure to return, thinking them long gone and wishing to know the fate of the king and his men.

And this they did. And at the end of that time the Knight of the

Lantern did indeed return. But when he saw the corpses that lay about in the hall as they had fallen, and then became aware of Galahad and his companion, he gave a great leap which took him into the clouds above the hall and none might know where he had gone. So in disappointment the knight and the dog departed. Having first set fire to the hall, they set forth again upon the sea.

V

IT IS NOT TOLD HOW LONG THEY SAILED or where they went, or what adventures overtook them. But when next we hear of them they were off the coast of Egypt, and when Galahad asked about that land the Crop-Eared Dog told him it was ruled over by a king who was father-in-law to the Knight of the Lantern (that was before he married the daughter of the King of Little-Isle, whom the dog slew). 'And further-more,' said the dog, 'the champion of this land, who is called Inneireadh, is the foster brother and friend of the Knight of the Lantern, and both were brought up by the daughter of the King of the Land of the Living, and the King of Greece, who is therefore their foster father.'

Then Galahad looked at the dog in silence for a time. Then he asked: 'I know not how you come to know so much of this knight and his family. Nor do I know aught of you. Now I would ask you, since we have been comrades this long time and have journeyed far together until I am quite worn out with it, tell me who you really are, and who put you in the form you now wear – for as surely as I know my own name I cannot believe that you were always in this form.'

'I do not like these questions', said the dog, 'but since we are comrades indeed I shall answer them. I am called Alastrann, and I am the son of the King of India and Niamh the daughter of the King of the Caolachs. Four sons she bore to my father, as well as myself, but then she died and the king my father took another wife, who was Libearn Lanfolar, daughter of the King of Greece. The Knight of the Lantern is her son, and thus my half-brother. And it came about that one day Queen Libearn was praising her son and telling him that he was the heir to vast lands and riches, when a passing youth answered that the king had other heirs indeed, to whit five sons. This made the queen angry, for she had known nothing of myself and my brothers. When the king returned that evening from the hunt she demanded to know the truth, and why it was that she had never seen these sons. The king told her that it was indeed true and that the reason why she had not seen his other sons was because they were all leading armies in different lands, and would not return unless he summoned them.

'So the queen pretended to be satisfied with this, but secretly she longed to destroy the king's other sons, so that her own child might rule

The Knight with the Sword

The Story of the Crop-Eared Dog

Sir Cleges

The Boy and the Mantle

India after him. And so she sent word to her father the King of Greece, asking him to come and visit her; and, just as she had hoped, when the king her husband heard of the army approaching he sent for his own sons, and their armies, to return home at once.

'And so it was that we were all foregathered to meet the King of Greece, and when the gathering was complete there was no one who spoke more highly of us than the queen. But secretly she spoke to her father and told him that unless we were killed her own son would not inherit the kingdom. And the king her father thought on this and deemed it right. And therefore he pretended that a great war had broken out in his lands between himself and the King of France, and he asked our father to accompany him with his army and fight at his side. And he advised that we should be left at home with the queen to care for the land.

'To this our father agreed, and set forth with the King of Greece, as he thought, to war. And as soon as he was safely gone Queen Libearn ordered a great feast in our honour. But in truth she drugged us all and made us drunk. Then, while we slept, she used her magic to put upon us the shapes of dogs.

'Well, when we awoke, it was a desperate case! We ran away from that place and began to wreak great damage upon the lands around there. But in a while we realized that our enemy was the King of Greece, and so we went and began ravaging the lands until news of us spread far and wide and the king's councillors advised him to gather as many dogs as he could and to set them upon us, to hunt us down and destroy us before we destroyed all the wealth of Greece.

'Now at this time we were living in a valley which had become known as the Valley of the Rough Dogs because of us. And there the hosts of our enemies came and found us, and there was a great battle between them and ourselves, and all my brothers perished. I myself almost lost my life for having retreated to a certain cave, I was surrounded and the host was set to burn me out. But I grew angry and despairing at this and, drawing upon all my strength, I ran forth and attacked my enemies. I can tell you that I did great damage to them in that place, and in the end I escaped and ran straight to the King of Greece and threw myself down before him. He in his wisdom decided to spare me when he heard me speak, and so he took me home with him to the city of Athens and put this great chain around my neck.'

Sir Galahad marvelled greatly at this strange and terrible tale. And when the dog fell silent he asked him how he came to lose his ears and tail.

'I will tell you,' said the dog, 'even though it is the saddest story of my life. The King of Greece soon saw that I had human sense, and even I think divined that I was under enchantment. And for this reason he saw to it that I was well cared for and guarded against attack by people of ill-will. But one day, as I had known he would, the Knight of the Lantern came to court, and when he learned of my existence he quickly realized that I was one of his half-brothers, and so he wished to kill me. But the king had seen to it that I was well protected, and so my evil foe set about another scheme. He spoke to the king's daughter, who was his own mother's child, and persuaded her, with great cunning, to have me killed. And so one day, when I lay dozing in the garden, she came and laid a spell of sleep upon me. Then she took a sharp knife, meaning to wound me, but all she could do was cut off my ears and my tail. At that I awoke and with a great howl I struck her down dead upon the ground.

'Then you may imagine there was a great outcry, and soldiers and warriors came at me from every side, but I defeated them all, and in the end I fought with my former protector, the king, who was wild with grief at the death of his daughter. Well, I slew him as well, and countless numbers of his guard, and I pursued the Knight of the Lantern from that place and I have been in pursuit of him ever since until we met. And now you have all my story,' said the Crop-Eared Dog.

'Never did I hear a stranger or sadder tale,' said Galahad. Then the two companions went ashore in Egypt and the king of that land, when he heard that the Crop-Eared Dog was come into his lands, sent messengers to welcome them and bring them before him. And he greeted them both with kindness for, as he said, the Knight of the Lantern was no friend of his since he had divorced his daughter and married another – namely the daughter of the island king whom the dog had slain. But when they asked for news of their quarry the king could tell them nothing. 'However,' said he, 'it may be that my daughter, who was once his wife, may know more. She lives now in seclusion in a distant part of the land, in a place called the Fortress of Obscurity. Go to her and it may well be that she can help you.'

VI

EARLY NEXT DAY THEY SET OUT and soon arrived at the Fortress of Obscurity, where they were made welcome, for the king's daughter had no love for the Knight of the Lantern, and wished him nought but ill fortune. And when she heard how they were purusing him she said: 'I believe the wretch is in a place called the Tower of the Three Gables, far to the west of here. There is only one way into it and that is through a dark cavern that has a most sinister reputation. He is there now, I am sure, with my brother, the champion Inneireadh.'

So they set off at once, and when they reached the tower the Crop-Eared Dog turned himself into a white dove and flew in at the window. And there he saw the Knight of the Lantern playing chess with Inneireadh; and when the knight saw him he turned himself and his companion into two gnats and flew out of the window. But in his haste he left behind his lantern, and the Crop-Eared Dog took it with him and returned to Galahad. 'Now we have an even greater part of the knight's power,' said the dog. And Galahad looked at the lantern and asked how the knight came by it and therefore by his name.

'I will tell you,' said the dog. 'The King of Scythia had two daughters, Beibheann and Beadhchrotha were their names, and both of them very fair indeed, so that many kings and princes fought over them. But Beibheann declared that she would only marry the man who could bring the lantern of Bobh of Benburb in the lands of Cruithneach. And the property of this lantern was that if he who possessed it should be wounded, he had only to look upon it and he would be healed.

'Well you may be sure that the knight set out at once to get the lantern. He went straight to the land of Bobh and demanded to borrow it. "For if I do nor have it, I shall take it by force of arms." Bohb's porter laughed at this, but went and fetched his master. And Bobh came forth in all his battle array and they fought a great battle. Then as he suffered many wounds Bobh turned his back to return to his house and look upon the lantern, and at that the knight leapt after him and cut off his head. Then he went within and took the lantern, and no one to gainsay him. And he returned to Scythia with the lantern. But when he arrived there he heard a strange and terrible tale. For the two sisters had both desired him so greatly that the elder had taken a knife and murdered the younger. And for that crime she had been burned at the stake. So both of them were dead and the Knight of the Lantern left there and returned home with his prize.

'And so you see,' concluded the dog, 'that no good comes of anything to which he sets his mind.'

'That is a terrible tale,' said Galahad.

VII

THUS THEY LEFT EGYPT AND SAILED ON until they reached an island called the Island of Light. 'But I expect to get no word of our quarry there,' said the dog, and so they sailed on until they reached another island, and the name of that one was the Black Island.

'Once its name was the Island of the Sun, because the sun always used to rise above it every morning,' the Crop-Eared Dog told Sir Galahad, 'but now it is called the Black Island because the Knight of the Lantern came here and fought with the champion of the place and slew him. And thereafter the sun did not rise here and so it gained a new name. Now I know that there is a place along the shoreline called the Red Cave, and when he is here the Knight of the Lantern lives there. I believe that he is there now, with the champion Inneireadh. If you go there alone while I conceal myself, they may be lured to come forth. Then I shall fall upon them also, and together we may defeat them.'

To this the two companions agreed. But they knew not that the Knight of the Lantern had overheard their plot, and that he had at once devised one to defeat them. For he had four rods of magic power which he had taken from the champion of the island, and they had the power to put anyone to sleep for a day and a night if they were set about him. And this is what the Knight of the Lantern did: he waited until the dog had hidden near the mouth of the cave and then he crept up close behind him and set out the four rods so that he fell at once into a deep sleep. Then the knight rejoined the champion Inneireadh and together they went out and confronted Sir Galahad. And so began a terrible battle with the two of them against the one of him, and the Crop-Eared Dog slept on. But we shall say no more of these events, but turn instead to King Arthur and his people.

VIII

NOW A WHOLE YEAR PASSED AFTER GALAHAD departed, and in that time the king and his court felt no pleasure. For they had no news of Galahad and wondered often where he was or if he was still alive. And so at the end of the year the king dispatched ten ships to search for them. And the expedition included many of the greatest knights of the Round Table, including Sir Lancelot, Sir Galfas, Sir Libnil, Sir Bobus, the White Knight and the Black Knight and many more.

The story does not tell of their adventures, but they followed the path of Galahad and the Crop-Eared Dog throughout all the lands where their adventures had taken them. And fate so decreed that they arrived on the Black Island the very same day and the very same moment when the dog lay in enchanted sleep and Sir Galahad himself was being hard pressed by the Knight of the Lantern and his ally.

And when he saw the warriors of Arthur coming, the Knight of the Lantern leapt up high into the air and vanished into the clouds, leaving the champion Inneireadh to fight on alone. When he saw this Galahad's spirits rose in him and he renewed his attack and slew the champion in a moment. Then he greeted Arthur's knights with extreme gladness, and together they went in search of the Crop-Eared Dog and released him from his enchanted sleep.

'Now is the last of the knight's druidry taken from him,' said the dog when he saw the silver rods. 'If we can catch him now we can easily overpower him.' And, though Arthur's warriors were eager for them all to return home together, neither Galahad nor the Crop-Eared Dog would hear of it, but must pursue their quarry again. And so they bade farewell to their fellows and set forth once again upon the ocean.

IX

NINE MORE DAYS AND NIGHTS they were sailing, until they sighted a fair and bountiful land that was called Sorcha. 'The king of this land is friendly to me,' said the dog. 'Let us go there and ask for news of the knight.'

The King of Sorcha greeted them warmly and with great hospitality, for word of their great quest had gone throughout all the world and he knew of their might and prowess. Indeed he was somewhat fearful of them, and that night he made certain that both were given as much to drink as they could until, indeed, they both fell into a drunken stupor. And so it was that in the night the Crop-Eared Dog was taken away, and when Sir Galahad awoke with a headache in the morning no one could tell him anything of the dog's whereabouts. Then Galahad was angered and made a sudden leap at the king and held him powerless and would have cut off his head.

The king cried out for mercy then, and offered Sir Galahad all the gold he could carry and his own daughter for wife. And when he thought about this Galahad knew that he must be cunning. So he agreed to marry the king's daughter, and the wedding took place at once. But Galahad could not forget the Crop-Eared Dog, and ever he sought to discover by secret means what fate had befallen his old comrade.

X

THEN ONE DAY AS SIR GALAHAD WAS WALKING in the garden of the king's palace, he suddenly saw coming towards him the Crop-Eared Dog himself, and with him the Kinght of the Lantern, bound and fettered as a prisoner. Then was the knight astonished and demanded to know what had happened to his comrade.

'That is a long tale,' said the Crop-Eared Dog, 'but I will tell it briefly. It was Abhlach, the daughter of Fergus the White, who took me away while we were both too drunk to notice. She laid a spell of sleep upon me and when I awoke we were at sea. I rose up in a rage and struck the druidess with a single blow that laid her out dead upon the deck. Then I jumped overboard and swam until I came to the Island of the Speckled Mountain, for there I judged I might find the Knight of the Lantern, since the champion of that island was a great ally of his. But I found only the champion, and so I fought him and slew him and jumped in the sea again. And this time I swam for seven days until I arrived at the Island of the Black Valley. But the knight was not there either, so I killed that champion also, and swam on. This time I did not stop until I came to the Island of the Naked Monks, for it was there that the Knight of the Lantern first learned his druidry. But he was not there, and the monks, they all fell upon me, so that I was forced to defend myself and kill them all. Then, when I had rested a while, I set myself to swim on once more.

'This time I did not stop until I reached the Isle of the Dead, which is so called because any man or woman who comes ashore there, and falls asleep, in the morning is found dead. But those who lived there already – who, by the way, were all women – were not affected at all by this.

'Well, to tell it shortly, I came there and went to the cave where the women of the island were wont to sleep, and there at last I found the Knight of the Lantern, and he took the form of a lion and fled from me. But I chased him and caught and bound him. Then I went back to that cave and slew all the women in there.

'When I had done that I found the knight had regained his own form, and then he pleaded with me, and spoke of our kinship, and begged me not to kill him. For, he said, if I spared him he would restore me to my rightful shape and do whatever else I wanted until the end of my life or his. And so I made him swear an oath to this, by sun, moon and stars, and by every creature in the world that would bear witness. And now I am here, and here is the Knight of the Lantern, who will do no more evil.'

XI

THEN WITH MUCH JOY AND DELIGHT they went before the King of Sorcha and told him everything and showed him the Knight of the Lantern, who was much cowed. And that night they dined royally, and in the morning took their leave of the king, whose daughter, now the wife of Galahad, went with them. And they set sail at once and went to the island that is called the Isle of Shaping, for there everyone receives the very best form they might have. And there the Knight of the Lantern gave back to the Crop-Eared Dog his own shape, which was truly the finest that might be seen upon any man from the rising of the sun to the setting of the moon.

After that they returned to the Fort of the Red Hall, where King Arthur and all his great fellowship came forth to greet them. Then all their long story was told, and a great celebration was held in which even the Knight of the Lantern took part. And afterwards it is said that he mended his ways, and became the first lieutenant of Alastrann when he inherited the crown of India. And as for Sir Galahad, he sorely missed his old friend the Crop-Eared Dog, and went often in later times to visit him. And in due time he inherited his father's lands in Lochlann, and even, it is said, the Fort of the Red Hall after King Arthur. But of this the story tells no more.

5

Sir Cleges

SIR CLEGES is an unusual and charming story which is based on a theme usually found in saints' lives. It is one of the few tales set not in Arthur's own time but in that of his father, Uther Pendragon – though it assumes the existence of the Round Table even this early on in the cycle of tales. It is an English story, dating from a single fifteenth-century manuscript preserved in the Advocate's Library in Edinburgh. It may be the work of a cleric with a sense of humour – presenting an unusual slant on the life of a knight. It is a Christmas tale with a long history, dating back to an earlier period of the Middle Ages, if not before. It probably derives in part from the famous 'Cherry Tree Carol' in which the Virgin asks Joseph for a cherry in mid-winter and the tree obligingly flowers in order to provide the fruit. Not strictly a romance, it falls more into the genre of a 'lay', a shorter poem aimed at a courtly audience – though it seems likely that *Sir Cleges*, with its emphasis on the home life of the knight, was meant for a more homely listener. There are thus a number of anomalies to this work, which is nevertheless worthy of rediscovery by a new readership.

I have made one very minor amendment to the story. The original text mentions that Uther gave some of the cherries to a certain lady of Cornwall. I could not help but wonder if this might be Igraine, the future mother of Arthur, whom Uther woos, thus instigating a war with the lady's husband, and inadvertently bringing the entire epic of Arthur into being.

Sir Cleges has been edited several times, notably by George H. McKnight in *Middle English Humorous Tales* (Boston, Heath, 1913), and retold in a modern English version by Jessie L. Weston in her *Sir Cleges and Sir Libeaus Desconus: Two Old English Metrical Romances Rendered into Prose* (London, David Nutt, 1901.)

Y LORDS AND LADIES, LISTEN and I shall tell you of a story that took place in the time of King Uther Pendragon, that was father to King Arthur. In those days there lived a knight named Sir Cleges, and a right fair and noble man was he indeed: open of hand, fair of face, and courteous to all men.

Now this knight had a wife, whose name was Clarys, who was as good and true a lady as ever lived, joyful of heart and generous to all who came to their house seeking succour. Indeed, no man, rich or poor, was ever turned away from their door, and thus they were well liked by all who knew them. In time the good knight's lady gave him two children, who were both fair and merry, and who loved their parents as much as any child ever could.

Every Christmastide Sir Cleges held a great feast in honour of the day. Everyone was welcome who cared to come, and there were minstrels to entertain, food for all, and a warm bed for those who required it. Nor, when the feast was ended, did any guest go away without a rich gift, be it a horse, a robe, a rich ring or a silver goblet. Whatever they could afford, Sir Cleges and his lady gave.

But after ten years the knight's coffers were almost empty from this generous manner of gifting and hospitality to all. However, nothing would dissuade Sir Cleges from holding his Christmas feast, and thereto he pledged his manors in the belief that he would soon redeem them. Thus the feast that year was as generous as ever, but when it was over and the new year dawned Sir Cleges and his lady found that all their money was spent and that they had but few goods left. Indeed, they were soon reduced to living on one last estate, which was too poor to support a large household and thereby Sir Cleges's men began to desert him upon every side, seeking employment elsewhere with other noble lords.

Thus the year passed in less happy state until it came round to Christmas Eve, and then Sir Cleges heard that King Uther was to hold court that year in Cardiff, which was close by his own lands. And every high-born man and woman in that part of the land of Britain was invited, save Cleges himself, who in truth the king believed dead, so many years had passed since he had heard from him. And this sorely grieved the knight, for as the feast of Christmas approached, for the first time in many a year he was not able to celebrate the birthday of Our Lord as he was wont. As he stood at the door of his house he could hear the sounds of revelry come drifting along on the wind, songs and carols and the tuneful sounds of pipe and harp, lute and psaltery. Then was Sir Cleges utterly cast down, and prayed aloud to God to forgive him for failing to celebrate the birthday of His Son in fitting manner.

Then came his good wife Clarys and embraced him and told him to weep no more. 'For this is no day upon which to grieve, husband. Rather come you in and eat the meat which the good Lord has provided, and let us be blithe and joyful as best we may.'

'That will I,' said Cleges, and did all that he could to be cheerful. Thus they went inside and washed and sat down to eat what fare they could find, and spent the rest of the day in joyful mien, playing with their children and making good sport until night fell. And if Sir Cleges continued to feel sorrow within, yet he hid it manfully, and showed the best face that he might.

Next morning they betook themselves to church, and there Sir Cleges knelt down and prayed that whatever befell him his wife and children might be spared from strife. And in like wise Dame Clarys prayed that her husband should find peace and contentment and put aside the sorrow that darkened his life.

When mass was ended they went home again, and Sir Cleges went apart into a little garden where he loved to sit on sunny days, and there he prayed again most devoutly, thanking God for his wife and children, and for the poverty that had been sent them, 'For in truth I believe that if was pride that led me to hold such splendid feasts, and thus to spend all that I had good fortune to possess.'

Now Cleges knelt beneath a cherry tree to pray, and as he stayed there a bough broke off and struck him on the head. At once he leapt up and took the branch in his hands. Then he saw that there were green leaves and fruit upon it, fresh as in the season of summer, and when he looked at the tree he saw that it bore a heavy crop of fruit, which glowed in the dim light of the day like a torch. Then Cleges was astounded.

'What manner of tree is it that bears fruit at Christmas?' he cried. Then he took one of the cherries and ate it, and lo! it tasted better than any fruit he had ever eaten.

Sir Cleges hurried inside and showed the branch to his wife. 'See what a marvel I have found in our garden!' he cried, and the lady was as astonished as he. Then she said: 'Husband, let us gather more of this wondrous fruit and take it with us to Cardiff as a gift for the king. It may be that we shall have better fortune from this moment.'

On the morrow Sir Cleges set forth with his eldest son on the road to Cardiff. They must needs go afoot as the knight no longer had a horse to ride, but took instead a sturdy staff to be his support. And they carried with them a basket filled with cherries from the miraculous tree.

So they went their way until they reached the gates of the city, which was full of people come for the feasting which would continue until the Twelfth Night. There, at the entrance to the hall where King Uther held court, the porter looked at the poor knight, clad in rough clothes and carrying only a staff, and bade him join the line of beggars who awaited the king's largesse.

But Sir Cleges held his ground and spoke firmly. 'See,' he declared, 'I have brought the king a gift such as only God himself could send.' And he showed the porter the basket. He, looking within, saw that this was indeed a rare gift, and being a greedy man he said, 'I shall let you pass, but you must promise me a third of whatever the king gives you.'

To this Sir Cleges agreed, and thus was allowed into the hall. There he met the royal usher, who raised his staff and threatened to strike him if he did not leave. But again Sir Cleges held his ground, and opening the basket, allowed the man to look within.

Then it was as it had been with the porter. The usher saw the sparkle of the fruit and agreed to admit the poor knight if he promised a third of whatever reward the king gave him. And again Cleges agreed, and was allowed to pass.

Now he met a third man, who was the king's steward, and all followed on as it had twice before. The man was about to throw Sir Cleges out, but when he saw what the basket contained he at once agreed to let the knight and his son pass if they promised him a third of whatever bounty the king might give them. Then Sir Cleges sighed, for he saw that whatever good might come from his gift he had lost all of it between the three men. But he nodded all the same, and was allowed to go forward.

He knelt before King Uther and uncovered the basket. 'Sire,' he said, 'I bring you this gift which is surely from heaven itself.'

The king took the basket and looked upon its contents with wonder.

'This is indeed a marvellous gift,' he said, and bade Sir Cleges (whom he had not recognized, so changed was he) sit down with his son at one of the long tables at one side of the room, meaning to speak with him later.

Then the feast began, and the king was very glad to be able to send some of the cherries to a certain lady of Cornwall whom he much wished to impress. (And it is said that much came of this gift, but that is another story entirely!)

When the feast was ended the king called to Sir Cleges to come before him again and asked him what was his will. 'For such a fine gift as that which you brought deserves a rich reward.'

Sir Cleges bowed low before the king and said: 'Sire, I ask only that you give me twelve strokes, and that I may be allowed to distribute them as I think fit.'

'What is this?' demanded Uther, frowning. 'I never heard of such a request. If you are jesting, it is a poor jest, I think.'

But Sir Cleges held his ground and with a shake of his head the king assented to his request.

Then Sir Cleges went through the hall seeking out the three men who had challenged him the right to enter, and to each of them he administered such buffets that they remembered them long after. And you may be sure that none of them behaved thus again to anyone who craved admittance to the king!

Meanwhile Uther had withdrawn to his parlour, and there held court with much mirth. And it happened that a minstrel sang a song in praise of Sir Cleges. When he heard this the king took to musing what had happened to this good knight, who in the past had been much wont to visit his court. When the minstrel fell silent Uther asked if he knew aught of the man about whom he sang.

'Nay, sire,' replied the singer. 'He is sorely missed by all who make mirth and joy at Christmastide, yet I hear that he has departed from this land.'

'That is a pity,' said King Uther, 'for he was a good man and true, and I wish that I might see him again.'

Then Sir Cleges, who had been standing near and heard this, came forward and knelt again before the king and thanked him for the gifts he had received.

Uther looked at him in some wonder and asked him how he intended to use the gifts. Then Cleges told him all that had occurred and how he had doled out the twelve buffets. When he heard this the king and all those present began to laugh right heartily. 'Now by my faith,' said the king, wiping his eyes, 'tell me your name, fellow, for I like you right well.'

Sir Cleges looked at the king and smiled. 'Sire, I am Sir Cleges, that was formerly your knight.'

Then the king was astonished, and bade him sit down. And, when he heard how the good knight's circumstances had changed because of his generosity to all men, he at once ordered his coffers to be opened and gave back all that the good knight had lost, and restored to him his lands and more. 'For,' said he, 'if I had a hundred knights such as you, Sir Cleges, I should be a rich man indeed.'

Then Cleges and his son returned home, riding on fine horses and dressed in good clothes, and told the lady Clarys all that had befallen them. And you may be sure that she was glad indeed, and that thereafter they lived a joyful life, and that every Christmas Sir Cleges held as brave and splendid as feast as might be seen anywhere in all the land of Britain.

6

The Boy and the Mantle

THE story of *The Boy and the Mantle* has appeared in numerous versions and in several languages, from which we may assume that it was a popular story – doubtless one of many which, under the guise of chivalric fiction, poked fun at both the institution of chivalry and, by inference, at the moralizers who looked upon such tales as either frivolous or immoral.

Today we may well find this tale less to our liking than the medieval audience for whom it was written. But it is still a timeless story, since most men are jealous at heart, and the true hero, Sir Caradoc, is the only one with the faith not to care about the outcome of the test. Indeed, the fidelity and worth of his lady is borne out elsewhere, in *The Story of Caradoc* (pages 13–29). (In this tale both feature as leading characters, and the lady saves her husband with great courage.) It is also worth noting that all the women, wives and sweethearts are tested alike – this is not a test of fidelity to the vows of marriage, but to the love of man for woman and woman for man.

As so often in these tales the character of the boastful Sir Kay is contrasted to that of the nobler Sir Gawain (though even he is cast in a less sympathetic role here), while the attitude of the misogynist Geres the Little makes him the least sympathetic character of all. Griflet, who appears in several other Arthurian romances, is generally presented as a knight of courage and chivalry; here he is a jester figure, much like Malory's Dagonet, given to uttering home truths from the privileged position of courtly fool.

Earlier versions of the story exist in which the mantle is replaced by a horn; those who drink from it – generally the wives of the Round Table knights – are unable to help spilling its contents over themselves, and it is in this form that it appears in *The Story of Caradoc*. In yet another variation, the mantle is poisoned, and anyone who wears it is at once struck dead or consumed by fire. Malory tells a version of this in Book 2 of *Le Morte d'Arthur*.

Generally, however, the object is to show up the hero's wife as both faithful and modest, always at the expense of the other noble ladies, who are forced to admit their own infidelities when they try on the all-revealing mantle. I have suggested that the lady who sends the youth to Camelot may well be the same as she who made it – an otherworldly woman of the type found extensively in Arthurian romances. Her function is ever, as here, to test the strength of Arthur's knights, not only in the physical realm, but in the moral as well.

The version used primarily in the writing of this story is the Old Norse 'Saga of the Boy and the Mantle' translated by Marianne E. Kalinke from her own edition of the text, *Mottuls Saga*, and included in *The Romance of Arthur III* edited by James J. Wilhelm (New York and London, Garland Publishing, 1988). I have also made use of the fifteenth-century ballad included in *The Reliques of Ancient English Poetry* edited by Bishop Thomas Percy (London, Dodsley, 1765), and the Old French *Le Lai du Cort Mantle*, (Lay of the Short Mantle), which was also included in Dr Kalinke's edition.

Y LORDS AND MY LADIES, LISTEN and I will tell you the
story of an adventure that took place one year in King Arthur's
great city of Camelot. Never was there a more splendid place
than this; nor could you find finer knights and ladies than
those who attended at the feasts which King Arthur and Queen Guinevere
gave. Everyone was invited, from the four corners of the realm, for Arthur
loved to know all that happened in his lands, and in this way he learned
of many things that might otherwise have passed unnoticed. To everyone
who came he gave the richest of gifts, armour and weapons to the knights
and horses and hounds to the ladies; and the queen likewise had all of
the ladies visit her in her own suite of rooms, where she gave them fine
silks and samites, as well as rich and costly jewels.

And so it came about that on a day at the beginning of the feast of
Pentecost, when the court was especially brilliant, the king and queen
and all their guests went to mass in the morning and then returned to
the great hall for dinner. But, as was his custom, King Arthur refused to
sit down and eat until he had heard of some new wonder. Sir Gawain,
who was serving as chief steward at that time, did his best to persuade
the king to dine, but Arthur was adamant. At that moment a young
man was sighted approaching Camelot on a horse that had clearly been
ridden hard.

'Now by my faith,' said Gawain, 'I believe we may be able to go in to
dine; for unless I am mistaken, this youth is the harbinger of a new
wonder.'

'Well, we shall see,' said the king.

The youth entered the hall and was stopped by Sir Kay who demanded
to know his business.

'As to that,' the youth replied, 'I shall speak to no one but King Arthur
himself of this.'

'He is there,' said Kay, and showed the youth where the king sat on
his throne, dressed in splendid robes.

At once the youth made his way through the courtiers who thronged
about the king, and all made way for him. He made a gracious bow to the
monarch and said: 'Sire, I have come on behalf of a lady to ask of you a
boon. But I must tell you that I may not say who the lady is or what it is
she desires until you have agreed to grant her wish. Yet I will say that it
shall bring no ill-repute to either you or your court.'

'That is well said,' Arthur replied. 'Speak now, and tell me of your
lady and her wish.'

By way of answer the youth took from out of a little pouch that he
carried at his side a most beautiful and remarkable cloak. If I tell you that
no finer had ever been seen in that hall then you will know that I speak
the truth and that it was truly remarkable. It seemed to shimmer as one
looked upon it, and where it was embroidered with a shifting pattern of

leaves, they seemed to be living rather than made with human artifice. And the strange thing was that the harder one looked at the mantle to see how it was made the harder it became to see it.

'Sire,' said the youth, holding up the mantle, 'this is a magical garment, woven by an elf-woman in a far-off place. It has this property: let any maiden or gentlewoman wear this and if she has done aught to be ashamed of the mantle will reveal it in this wise: either it will become too long or too short. Only she who is of the noblest and most innocent nature and true to her lover will find that it fits her exactly. This is the boon I ask, for the sake of my lady: that all the women of your court be asked to try this mantle, and that they be not told about its properties until they have done so. For I have heard that only the fairest and most illustrious of women are to be found at this court, and I would see for myself if it be true or not.'

Now at this King Arthur looked askance, as did many of the other nobles gathered about him who had heard the words spoken by the youth. Only Sir Gawain laughed and said this test was surely worth the sport it might bring.

And although he was reluctant to play what seemed to him an unknightly trick, the king had given his word. So he sent Sir Gawain, together with a page named Meon, to the queen's rooms to summon her and all her ladies. This is how Sir Gawain spoke to her.

'Madam, the king asks that you join him in the great hall, and that you bring with you all your gentlewomen and all the noble ladies who are our guests. For there has arrived a handsome young man who has brought a wondrous gift, the fairest mantle that ever was seen. The king has promised that whichever lady it best fits shall have it to keep. It is my belief that it is made by no mortal hands.'

'Surely this is a great wonder,' said the queen, and without further delay she ordered all the ladies and gentlewomen to accompany her, and like so many lovely birds they made their way to the hall.

There the king showed them all the mantle, which sparkled and shimmered with unearthly light. All who saw it desired it greatly, but the first to try it was the queen herself. Imagine her displeasure when, on settling it around her shoulders, she saw it was too short by several inches.

At that the queen changed colour, and bit her lips with annoyance. Meon the page, who was standing by, said to her, 'It seems a little short, my lady, but here is the maiden who is beloved of the noble Aristes. She is less tall than you. Surely the mantle will fit her.'

The queen handed the mantle to the maiden who stood beside her, but when that lady put it upon her it seemed even shorter, barely covering her calves.

'Now it seems to me,' said Gawain, straightfaced, 'that this mantle has grown shorter, even though it has not been worn long!'

'My lords,' said the queen, 'I am sure the garment was longer than this. Am I wrong to think so?'

Sir Kay said, 'I think you are more faithful than this other lady, at least by as much as a few inches!'

The queen turned to King Arthur. 'What manner of garment is this? It seems to me that is has some power of which you have not spoken.'

Then the king somewhat shamefacedly told her everything about the mantle. And as she listened the queen went first white then red, but at last she laughed, turning her embarrassment to jest. 'Now surely,' she said, turning to the rest of the women who were gathered there, 'every one of you will try this garment since I have done so first.'

'Then on this day shall the faithfulness of all of you be proven once and for all,' said Sir Kay spitefully. 'For I dare say there is not one of you here today that has not sworn that she was faithful, or chaste, or true to her lover.'

And when they heard this there was not a single woman there who would not as soon have remained at home that day and kept her honour intact; none of them wished to go near it or touch it. Then King Arthur said that he would return the mantle at once to the youth.

But the young man said that this was not fair, according to the promise the king had made. 'For I shall be by no means satisfied until every maiden or gentlewoman present has tried the mantle. Such was our agreement, and I see no reason to rescind it.'

'You speak the truth,' said the king, 'and I am ashamed to have thought thus to avoid the matter. I promise that every lady here shall try the mantle.'

Then Sir Kay spoke up, addressing his own lady. 'Beloved, do you try the mantle, for I know of no one more faithful than you. Together we shall carry off this prize.'

But the lady looked at the floor and said she would as soon not, for there were many more here whom she knew would fail this test if they were put to it.

'Ah-ha!' cried Sir Kay. 'It seems to me you are afraid, and I would know why!'

'It is not that I am afraid,' replied the lady, looking up and blushing rosily. 'Rather it is that there are many more noble ladies than I who should try this first. I would not put myself forward ahead of them.'

'You have no reason to fear,' said Kay sharply. 'Since no one seeks to put on the mantle, I am sure no one will object if you are the next to try it.'

Biting her lip the lady took up the mantle and arranged it about her. But alas! it came scarcely to her knees at the back and in front rode even higher.

Now it was Sir Kay's turn to change colour, while the lady herself fled from the hall, pursued by the laughter of both knights and ladies.

'Now I dare say,' said one of the knights to Sir Kay, 'that you may boast of your deeds done in honour of this lady' (for Sir Kay was known for a braggart) 'as much as you like, for we know now that there is not another like you in all of Britain!'

And Sir Yder said, 'Surely you have derided enough of us in the past; now it seems only fair that such words should be said of you!'

Angrily Kay said, 'Don't be so hasty to speak of my lady. It remains to be seen how your own loves will fare!'

Then one of the squires, a lad named Bodendr who was known for his courtesy, said innocently enough, 'Surely we are going about this in the wrong way, my lords. Sir Gawain's lady is by far the loveliest among us – surely she should have tried the mantle after our lady the queen?'

'I shall be glad to have that happen,' said Gawain at once, and called forth his own sweetheart, who was widely believed to be faithful and true. However, once she had put the mantle about her it was so long at the back that it dragged on the ground, while in front and to one side it hung most crookedly.

Both the lady and Sir Gawain were put out by this, though the latter made light of it, seeing that his own reputation was far from unspotted. However, Kay would not let matters rest, but exclaimed that he was glad that he was not alone in feeling disgrace on this day. 'Shall I send you to join my lady?' he asked of Gawain's love, but she only hung her head and answered nothing.

Then King Arthur turned to the lovely daughter of King Uriens, a powerful lord and ally who often rode to the hunt with him. 'I have heard only good things of you, my lady,' he said. 'Will you try the mantle next?'

And this she did, but as with the rest it proved ill-fitting, being both over long on one side and too short on the other. Then one of the knights, who was named Geres the Little and who was known to have no good opinion of women, said loudly: 'Now we see how foolish it is to put trust in any woman! They are all too quick to discard a husband or a lover once they tire of him. Indeed, they love the novelty so much we can never trust them. It seems clear to me that the mantle is long on one side because the lady will not hesitate to lie upon that side; while it is short on the other because she does no care if her skirt be lifted!'

At this many people murmured aloud their agreement or disagreement with these words. The maiden herself looked furiously at Geres, while Gawain stared at him so hard that it seemed he would consume him with the look.

Then the king sighed heavily and called forth the beloved of Sir Paternus. 'My dear,' he said, 'will you be next? For surely you are the kindest and most true among us.'

But Griflet, the king's fool, spoke up. 'Sire,' said he, 'don't be so quick to judge before you know the truth. The day may well be praised, but such praise is best left till evening!'

Sir Paternus' love, though she trembled to do so, did as the king bade her; but before she could even arrange the mantle about her the ties which held it at the neck broke off and fell rustling to the floor. At which the lady began to weep and wail and to curse the mantle and he who had brought it. And indeed there were others who looked upon the stranger in their midst with less than friendly mien.

He, however, with scarcely a look at any of them, took up the mantle from where it had fallen and attached fresh ties. Then he turned to King Arthur and held up the mantle again. Suddenly now the king was angry. 'Why are we fasting for so long.' he demanded. 'What is the matter with you all? Let us get this matter over with as quickly as may be.'

But Griflet the fool spoke up again: 'My lord, I love a joke as well as the next man, but surely this has gone far enough. It seems to me that every lady here might as well admit her faults to her husband or love and have done with it.'

To this Arthur would have gladly assented, but the youth who had brought the mantle spoke up: 'My lord, this is scarcely in keeping with our agreement. Besides, what would all those whose ladies have not been tested think of those who have? Do you want to divide your court?'

Then Yder turned to his lady, who stood close by his side. 'My love, let you try the mantle next, for only this morning I boasted of your loyalty to me in front of Sir Kay here, and now I am wondering if I was right to do so.'

And so the lady obeyed at once, and on her the mantle covered her at the front, but at the back it rose almost to her waist, at which Griflet was heard to murmur that he thought this must mean she liked to be had from behind!

His face dark with anger, Yder tore the mantle from the lady's back and flung it on the floor in front of the king. Kay meanwhile led the lady to sit with those who had already tried the fateful garment, muttering that there would soon be a fine large gathering there.

Now it became clear that there was nothing more to do but to have every woman there, young or old, maiden or wife, try the mantle as soon as might be. But there were none that it fitted, and pretty soon the circle of ladies who had failed grew large indeed, while their husbands or lovers stood by with ever more crestfallen faces.

Then Sir Kay said, 'Do not be put out, friends, for at least we are all together in our disgrace.'

To which Sir Gawain answered, 'Nor should we forget the ladies themselves, for it seems we are too concerned with our feelings at the expense of theirs.'

At this the youth with the mantle spoke up, addressing the king. 'Sire, it seems I shall have to depart without bestowing the mantle upon anyone here, though I must say that I find it astonishing that not one lady in all of this great court can be found whom it will fit. Are you certain there is no one else that has been forgotten?'

'He's right,' said Gawain. 'Let every room be searched to make certain there is no lady missing from our gathering.'

King Arthur forthwith ordered the castle to be searched, and Griflet the fool, who had been glancing around all the while, went at once to the chamber of a certain lady who he had noticed was absent. There he found her abed, for she was unwell that day. But Griflet said to her, 'Ah, maiden, you must rise and come into the court, for there is such an adventure as ought not to be missed!'

Then the lady rose and dressed herself in her finest clothes and went into the court, and the brave knight Sir Caradoc, whose love she was, grew pale when he saw her, for he had secretly been glad that she was not present, since he loved her greatly and was ill-disposed to see her perhaps humiliated before all. At once he called out to her, 'My love, do not go near this evil garment, for I care nothing for any misdeed you might have performed, save only that our love is stronger than any such thing.'

'Ha!' said Kay. 'Why do you speak thus? No man wants an unfaithful woman. It's better to know the worst and be done with it.'

But the lady herself spoke out: 'I am not afraid to try the mantle, so long as my love does not care about the outcome.'

'I believe that you are true to me in all things,' said the knight, 'and I care nothing for this paltry test.'

At this the lady took up the cloak and put it on – and behold it fitted her perfectly both back, front and sides. And very well she looked in it too, for it had the property also that it made even the fairest of women seem more lovely than they had before.

Then the youth said: 'Now I think that here is a lady fitted to wear the mantle, and I ask that she keep it. And as for you, sir knight,' he added, turning to where Caradoc stood smiling with joy, 'I dare say you are the most fortunate man in this world. More than seven courts have I visited and in not one of them have I found a lady who was so true and gentle that the mantle fit her so well. Truly has she earned the right to wear it.'

'Madam,' said the king, 'you have upheld the honour of my court where no one else could so do. I gladly give you the right to wear the mantle.' Then he turned to the rest of the court and said, 'And now let us go in to meat, for we have been kept waiting a long time today.'

Thus the court went in to dine, and the young man who had brought the mantle took his leave and hurried away back to his mistress to tell her of the events at Camelot. And if she was not of this earth I should not be surprised, for women of the faery race love to play such tricks upon mortal folk. But this I will say: from that day came much sorrow and unrest, for many of the knights foreswore their loves that they no longer believed in, and those who had loved a long time were filled with unease about their loves. But Caradoc and his lady were most happy, and when they left the court they placed the magic mantle in a monastery for safe keeping. I have heard it said that it is still there, and that the one who owns it now will soon be setting forth with it to test the faithfulness of women everywhere. Perhaps he will come to this court one day – who can say? But for now, gentle lords and ladies, my tale is ended.

7

Sir Gawain and the Carl of Carlisle

THE many tales which have survived that feature Gawain as the hero demonstrate the importance of his character throughout the early stages of the Arthurian cycle. Before Lancelot became the premier hero of the later medieval epics Gawain was the first of Arthur's knights. As the king's nephew, and the son of a king, he had a privileged place at the court, and was besides recognized as a champion of great power. He was also noted for his courtesy, and for his love of women – a fact which later on caused him to be dubbed a libertine. Indeed, as Lancelot's star rose so Gawain's fell, though the reasons for this go deeper than the fickle wind of fashion. The later writers of the Arthurian cycle, who sought to Christianize what were, essentially, pagan stories, recognized in Gawain the last of an earlier breed of heroes dedicated to the service of a goddess rather than a god. The two greatest tales in which he featured, *Sir Gawain and the Green Knight* and *The Wedding of Gawain and Ragnall* (see the version of the latter included in John Matthews' *The Unknown Arthur*, London, Blandford, 1995) both portrayed Gawain as the Knight of the Goddess, despite a veneer of Christian symbolism applied by the medieval authors. It was this which caused Gawain to be steadily demoted from the main hero of the Round Table to a blustering braggart and even murderer, in which guise he generally appears in Malory's version of the cycle. It was for this reason, perhaps, that the two shorter Gawain stories included here (see also *Gorlagros and Gawain* pages 114–27) were omitted from *Le Morte d'Arthur* –though Malory may simply not have known of them.

The two other heroes who appear in this story are not only important in their own right but serve as contrast to Gawain. The first of these is Sir Kay, who, like Gawain, was once both better known and better liked than in his later incarnations. He is listed among the first of Arthur's heroes in the early Celtic stories, and in the story of *Culhwch and Olwen* from the great Welsh mythbook *The Mabinogion* he has a remarkable set of abilities, including being able to hold his breath under water for nine nights and nine days, and being able to go without sleep for as long. In Malory's version of the stories he is a blusterer and a fool, mean-spirited and ill-natured. In the story told here he is somewhere between the two, capable of courage but contrasted by his failure with the more courageous Gawain.

The third of the trio of heroes, Bishop Baldwin, may well be the same as the 'Sir Baldwin of Britain' who features in another Gawain story, *The Avowing of Arthur* (retold in Matthews, *The Unknown Arthur*) where he again serves as a foil to the more aggressively inclined knights. Though he is, as he reminds the Carl in the story, 'in holy orders', he is a knight as well and follows all the adventurous pursuits of a knight. In the older Welsh stories he is known as 'Bishop Bidwini,' an indication of his long-standing association with the Arthurian cycles.

As for the Carl, he is really one of a number of such characters who appear scattered throughout the Arthurian corpus – generally as bold, rough-natured fellows who will just as soon deliver a buffet as a gift, and who possess some magical attributes. The word 'carl' is actually borrowed from Old Norse and meant simply 'man'; in English it becomes synonymous with the word 'churl' (from which we have 'churlish'). In the story given here he is under a spell in much the same way as the Green Knight or Sir Gromer Somer Jour are in the two great Gawain romances named above. In each case the villain is exonerated from his previous behaviour when all is finally explained.

The tale which follows here is a small masterpiece of storytelling excellence, which preserves Gawain's original qualities as a hero and as a courtly knight, contrasting him favourably with both Kay and the Bishop. The story also contains some of the elements of the *Green Knight* story, both in the episodes of the beheading of the Carl and in the feelings evinced by Gawain for his host's wife. Her behaviour, and that of his daughter, may seem odd or even repugnant to us today, but faithfully reflects the power of men over their wives and children in the Middle Ages.

The main source used here is an anonymous text composed somewhere between 1450 and 1470, which also exists in a later, sixteenth-century reworking. The episode of the beheading, which is missing from the fifteenth-century text, is here restored from this version, which in fact retains a number of features which are clearly from an older story. Both have been used in the writing of the story given here.

The best edition of *The Carl* is that by Donald Sands in his *Middle English Verse Romances* (New York, Holt, Reinhart & Winston, 1966). It had been translated by Professor Louis B. Hall in his admirable collection *The Knightly Tales of Sir Gawain* (Chicago, Nelson Hall, 1976) and the two versions were edited by Auvo Kurvinen in *Sir Gawain and the Carl of Carlisle in Two Versions* (*Annales Academiae Scientiarum Fennicae*, Series B 71.2, Helsinki, 1951.) There is a good commentary on the story by Robert W. Ackerman in *Arthurian Literature in the Middle Ages*, edited by R.S. Loomis (Oxford, Clarendon Press, 1959, pp. 493–5). For more about Gawain and his pagan origins see my *Gawain, Knight of the Goddess* (London, HarperCollins, 1990).

ISTEN, THEN, AND YOU WILL HEAR a good story of Sir Gawain, who, as everyone knows, was the finest and best of all King Arthur's knights. . . .

One day the court was in Wales, preparing for the hunt. Let me tell you who was there. Along with Sir Gawain were Sir Lancelot of the Lake, Sir Lanval, Sir Ewein of the White Hands, Sir Perceval, Sir Gaudifeir and Sir Galeron, Sir Constantine and Sir Raynbrown of the Green Shield, Sir Petypase of Winchelsea, Sir Grandoynes and Sir Ironside.

This last named was a noble man indeed. Ever he sought adventure, summer and winter alike. His armour was the best; his horse, Sorrel-Hand, was the strongest and fastest of any; he bore a shield of azure, blazoned with a griffin and a fleur-de-lys; his crest was a lion of gold. Giants he fought, and dragons, and he was as good at hunting as any king.

This day it was Sir Gawain's turn to gather the huntsmen and steward the pack. When mass was ended they set forth, and those I have named were among the first. King Arthur followed after with as many as a hundred more, but it was Gawain, along with Sir Kay and that great bishop, Baldwin of Britain, who led the way. From morning to midday they followed a huge stag, when the mist began to rise and they found themselves alone on the edge of a deep forest.

'We'll find no more game today,' Gawain said. 'Let's dismount and take our rest for a while. We can shelter beneath these trees.'

'Let's go on,' said Sir Kay, who was ever wont to take the opposite view of any man. 'Doubtless we shall find lodging near at hand.'

'True enough,' said Bishop Baldwin. 'I know of a castle near here. But we may want to think twice before we go there. Its guardian is a fierce wild Carl who may give us a rougher welcome than we like. I hear no one has ever gone there who failed to get a sound beating. Indeed such as go there are lucky to escape with their lives.'

'Let's go there,' said Sir Kay at once. 'I'm not afraid of this Carl. In fact, I'll beat him black and blue if he tries to stop me from entering. He'll wish he'd never seen us!'

'Enough of your boasting,' Gawain said. 'I'll not be any man's guest against his will. Let us go there by all means, but we'll ask politely for lodging.'

The three companions rode on until they sighted a fine large castle, where they knocked at the door. A surly porter answered and asked what they wanted there. Sir Gawain replied with courtesy, asking for food and shelter for the night.

'I'll take your message to my master,' the porter said. 'But you may not like the answer you get. My lord knows nothing of courtesy and will soon send you about your business, I swear.'

'Go, you oaf!' shouted Sir Kay. 'Or I'll have your keys from you and open the gate myself.'

Without another word the porter vanished from sight and went in search of his master the Carl. He, when he heard there were two knights and a bishop at the gate, was glad. 'Let them come in,' he said. 'I shall be glad to welcome them.'

The knights were ushered into a huge hall, where a fire burned fiercely in the centre. There stood the Carl of Carlisle, and a more fierce fellow you never saw. Twice the height of a normal man, with arms and legs like tree-trunks and massive hands and feet, he had a harsh face, broad and heavy, with a hooked nose and a wide mouth. A grey beard as broad as a battle-flag covered his chest and he was roughly dressed. But it was not the Carl that they noticed first, but the four beasts who lay about untethered at the edge of the fire: a huge wild bull that snorted and pawed the earth; a lion fierce as a coal; a boar that glared and whet its tusks; and a bear that rose on its hind legs and roared at them.

At once the knights prepared to draw their swords, but the Carl ordered his beasts back with a single word, and they obeyed him at once, cringing, it seemed, at the sound of his voice.

Then Sir Gawain bowed his knee before the Carl, as guest to host, but the Carl commanded him to stand up at once. 'I'm not about to knight you, fellow,' he said. 'No man kneels to me. I'm no lord, but a simple Carl who offers only a Carl's hospitality. Be welcome all.' So saying he called for cups of wine to be brought, and when they came, believe me, they were in vessels of gold that shone like the sun, and held at least a gallon of wine each. But this failed to satisfy the Carl, who called for his own cup, a massive vessel which held at least two gallons. 'Now let's really drink,' he said.

The knights began to feel happier at this, and joined with their host in drinking the sweet wine he offered them. Then, as the time for supper approached, they went out to see that their horses were being properly cared for.

The Bishop went first and found that all had been well supplied with fodder, but he noticed that a little foal was eating from the same trough as their own mounts. At once he pulled the small beast away, exclaiming that it should not 'eat from my horse's trough while I'm bishop here'.

At that moment the Carl himself came out. When he saw that the foal had been pushed to one side a dark look came onto his face and he demanded to know who had done this thing.

'I did,' the Bishop said.

'Then you deserve the blow I'm going to give you,' the Carl said.

'Let me remind you that I'm in holy orders,' said the Bishop.

'That may be, but you know nothing of courtesy,' said the Carl, and with one blow he felled the Bishop to the ground, where he lay unconscious.

Now Sir Kay came out to look to his own steed. He failed to notice the Bishop, lying where he had fallen, nor indeed the Carl, who stood to one side in the shadows, but he did notice the foal, which had moved back to feed again at the trough. With his usual brusqueness Kay slapped the beast across the haunches and drove it off. When he saw this the Carl stepped forward, and before Sir Kay could even raise a hand to defend himself, gave him such a buffet that he fell down senseless.

'You evil-hearted dogs,' the Carl said aloud. 'I'll teach you some manners yet.'

In a while Kay and the Bishop regained their senses and hobbled back into the hall, where they found Sir Gawain toasting his toes by the fire and drinking of the Carl's wine while he kept a wary eye on the four beasts, who had crept away under a table and lay watching him with less than friendly gazes.

'Where have you been, friends?' asked Gawain, eyeing his companions and noting their dishevelled appearance.

'Seeing to our horses,' said Kay. 'But we got sore heads doing it.'

Well,' said Sir Gawain thoughtfully, 'I will go and see to mine.'

Outside the rain fell lashing to the earth and a terrific storm had begun. As he drew near to the stable Gawain saw the little foal standing outside shivering in the cold. At once he led the beast inside and covered it with his own green mantle. 'Eat well, little beast,' he said, and then turned to his own mount. The Carl, who was hidden nearby, saw all this and smiled to himself.

As the time for supper drew near tables were spread with food and the Carl's servants showed the Bishop to the head of the table and Sir Kay to a place opposite the Carl's wife, who now came to join them. She was the fairest lady the knights had seen since leaving the court, as fair, indeed, as the Carl seemed foul, as richly dressed as he was garbed in rough clothes, as delicate and bright as a butterfly as he was rough and solid as a tree. Kay, staring across the table at her, could not help thinking what a pity it was that such a lovely creature should be wasted upon a man like the Carl.

Their host, who entered at that moment, closely followed by Sir Gawain, stopped by Sir Kay's chair and leaned over him. 'Watch what you think, my friend,' he growled, 'or be prepared to speak your thoughts aloud!' Then he turned to Sir Gawain, who had been left standing in the centre of the hall with nowhere to sit.

'Sir knight, do as I bid you,' he said urgently. 'Do you see that axe resting by the door to the buttery? Well, I want you to take it and cut off my head with it. Do as I say and all shall be well. Do not fear, for you cannot hurt me!'

Gawain, startled, none the less bowed his head and took up the axe, which was a magnificent weapon sharpened to the keenness of the wind. The Carl bowed down to the earth and with a single blow Gawain cut off his head. But the Carl did not fall dead as might have been expected. Instead his form wavered like smoke, and there, in place of the ugly, powerful fellow, stood a handsome man dressed all in fine clothes. Smiling he embraced Sir Gawain and thanked him.

'For now have you set me free from a spell of more than twenty years. In all that time I have done only evil to everyone who came here – for it was said that until I could find a man who would do everything that I asked of him, and behave with perfect courtesy, I should never be free. By your gentleness to my foal, and by your obedience in striking me down, I am released. My thanks to you, and my blessing!'

As the other knights looked on in astonishment the Carl escorted Gawain to the table and seated him next to his wife. When Sir Gawain saw her he was so enamoured of her beauty that his thoughts betrayed him. But the Carl, who despite being released from his spell which had bound him, still seemed able to read the minds of his guests, merely said, mildly enough: 'Be comforted, my friend. I know how lovely the lady is, but she is mine, remember. Drink up and eat heartily and put your thoughts to other things!'

Gawain blushed for what had been in his mind and applied himself to his food and wine. Then there came into the hall a lady who was it seemed even fairer than the Carl's wife. She sat down near the fire and proceeded to play the sweetest music on a harp of finest maple, the pins of which, I dare say, were of solid gold. And now it was at her that all three knights looked with equal longing – even the Bishop! And the Carl smiled and said: 'Sirs, this is my daughter. Never was there a fairer or more gentle girl in all the world.'

When supper was ended the Carl's servants came to escort the knights to their beds. The Carl himself, together with his wife, went with Gawain, and showed the knight into his own bedchamber, in which was a magnificent bed covered with a golden cloth. There a squire came quietly in and helped Gawain undress himself. Then the Carl turned to his wife and ordered her to get into the bed. To Sir Gawain he said, 'Now I command you to kiss my lady in my presence!'

Gawain turned a little pale, but steadily he said, 'Sir, I shall do as you ask, even though you strike me down for it.' So saying he took the lady in his arms and kissed her long and lingeringly on the lips.

The Carl stood by with an unreadable look upon his face. Then he said, 'Enough, Sir Gawain. More than this you shall not do. But, since you have done all that I asked of you without question I shall reward you.' Then he beckoned to his daughter, who had entered the room unseen, and bade her get into bed with Gawain. 'I give you both my blessing,' said the Carl. 'I am sure you shall have joy of each other!' Then he left the room and the two were alone together. They looked upon each other, and I must say that each liked what they saw and were well pleased. But as to what took place thereafter I shall not speak, for it is not too hard to guess!

And so we turn to the morning, when Sir Kay and the Bishop were up early. Sir Kay was all for fetching his horse and setting forth at once, but the Bishop said they must wait for Sir Gawain.

Soon the bell rang for mass, and Gawain came to join them, stretching and yawning, for he had slept little that night. And when mass was over the three knights prepared to depart, giving thanks to the Carl for his hospitality.

He, however, was not ready to let them go. 'First you must eat and then go on your way with my blessing,' he said. Then he took Gawain to one side and requested that he follow him. They went to a hut in the woods and there the Carl showed Gawain a great pit full of bones. 'Here are all that remain of the men who came asking for shelter. While I was under the spell from which you released me I could not help myself from acting in this way. Now I am free and I take God to my witness, and you Sir Gawain, that I shall make what amends I may for these evil deeds. From now on everyone who comes this way shall be greeted and entertained as warmly as I know how, and here I shall erect a chantry for the souls of those whom I killed, and a priest shall be brought hither and instructed to sing masses for them for as long as I live.'

Then they repaired to the castle again and sat down to a hearty breakfast. The Carl asked that the Bishop give them all his blessing, which that good man did. And in return the Carl gave him a golden ring, a splendid mitre, and cloth of gold. And to Sir Kay he gave a splendid blood-red steed, more fleet of foot than any that knight had ever possessed. But to Gawain he gave his daughter, and with her a white palfrey and a packhorse loaded down with gold, for she had expressed her love for Gawain and a fear that she might never see him again once he had left that place. And Gawain was glad indeed, for he too was struck by her beauty and gentleness, and was sorely grieved to leave her behind.

'Now go all of you with my blessing,' said the Carl. 'And greet me to your lord King Arthur and bid him come hither to feast if it pleases him.'

Then the knights took their horses and their rich gifts and rode away singing through the woods until they reached the place where King Arthur was encamped. And they told him all that had occurred and relayed to him the Carl's invitation to feast with him.

'I am glad indeed to see that you escaped safely,' said the king to Gawain. Hearing which Kay said, wryly, 'I too am glad to be safe! In fact I was never so glad of anything in my life.' And Arthur welcomed him also, and listened to them relate the whole story of their adventures.

Next day they rode to the Carl's castle, where they were greeted with the music of silver trumpets, harps, fiddles, lutes, gitterns and psalteries. The Carl himself knelt before Arthur and made him welcome. Then the whole party went into the great hall, where a magnificent feast was laid ready. Nothing was lacking, you can be sure! The tableware was of gold, the linens of the finest, and the food ... ah, lords, it was such as one may only dream of. Swans there were, and pheasants; partridges, plovers and curlews enough for all. Wine flowed in rivers into golden bowls and cups of finest glass. Not a single person was there who did not eat and drink to their fill.

So pleased was King Arthur with all of this that at the end of the feast he summoned the Carl before him and made him a knight and gave him all the lands about Carlisle to hold for the rest of his days. And so they feasted and made merry for the rest of the day, and repaired to bed that night. And on the morrow Gawain married the Carl's daughter, Bishop Baldwin himself conducting the ceremony.

Then the Carl was happy indeed, and decreed a further week of feasting and games. And in time after he built a fine palace and a rich abbey in the fair town of Carlisle, and there Franciscan monks sang masses for the souls of those the Carl had slain while he was under enchantment.

Thus my story is told. May all here find rest this night and every night. Amen.

8

The Lay of Tyolet

TYOLET belongs to the genre of works called *lais* – short, usually romantic poems intended for a courtly audience, but which often preserve material from an earlier period. It is these brief tales which constitute the raw material from which the great epic cycles of Arthurian romance were formed, and many of the stories told in this form turn up again, usually in a hugely extended and elaborated way, in the later romances.

Thus we can see echoes of the boyhood of the Grail hero Perceval in the story of Tyolet, while a thoroughly muddled version of the main story turns up, with Lancelot as the hero, in the vast *Vulgate Cycle*. It is generally acknowledged by the majority of scholars that the *lais*, especially the ones which originated in Brittany, as well as those by the acknowledged mistress of the *lai*, Marie de France, contain an extensive amount of Celtic material. They may well, indeed, be the descendants of the original stories, carried overseas by the Celtic bards fleeing before the Saxon hordes after the disappearance of Arthur in the sixth century. Planted in the fertile soil of Normandy, these tales returned to Britain, in the guise of the new courtly literature, in the eleventh century, and formed the basis of subsequent Arthurian epics.

Tyolet does not appear as a character in any other Arthurian tale though, as noted above, elements of his story reappear in different guise in various later romances. Indeed, it seems more than likely that the original story which inspired the anonymous author may have been the same as that upon which Chrétien de Troyes based his story of Perceval. *Tyolet*, however, is full of details which are missing from the latter, such as the teaching of the youth by a faery woman, and the transformation of the stag into a knight. The exchange between Tyolet and this character is both comedic and archetypal, and may indeed derive from a far more ancient question-and-answer sequence. The episode in which the hero gives the spoils of his adventure to another, who then claims it for himself, is found in the romances of Tristan among others.

The text, which dates from the thirteenth century, has been edited several times, notably by Gaston Paris in *Romania* 8 (1879), pp. 40–50. I have used the translation of J.L. Weston in her *Guingamore, Lanval, Tyolet, Bisclavaret: Four Lais Rendered into English Prose*. (London, David Nutt, 1900). An interesting commentary by Herman Braet, 'Tyolet/Perceval: the Father Quest', can be found in *An Arthurian Tapestry: Essays Presented to Lewis Thorpe* (Glasgow, French Department of the University, 1981).

HERE WERE FEWER PEOPLE IN BRITAIN in the time of King Arthur, but in spite of this the great king assembled a fellowship of knights the equal of which has not been seen before or since. Though it is true that there are brave knights in this land still, they are not as they were in those older times. For then the best and bravest knights were wont to wander through the land every day in search of fresh adventures, often finding none and being forced to sleep out under the stars with only their horses for company. When they did find adventures they pursued them, and afterwards returned to the court to tell what had occurred, so that it could be written down by clerks and retold in later times, whenever folk might like to listen.

One such tale is that which I am about to tell: of a brave knight named Tyolet, who was fair, proud, skilful and valiant. And this youth had a particular ability, which was that he could whistle and call up any creature of the woodland that he liked. It is said that a faery woman taught him this skill, and he used it well, for he lived in a distant and lonely tract of woodland, all alone with his mother, and whenever they needed meat Tyolet would go out and summon a beast and slaughter it for the table. But he never slew more than they needed, and indeed he loved the creatures of the wood as if they were his kin.

Tyolet's father had died when he was but a child, leaving his mother alone. She brought up her son in the woods and kept him from the world outside, though he was allowed to wander wherever he wished in the woodland. And thus he saw few other people, and grew towards manhood in ignorance of the world.

One day his mother asked Tyolet to go forth and kill a stag for the table. Straightway he set forth, and wandered the woodland until noontide without sight of a single beast. Then he was sorely vexed and thought to return home, when under a sheltering tree he saw a great stag with a mighty spread of antlers. And Tyolet drew his knife and whistled to call the proud beast to him.

Hearing his whistle the stag looked toward him, but it made no move to approach. Rather, it turned away, and went at a slow and stately pace in among the trees. Tyolet, in astonishment, followed it to a river bank and watched as it swam easily across. He himself dared not follow, for it was a wide and swiftly-flowing stream, and beyond it lay open country where he had never been before. Then, as he looked across at the stag, which stood as though waiting for him on the further bank, he saw a fat roebuck approach along the bank where he stood. At once he called it to him and dispatched it with a swift blow. Then, as he looked up, he saw that the stag had vanished, but that in its place stood a figure, fully armed, mounted upon a gallant war-horse.

Tyolet stared at the apparition with jaw agape. He had never seen anything like this in his whole life, and wondered what manner of creature it was. Then the knight called out to him across the water, asking him who he was and what he was doing there.

'I am the son of the widow who lives in this forest. I am called Tyolet. What do they call you? And, please, what are you?'

'I am called Knight,' said the figure.

'What manner of beast is a knight?' asked Tyolet. 'Where do you live and what are you for?'

'I am a beast that is much feared,' said the knight slowly. 'Sometimes I live in the forest and sometimes in the open lands. Sometimes I take other beasts and consume them.'

'You are a wonder indeed,' said Tyolet. 'In all the time I have spent in these woods I never saw a creature like you. I have seen lions and bears, and every kind of venison, and never one of them that I could not call to me. Tell me, knight-beast, what is that thing on your head and what hangs around your neck all shining and bright?'

'The thing on my head is called a helmet, and it is made of steel to protect me. That which hangs about my neck is called a shield. It shines brightly because it is painted, and banded with gold.'

'And that stuff in which you are clad, that seems full of little holes, what is that?'

'It is called a hauberk, and it is made of rings wrought to form what is called chain mail.'

'And those things on your feet. What are they?'

'Those are called greaves. They cover my legs and feet and protect them from harm.'

'And that long thing at your side. What is that?' demanded Tyolet eagerly.

'Why, that is my sword,' replied the other. 'It is long and sharp and fair to look upon.'

'And that long wooden thing you hold in your hand. Tell me what it is.'

'That is my lance,' was the answer. 'Now I have told you all that I may, and must be upon my way.'

'I thank you, O knight-beast,' said Tyolet. 'But before you depart I pray you tell me one more thing. Are there any more of you in the world? For I would dearly love to see them.'

'Indeed there are,' replied the knight. 'If you will wait here but a moment or so longer you shall see more than a hundred.'

As he spoke there came a great jingling of harness and a thunder of hoofs, and a great company of knights came into view. They were of the king's court, and had but lately attacked and destroyed a fortress of evil intent and were returning home.

When Tyolet saw them he cried aloud in amazement. 'How can I be like them?' he demanded. 'For never in my life did I wish for anything half so much as this.'

The knight asked, 'Are you brave and valiant?'

'I think so,' answered Tyolet. 'Certainly I should like to be.'

'Then go home, and when your mother sees you she will ask why you are so thoughtful. Tell her you have seen the knight-beasts in the wood and that you will never again be happy until you are like them. She will tell you that this makes her sad, and bid you forget what you have seen. Tell her that she will get no joy of you until you have your way. I promise you that she will go and get you just such mail and arms as you have seen me wear.'

Then Tyolet sped home as fast as he could and gave his mother the roebuck he had killed and told her all his adventures. And, just as the knight-beast had said, Tyolet's mother expressed her grief at what he had seen. 'For these beasts devour others,' she said, 'and how may that be a good thing?'

'Nevertheless, mother, I would go and be one among them, for if I do not I shall never more be happy.'

Then Tyolet's mother went to the chest in which she kept her dead lord's armour and weapons, and she brought them and put them upon her son until he seemed in very truth a knight-beast. Then she said: 'Son, this is what you must do. Go from here to King Arthur's court, which lies to the West, for there you shall find a good welcome and fair treatment. But remember to keep company only with men and women of good breeding. For you are of noble birth and should be with your own kind.'

Then she kissed her son and Tyolet departed and rode over hill and through valley and across plains until he came to the court of King Arthur. And he passed through the open gates and went within, to where the king was seated at high table for the evening meal. Tyolet rode right up to the dais, still clad in his armour, and there he sat, speaking not a word.

King Arthur looked at him kindly and bade him dismount and join the company and tell his story.

'Sire, my name is Knight-Beast, but once I was called Tyolet and I am the son of the widow who lives in the forest. I can catch any beast you like, and am skilled in hunting; but now I would learn the ways of the court and this thing that I have heard of called chivalry.'

'You are most welcome,' said the king. 'Come now and eat.'

Then squires came forward who unarmed Tyolet and put upon him a fine mantle and brought him water in which to wash his hands. Then he sat down to meat, staring all the while at the wonders of the court.

Then, as they sat at table, there came into the hall a very fair damsel indeed, riding upon a white palfrey and holding in her arms a white bratchet with a small bell of gold around its neck. Right up to the dais she came and greeted the king.

'What service may I or my knights do you?' asked Arthur.

'Sire, I am the daughter of the King of Logres,' said the maiden. 'I have come here to see if there is one among your company who will pursue and bring me the right foot of a certain white stag, the hair of which shines like gold and which is guarded by seven lions. Only he who is brave enough to do this may win my hand, for I will take no other but he for my lord.'

'Now by my faith,' said King Arthur, 'this is just such an adventure as is proper to my knights. Do you give your word that the one who succeeds in this task shall be your husband?'

'I do so,' replied the maiden.

And so it was agreed, and King Arthur looked about him to see who would undertake this adventure. You may be sure there was not a man there who did not leap up from his place and cry that the adventure be given to him. But one among them, Sir Lodoer, made the greatest plea, and to him King Arthur awarded the task.

'How shall I know where to find the white stag?' he asked, and the maiden gave him the white bratchet and told him that he should follow where it led. Thus he set forth and followed the dog, which led him through a wild land to the bank of a wide, fierce, greatly swollen water. There the dog leapt in and swam strongly, but Lodoer sat upon his horse and looked with dismay upon the flood and dared not venture into it.

Shortly the dog returned, and the knight took it up on his saddlebow and rode back the way he had come to the court. There King Arthur asked how he had fared, and if he had the foot. But Lodoer only shook his head and said that if another wanted to risk his life the adventure still waited. Then the other knights mocked him, but Lodoer merely said that they should go and try for themselves before they decried his efforts.

And so it was that many of King Arthur's knights set forth in quest of the white stag, but each one returned home empty-handed and was forced to admit that Lodoer was right. Then Tyolet, whom everyone had come to call 'Knight-Beast', came forward and begged the adventure for himself. 'Be sure that I shall not return until I have succeeded, or died in the attempt,' he said.

The king gave him leave to go, and Tyolet took the bratchet and departed as soon as ever he might. He followed the little dog to the side of the great flood and, when it plunged in, he followed, urging his steed into the racing waters. These proved to be less fierce than they had appeared, and both dog and knight soon reached the further bank. There the bratchet ran ever before him until it came to a broad meadow, where Tyolet saw the stag grazing in the shade of some trees.

At that moment there was no sign of the lions which guarded the prize, and Tyolet made good advantage of this, riding as close as he could

Gawain and the Carl of Carlisle

The Lay of Tyolet

and then whistling as he had been taught to draw the beast to him. After he had whistled seven times the stag came and stood submissively by, and Tyolet took his sword and smote off its right foot and hid it in his shirt. Then the stag cried out in pain, and the lions, who were near at hand, came in haste to defend it.

The first leapt at Tyolet's horse and wounded it terribly, tearing the flesh from its shoulder. Tyolet struck it such a blow in return that it fell dead, but his mount now fell upon the earth, and he was thrown clear into the path of the rest of the pack, which attacked him from every side.

A terrible battle now ensued, in which Tyolet received wounds on his back and ribs and shoulders. But in the end he slew all of the lions before falling unconscious from loss of blood. And as he lay, there came a knight who was not known to him, who looked upon his wounded body and deemed him almost dead. But Tyolet roused himself enough to draw forth the stag's foot and proffer it to the stranger, bidding him take it to King Arthur and tell him all that had befallen.

The knight took it with secret delight, for he knew the story of the quest for the white stag, and had longed to succeed in it. Now the chance had come that would enable him to seem successful. Therefore he took the foot and made to ride off, without even a thought for the wounded Tyolet. Then he bethought that if the youth should survive he might return to claim his right, and so he turned back and drawing his sword plunged it into the youth's body. Then he rode on and found his way back to the court, where he showed the foot to King Arthur and claimed the hand of the maiden.

But he failed to bring back the bratchet, for in truth he knew naught of it. And indeed it had returned alone some days earlier, and King Arthur, deeming this a sign that Tyolet had perished, had sent the good knight Sir Gawain in search of his body. Thus, being wise in the ways of men, and wondering at the success of the strange knight, the king sought to delay matters for a further nine days, giving as his reason that he must summon his court to witness the wedding of the knight and the maiden.

Gawain meanwhile followed the bratchet, which led him to where Tyolet lay as though dead. And Gawain saw the bodies of the lions and the dead horse and the dreadful wounds that were upon the youth, and he mourned greatly. But as he knelt by the body, Tyolet opened his eyes and, in the merest thread of a voice, told what had happened. Then as Gawain gave thought to how he might aid the wounded knight, there came in sight a damsel mounted upon a white mule, and Gawain recognized her as a messenger of the Lady of the Lake, whom he had helped on other occasions. And he called out to her to help the wounded man, and she greeted him well and they embraced. Then the damsel and Gawain took council together, and decided to take the wounded man to the leech of the Black Mountain, who lived nearby. 'For, if anyone can help this good knight to recover his health it is he,' said the damsel.

Then they lifted Tyolet onto Gawain's horse and took him to the healer, who washed and cleaned his wounds and searched them and then declared that he would live and be as strong as ever within a month. And very gladly indeed Gawain made his way back to the court, where the false knight was about to wed the maiden. But Gawain burst in and cried that the knight was false, and that he had stolen the right of Tyolet to be acknowledged the successful contender in the matter of the white stag.

Angrily the traitor protested his innocence, and sought for reparation at the hands of his accuser. And so a day was set when he and Sir Gawain should meet on the field of battle to decide the matter. But before that day could dawn Tyolet himself returned to the court, pale and drawn from his ordeal, but hale enough to ride a borrowed mount. And when he saw him the traitor turned first red and then white in turn, and began to bluster and cry out that his was the right to wed the King of Logres' daughter. But Tyolet turned from greeting the king and all the knights who had rushed forward to embrace him, and asked, mildly enough, on what grounds he made this claim.

'Why, because it was I who took the stag's foot!' cried the false knight.

'And who then slew the lions that were its guardians?' asked Tyolet.

The knight grew red, and waxed wrathful, but he had no words to answer.

'Then tell me who was the one smitten with the sword and who the smiter. For in truth I believe the last was you and the first myself.'

Then the knight looked away in shame, and Tyolet demanded to know if he would deny the charges. 'For if so then I offer my gage to you in King Arthur's name and promise to prove the truth of this before all.'

Then the knight began to fear for his life, and there before all he fell down on his knees and confessed his crimes and begged for mercy. At which Tyolet, looking upon him with gentleness, pardoned him, so that the knight fell down and kissed his feet. And Tyolet raised him up, and kissed him, and from that day they spoke no more of the matter. But Tyolet took back the stag's foot and gave it to the maiden, who blushed with all the beauty of a new-blown rose. And there and then did King Arthur marry them, and afterwards they returned home to the maiden's own land, where upon the death of her father they became king and queen and reigned long and wisely together. And here the lay of Tyolet has its end.

9

The Rise of Gawain

De Ortu Waluuanii nepotis Arturi, or *The Rise of Gawain, Nephew of Arthur*, is one of the few surviving Arthurian romances (excluding pseudo-historical works such as Geoffrey of Monmouth's *Historia Regum Britanniae*) written in Latin. It dates from the end of the twelfth century, although the unique manuscript, Cotton Faustina B, held by the British Museum, dates from the beginning of the fourteenth century. It has been attributed, with some caution, to a writer named Robert of Mont St Michel, a Benedictine abbot from the school of Bec, who is the author of a number of theological works.

The story it tells is unique in the annals of Arthuriana, in that it describes Gawain's whole early career, from birth to his establishment as Arthur's nephew – a fact which, as the title suggests, was an important aspect of the story, even though he is not officially recognized as such until the end of the romance. For the rest, Gawain's visit to Rome, and his meteoric rise to fame and fortune, makes a fascinating tale with many original and interesting facets. To my mind it further demonstrates a fact which is already evidenced in the surviving stories which feature Gawain, namely that his position as an Arthurian hero was at one time pre-eminent, far above that of Lancelot or Galahad or any of the better-known knights of the Round Table. Gawain indeed remains a central character in the drama of Arthur's days, but he becomes steadily demoted until, by the time Sir Thomas Malory composed his great book, the character of the king's nephew had been debased to little better than a lecher and murderer. I have traced the course of this descent

in my book *Gawain, Knight of the Goddess* (London, Thorsons, 1991), pointing out there that the systematic blackening of Gawain's character derives from his long association with paganism. Thus his devotion to the Great Goddess, and through her to all women, becomes, in the hands of the monkish writers of the medieval Arthurian romances, a very human, libidinous, trait, which put Gawain beyond the pale. (The fact that Lancelot is the lover of Queen Guinevere is passed over in spite of this.)

In the *De Ortu* none of this stigma is present. Gawain is, purely and simply, a hero *par excellence*, whose natural inheritance shines through his lowly upbringing, and proves that 'blood will out'. There is something, too, about the message which reaches Gawain and sends him back to Britain as he is about to assume the highest office, which smacks of a genuine historical tradition. If, as has been suggested by other authorities over the years, the Romano-British people did send to Rome for help against the Saxons, it would have been just such a response which might have gone out from the Empire to its old colony. Though we have no direct evidence for this, it makes a fitting climax to a powerful story.

I have compressed part of the action considerably to be able to include the whole of the story. In particular the sea battle, which is long and fascinating, has had to be much abridged. It contains a detailed account of medieval maritime warfare, including several pages on the making and uses of 'Greek Fire', an early incendiary device which was often used to turn the tide of victory in such conflicts. Indeed, the author shows some not inconsiderable knowledge of siege warfare as well as battle at sea, a fact which seems to give the lie to the suggested author being an ecclesiastic.

The text was first edited by J. D. Bruce in 1898 ('De Ortu Waluuanii' in *Publications of the Modern Language Association*, vol. 13, pp. 365–455). Its most recent editor, Mildred Leake Day, also included an excellent translation, which I have followed in making my own rendition of the story (see *The Rise of Gawain, Nephew of Arthur*, New York and London, Garland Publishing, 1984).

N THE TIME OF UTHER PENDRAGON, who was the father of the great King Arthur, a number of royal children lived at the British court. Uther had them there as hostages for the good behaviour of the neighbouring kings over whom he held sway. One of them, Lot of Orkney, nephew of King Sichelm of Norway, was a youth of such outstanding qualities that he became familiar with Uther and his family, and was often to be found in their private quarters.

Now it so happened that Uther had a daughter named Anna, who was still very young and lived with her mother. She and Lot were often together, laughing and joking, and no one thought more of it. But the truth of the matter was that they had fallen in love with each other, and that after a period of shyness, they both gave way to their impulses, with the result that Anna became pregnant.

By means known only to her she managed to conceal the fact of her condition to everyone save her most trusted lady in waiting, and when the time came for her to give birth she feigned illness and retired to her chamber with only her lady as companion. And there, in due time, she gave birth to a male child of surpassing beauty.

Now, with the help of her lady in waiting, she had previously made contact with certain wealthy merchants, whom she had bribed with much gold to take care of her child and bring it up in secret in a foreign land. When she entrusted the child to them, she also gave them, in keeping for her son, a rich cloth of gold, an emerald ring which had belonged to her father, and a scroll sealed with the royal seal which offered proof that the child, whom she had given the name Gawain, was the son of herself and Prince Lot.

Thus the merchants took charge of the infant and took ship for Gaul, where they had business. They landed near the city of Narbonne and travelled inland, leaving the ship to ride at anchor with only a single boy to watch over their merchandise and the child who had been placed in their care. And here by chance came a merchant named Viamundus, a man of noble birth who had fallen on hard times. When he saw the apparently deserted ship anchored close to the shore, he went aboard, finding only the sleeping servant and the child, along with many riches. Struck by this piece of good fortune, Viamundus decided that the fates were smiling upon him, and he took as much gold and other riches as he could carry – and also the child, along with the chest containing all the things pertaining to its birth and station. Then he went home laden to his wife and gave her the infant to nurse.

In a while the merchants returned to their ship, and were horrified by the loss of the child and their goods. At once they sent messengers to go through the land around Narbonne to search for any news of the theft. But they returned in a few days with no word, and sadly the merchants were forced to continue on their way, not daring to announce to the world the true nature of their loss.

Viamundus, meanwhile, hid his stolen wealth with as much care as he hid the child. He dared do nothing while questions were being asked about the crime, for which, if the truth be known, he felt considerable guilt. Indeed he pretended that nothing had happened, spending only a little of the money he had acquired, and that with great circumspection. And thus seven years passed, during which time, both Viamundus and his wife became very fond of their unlawful child, and came in fact to think of him as their own offspring, which all in that neighbourhood believed as well.

At the end of this period, Viamundus decided to pack up everything he had and make the journey to Rome. In part this was because he wished to expiate himself for the theft of the child and the gold – though a more shrewd part of him knew that he could improve the lot both of himself and his family with the money he had kept hidden for so long.

And so, accompanied by his wife and 'son', he set out and soon arrived in Rome, which in this time had been repeatedly sacked by barbarians, and was looking as poor as it ever had in several centuries. However, a new emperor had recently been crowned there, and was exerting himself to restore the city to its former glory. And when he heard of this Viamundus hit upon a scheme whereby he might establish himself in the emperor's favour. To this end he retired outside the city and there acquired a number of slaves and much fine raiment. Then, dressed like a prince, he entered the city and sought an audience with the emperor. Claiming to be a former military governor from Gaul, he offered whatever aid he might in terms of money and men. Delighted and impressed by the dignity of Viamundus, the emperor made him welcome and offered him great estates both in and around the city.

From this moment onward, the career of Viamundus was that of a noble and popular man. Swiftly elevated to the rank of senator, he conducted himself with such kindness and nobility that soon he came to be regarded as one of the most important men in Rome. He was often consulted by the emperor on matters of state, and personally endowed many new buildings in the gradually restored city.

At the same time, the youth whom everyone believed was Viamundus' son grew towards manhood and was as well liked and popular as his adoptive father. He spent much of his time in and around the emperor's palace, and became fast friends with several of the noble youths who dwelt there.

Then, when Gawain was in his twelfth year, Viamundus was stricken with a fatal illness. Realizing that the end of his life was near, he begged the emperor and the pope (Sulpicius was pontiff in those days) to attend upon his death bed and hear what he had to say. And, because of the great love and respect they bore him, both the great men agreed to come.

When they were present Viamundus told them everything about his past: how he had come by his wealth, and, most importantly, that the youth whom everyone called his son was in fact stolen away by him as an infant.

'My lords,' said the dying man, 'I have delayed almost too long in telling you these things – though I have often longed to do so. Now that my time on this earth is almost over, I ask this of you. That you, my emperor, care for the future of the youth, and see to it that he receives an education in chivalry and the ways of knighthood. For I will tell you now, and I ask you, the pope of all Christendom, to bear witness, that this boy is indeed the nephew of the renowned King Arthur, of whom so much praise is spoken in this time. I am sure that in time he will be recognized and reclaimed by his true parents, though I do not know how this will happen. Meanwhile I ask that you speak to no one of his true identity, least of all to the child himself, but to keep these things that I have told you secret until the right time. Then, when he reaches full manhood, let him be sent home, with the proofs which I will show you, and a letter explaining all that has occurred.'

Having heard this in some wonder, the emperor gave his word. Then the boy was sent for and heard his dying father give him into the care of the master of Rome. And he wept to see his father so close to death, until the old man reassured him that he was dying happy in the knowledge that his son should enter the household of the emperor. Then, having received the Last Rites, and with the emperor at his bedside, Viamundus died.

Thereafter the youth became part of the emperor's court, and was treated much as were his own sons. And when, three years having passed, he attained the age of fifteen, the emperor himself invested him with his arms. At that time there were a number of other noble youths due to receive the accolade of knighthood. All were tested in the Circus, where once chariot races had been held, but which now served as lists to the knights of Rome. In the trials which followed the youth outmatched all his peers, and shone so greatly in the field that everyone agreed that he was the finest young knight they had ever seen.

At the end of the trials the emperor awarded the first place to the young man, and gave him as tokens a circlet of golden oak-leaves, and a tunic of crimson silk, which the bold youth declared he would wear with pride for all of his days. Then he asked, by way of a boon, that he be permitted to undertake the first single combat required by the emperor against any enemy who might come forward in the future. To this the emperor agreed, and the youth was much praised. In the days that followed, he became known by a new title, 'the Knight of the Surcote' because of the splendid garment the emperor had given to him. And this name replaced his own for a time, so that the name Gawain was seldom if ever heard in the halls of the imperial palace.

At about this time war broke out between the Persians and the Christians remaining in Jerusalem. Each side was eager to join in battle, but their leaders were wiser and sought to end the affair through single combat. A truce was arranged while the Christians sent word to Rome asking for a champion. Hearing of this, the emperor called a council to discuss the matter, and it was here that the Knight of the Surcote came bursting in, begging the emperor to forgive him for the interruption, and reminding him of his promise to allot the first single combat to him.

At first the emperor was reluctant to give the task to so young and untried a knight, but he could not foreswear his promise, and his councillors reminded him of the prowess displayed by the youth in the lists. And so the emperor gave his consent, and the Knight of the Surcote set forth, accompanied by an escort of one hundred knights under the command of a centurion.

They took ship as soon as was possible and set sail for the Holy Land. For twenty-five days they were tossed on the backs of great waves, then a storm blew up and drove them off course, bringing them to shore at last on the shores of an island ruled over by a cruel and powerful lord named Milocrates. This same man had recently abducted the emperor's niece, who had been betrothed to the King of Illyricum. It had so far proved impossible to rescue her, owing to the heavy fortifications with which the island was guarded, and the overwhelming fierceness of Milocrates' followers.

The Romans came ashore on the far side of the island from its strong forts, in a part heavily forested. Wild animals were to be found there, but were carefully protected because of their scarceness. In fact they were intend for Milocrates' table alone, and fearsome punishments were meted out to anyone who hunted there without leave. The Romans of course knew none of this, and since they required food they went ashore and began hunting. Under the leadership of the Knight of the Surcote they soon took six stags. They were in pursuit of a seventh when they were met by the guardian of the forest, along with fourteen knights, who demanded by what right the strangers hunted the royal preserve.

'We have taken only what we needed to save our lives,' said the Knight of the Surcote.

'That is not good enough!' bellowed the forest warden, and he demanded that they lay down their arms and place themselves in his custody.

'That we shall never do,' replied the young knight, and flung his spear at the warden, who received it in his shoulder. Crying out in agony, he none the less pulled out the spear and flung it back at the youth. It narrowly missed him and stuck in a tree. This was the signal for general fighting to commence, and despite the fact that the Romans were without armour, while their adversaries were fully armed, under the leadership of the Knight of the Surcote, they soon killed them or put them to flight.

Of those who escaped, one went straight to Milocrates, where he was staying in a nearby city, and told him of the strangers. Now word of the Roman champion and his followers had quickly spread through the lands around the Aegean Sea, and all who sided with the King of Persia had been warned to look out for their coming and to do all in their power to prevent them reaching the Holy Land. Thus, when he learned of the strangers who had raided his hunting lands and defeated his men, Milocrates at once guessed who they must be and forthwith summoned an army.

The Romans, meanwhile, returned to their ships, where the Knight of the Surcote was much praised for his courage in leading the foraging party. They now prepared to up anchor and depart, but contrary winds soon made it apparent that they were not destined to leave just yet. The centurion in charge of the Roman knights expressed his concern that their enemies would, by now, know of their presence and were probably even then assembling a force to attack them.

'We must,' he said, 'send spies inland at once to get some idea of their numbers and disposition.'

Two men were chosen for this: the Knight of the Surcote and an officer named Odabel, a blood-relative of the centurion. While they were still preparing to depart an outcry announced the discovery of scouts sent out by Milocrates. These were soon brought before the centurion and, through a mixture of threats and bribes, the Romans acquired much information, including the knowledge of whom they were soon to face in battle.

Now the two spies set out together and journeyed inland to the city where Milocrates was assembling a huge force to attack the Romans. Owing largely to the number of soldiers and knights who were gathering there from all corners of the island, the two Romans were able to mingle with their enemies and enter the city itself. There they learned that reports of the Roman force had been so exaggerated that Milocrates believed a much larger force was arrayed against him. He therefore elected to hold off the attack until his brother, Buzafarnan, could arrive from a nearby land, bringing an even larger army. All of this the Knight of the Surcote heard and committed to memory.

But spying out the strength of the enemy was not all that was in the young man's thoughts. He had in mind a daring plan to rescue the emperor's niece, news of whom had been obtained from the captured spies. Now the Knight of the Surcote slipped into the palace, mingling easily with the enemy and seeking the way to the king's own suite of rooms, where the captive princess was held.

As he made his way through the corridors, the Knight of the Surcote espied a man he recognized, a knight named Naboar, whom he had known at the emperor's palace in Rome. This man, he remembered, had been captured along with the princess, and was now likewise held in captivity. With great daring the Knight of the Surcote attracted Naboar's attention, and when the two men had embraced and exchanged news of each other, they spoke of the princess.

'She is indeed in this very palace,' said Naboar, 'and what is more she has heard of you.'

'How is that possible?' asked the youth.

'Your fame has gone before you more than you may realize.'

'Then do you think she would be willing to be aided by me?'

'Indeed, I believe you would find her most willing. For though it is true that Milocrates has honoured her greatly, she cannot forget that she was abducted by force.'

With the help of Naboar, who was a familiar figure about the palace, the Knight of the Surcote made his way to the chambers occupied by the emperor's niece. As Naboar had suggested, when the youth revealed his identity, he found her eager both to escape but also to help the Romans in any way that she could. It had quickly become clear that the force which Milocrates was assembling was far superior to their own, and that they had little chance of victory without considerable luck. Therefore they set about devising a plan. With all the preparations for battle going on everywhere, it should be easy for a small contingent of the Roman force to lie hidden just outside the city walls Then, when the army of Milocrates set forth to overwhelm the Romans, the princess could open the gates and admit the hidden contingent, who would capture the city itself and set it ablaze, thus distracting Milocrates and convincing him that another large force was behind him.

To this the Princess most willingly agreed, and to further aid the Knight of the Surcote she gave him a sword and armour belonging to Milocrates, of which it was said that if another wore it then its real owner would soon perish. With these gifts, and strengthened by the compliance of both the princess and Naboar, the young knight slipped out of the palace and having rejoined Odabel, who had been spying out the size of the enemy force, the two left the city and returned to their own camp.

The centurion heard their news with elation. He quickly dispatched Odabel, with a small force, to await the signal to enter and possess the city. Then he gathered the rest of the Romans and went forth to meet Milocrates. The latter had divided his army into two forces. One, under the command of his brother, was to attack from the sea; the other, under his own leadership, marched towards the place where the Romans were encamped.

As for Milocrates himself, he was filled with fear and had little expectation of victory, despite his army's superior numbers. For that morning he had gone in search of the armour which gave him greater strength, only to find it missing. So filled with despair was he at this, that even though he did not know that the enemy had somehow succeeded in stealing it, he became fearful of the prophecy against himself. When he reached the field of battle and saw that the Knight of the Surcote – whose prowess rumour had already exaggerated – was wearing his missing armour and carrying his sword, Milocrates wished that he might turn and flee. However, it was too late to stop what he had begun, and so battle was joined.

At first there seemed no movement on either side. The Romans, though outnumbered nearly twelve to one, fought with such heroism that they held the enemy at bay. Then, as the plan devised by the Knight of the Surcote began to be put into operation, smoke was seen to arise from the city. At once panic ensued among the followers of the king. Milocrates' entire force turned tail and fled back towards the city. There they found the gates closed against them, and thus caught between their own walls and the attacking Romans, they were cut to pieces.

When he saw the slaughter Milocrates rallied his forces and, in a brave attempt to reverse his fortunes, attacked the centre where the Knight of the Surcote was fighting. Inevitably the two came face to face, and at their first encounter the knight unhorsed the king and sent him stunned to the ground. The battle raged on around them, as Milocrates regained his feet and struck out at the young knight. A lucky blow opened a wound on his brow, and as he felt the blood flowing down into his eyes, he struck out furiously, severing the king's head from his shoulders.

When they saw that the last resistance among Milocrates' men failed and they threw down their weapons and surrendered on every side. Thus the battle ended and the prophecy that the king should die at the hands of the man who wore his armour was fulfilled. The Romans took possession of the city and were welcomed by the emperor's niece, who gave orders for the dead to be buried and the wounded cared for.

And so it seemed that the battle was over. The centurion secured the island and placed a governor loyal to Rome over its people. Then he dispatched a company to escort the emperor's niece to her rightful lord, the King of Illyricum. Then, with an additional levy of soldiers from Milocrates' own guard, the fleet prepared to set sail to their original destination.

However, they had reckoned without the dead king's brother, who had been sailing up and down the reaches of the coast all this time, blown hither and thither by the winds which had kept the Romans from sailing. Now he saw the Roman fleet approaching, and at once attacked.

A pitched battle now ensued, with ships ramming each other with their iron prows, smashing great holes in the sides of their adversaries and causing great loss of life. The Knight of the Surcote himself was in charge of one of the most powerful of the ships, and wreaked great havoc wherever he sailed. Grappling irons were flung against the sides of the enemy ships and the knight himself led the way aboard more than a dozen of them. At one point the enemy surrounded him and flung Greek Fire onto the deck of his craft. This evil weapon, which clung to everything it touched and consumed it upon contact, seemed as though it would overwhelm the Romans. But thanks to the Knight of the Surcote the tables were turned. Single-handedly he took the assault to the enemy ship, leading his own men aboard, where they swiftly overcame their adversaries and took possession of the craft. While their own ship sank burning beneath the waves, the knight turned the enemy's weapons against them. In less time than it takes to tell, the enemy were routed, with more than twenty ships captured and dozens more sunk. Milocrates' brother was himself captured, and the centurion sent him in chains to Rome before turning once again for the Holy Land and the completion of their original mission.

With prevailing winds they reached Jerusalem in a matter of days, and were received with joy and expectation. The Christian forces had placed all their hopes of peaceful outcome on the person of their champion, and if some were concerned by his youth, all were impressed by his bearing and by the word of his battle against Milocrates.

So, on the day appointed, the two armies began to assemble on the plain outside the walls of the city. The Knight of the Surcote now learned for the first time something of the adversary he would soon be fighting. The Persian champion was named Gormundus, a huge man, almost a giant, with tree-like limbs and immense strength. So large was he, indeed, that no horse could be found to carry, him; therefore the combat was destined to take place on foot, a fact which many deemed a disadvantage to the Knight of the Surcote.

Having prepared themselves, the two champions advanced together and met with a fearsome clash in the midst of the field. Blows and taunts were exchanged and blood was shed, but neither could gain the advantage. Like two great boars they rushed upon each other, hammering at their mail-clad bodies with all their strength. The Knight of the Surcote, the lighter of the two by no small measure, danced around his opponent, causing him to work harder at his task. Gormundus, for his part, delivered slow and ponderous strokes which, when they connected, slowed down the Christian champion considerably. Thus the two fought on wearily throughout the long hours of the day, and when sunset fell neither had succeeded in inflicting any serious wounds upon the other. The day ended in uncertainty for both sides, for no one could say how the battle would go on the morrow.

The next day the combat recommenced, with both champions striving ever more valiantly for supremacy. Sparks were struck from their swords and it was a wonder to all that their armour did not crack from the blows they rained down upon each other. Yet as the day advanced neither could be said to have gained an advantage. Then the Knight of the Surcote, plunging in past his enemy's guard, struck him in the mouth, knocking out two teeth and breaking half his jaw. It was not a serious wound, but it stung Gormundus to rage. He pressed his attack with even greater force, and delivered a blow under which the knight's sword broke off near the hilt. The knight himself was now in the weaker position, and gave ground swiftly. A great roar went up from the Persians. Gormundus pressed home his advantage, but as the prospect looked black for the Knight of the Surcote the sun dipped below the horizon and the combat was at an end for that day.

Next morning there was some argument over whether or not the knight should be permitted to use a new sword, but in time agreement was reached and the combat began again. By this time the two men had gained a measure of each other, and as they renewed their onslaught upon each other they struck ever more cunningly, inflicting countless minor wounds. But in time the Persian champion began to weaken, driven back before the sheer force of the younger knight's attack. His people cried out in alarm at this, encouraging him and taunting him at the same time until, driven half mad with pain and shame, he struck such a blow that he brought the knight to his knees.

Then the young champion sprang up, and with great fury and passion renewed his assault. Lifting his sword high he cried: 'Here is the blow that ends it all!' Then he struck such a blow that it penetrated the helmet and brain-pan of Gormundus and felled him to the earth stone dead. A great moan went up from the Persians, soon drowned by the cheers of the Christians.

Thus war was averted, both sides abiding by their agreement and proceeding to exchange prisoners, pay dues and agree the reparation of goods. The Knight of the Surcote, needless to say, received praise and gifts from all sides, and returned to Rome in triumph. There, the emperor himself welcomed him and awarded him with the highest rank and titles.

But the Knight of the Surcote was already restless for further acts of adventure, and began actively to seek about for word of conflict in which he might join. Word came to him of the renowned King Arthur (his own uncle, though he knew it not), whose knights were said to be the best in all the world, and whose court offered more adventures than any other.

And it was said that in this time the Kingdom of Arthur was under attack from many hostile forces, and that he was much in need of knights. At once the young hero desired to go there, and, believing that this might in time bring the old province of Britain, long separated from the Empire, back into a relationship with Rome, the emperor agreed.

Before the knight departed the emperor summoned him and gave him certain gifts. Then he handed to him the chest which Viamundus had given into his keeping, instructing him not to look within it but to present it to King Arthur himself and none other. Then the Knight of the Surcote took his leave of the emperor and set out upon the long journey across the Alps, through Gaul, and across the Narrow Sea to Britannia. There he enquired after the whereabouts of King Arthur and was told that he was at present in the city of Caerleon.

The hero set out at once in the direction of the River Usk, but when he was still several miles from his destination a sudden violent storm struck, driving him from the road to seek the shelter of a nearby grove of trees.

Now it happened that King Arthur and his queen, Gwendoloena, were abed at this time, and discussing matters of note to do with the kingdom. The queen was not only one of the most beautiful women in the kingdom, she was also wise in the ways of magic and she often prophesied events that subsequently came about as she had foretold. On this occasion, after they had talked long into the night, the queen suddenly said: 'Arthur, you are often said to be one of the best knights in Britain, at least as strong as your own followers. Do you believe this to be true?'

'Of course,' replied the king. 'Do you not feel it in your own heart?'

'Indeed I do,' said Gwendoloena. 'But, there is even now approaching the town of Usk a knight of Rome who is of boundless strength. By mid-morning tomorrow he will send to me a gold ring and two horses. I do not say that he is stronger than you, but he is certainly a very powerful champion.'

The king said nothing to this, but as soon as the queen was asleep he rose from his bed and went quietly outside, calling his squire and servants to him and instructing them to bring his armour and weapons and to prepare his horse. Then he summoned his seneschal and friend Sir Kay to accompany him, and shortly after the two rode forth secretly, telling no one in the castle.

Soon they arrived at a tributary of the river Usk which was swollen by the storm, and there they found the Knight of the Surcote, casting about to find a crossing place.

'Who are you, who wanders the country in the dead of night?' cried the king. 'Are you a spy or a fugitive?'

'I am neither,' called back the knight. 'I wander because I do not know the way.'

'You are quick to defend yourself with your tongue,' replied Arthur. 'Let us see if you are as good with a lance and sword.'

'If you will,' said the young knight, and lowering his lance charged to meet the king.

They met in the middle of the stream and King Arthur flew from his horse's back and landed in the water. The knight at once reached out and securing the mount's reins returned to his side of the stream.

When he saw this, Sir Kay issued his own challenge and rode to meet the stranger. The Knight of the Surcote dealt with him as easily as he had the king, and Kay quickly joined his master in the river. As before the knight scooped up the reins of the riderless horse and secured both. Then he took the path away from there, leaving the king and his seneschal to walk home.

When he arrived back at the castle King Arthur hastened to bed to get warm. The queen, stirring at his arrival, asked why he was so wet and cold. 'I thought I could hear noises outside in the courtyard,' said Arthur hastily. 'I thought it might be some of my men fighting and went out in the rain to see.'

'Well,' said the queen sleepily, 'we shall see what news my messenger brings in the morning.'

The Knight of the Surcote, meanwhile, continued on his way with the two captured horses and found lodging nearby for the night. When day dawned he rode on towards Caerleon, and on the way he met a boy wearing the royal arms.

'What is your duty?' asked the knight.

'Sir, I am the queen's messenger.'

'Then if you will I bid you take a message to the queen from me.' And he gave the two horses into the care of the boy, along with his ring and a gold piece for his trouble.

Queen Gwendoloena, meanwhile, knowing what to expect, watched the road leading to the castle, and when she saw the messenger approach, leading two horses, she went down to meet him. The boy explained that he had met a knight on the road and gave the queen the ring. When she heard the name of the knight, she smiled and then went at once to where King Arthur lay still abed and woke him.

'My lord,' she said, 'lest you doubt my words to you last night, here is the ring which I was promised, and outside are the two horses which I foretold. They are all sent by the knight whom I described. It seems that he overthrew their riders last night at the ford.'

Shamefacedly, the king rose and looked out of the window. Of course the horses were his own and Sir Kay's, as anyone could see at once. Then Arthur laughed and ruefully confessed all to the queen.

Later that morning the king held an assembly of his nobles which, due to the fine weather, took place under a certain ash tree in the gardens of the castle. And here, as they sat in conference, the Knight of the Surcote arrived and rode right up to where the lords of Britannia were sitting on the grass.

Arthur, not knowing who he was, addressed him sternly for interrupting. The youth held his own, however, and declared that he was a knight of Rome who had learned of the problems facing the king of Britannia and had come to offer help. He announced that he brought mandates from the emperor himself, and forthwith handed over the sealed casket.

Arthur, knowing now that this was the knight who had defeated him, spoke more gently and ordered the youth to be received and bathed and rested whil he studied the emperor's communication. However, when he opened the casket and read the documents it contained he was overwhelmed to find that not only were there letters of greeting and friendship from Rome, but also proof that the Knight of the Surcote was his own nephew. Full of wonder he sent for the parents, Lot and Anna, who were there with the rest of the nobles, and questioned them rigorously. Both were relieved to confess, and in the joy of the moment could scarcely believe that the renowned knight was indeed their own child. Arthur too was glad, but made them swear not to speak of these matters until he had further tested the prowess of the knight.

Then he called the knight before him and said that, while he appreciated his coming and the letters from the emperor, at that time he had no need of more men. 'I have such a great fellowship of knights around me – most of whom serve me without stipend – that I must be careful whom I admit to their ranks. I can hardly invite you, an untried youth, to be part of my chivalry.'

When he heard this the Knight of the Surcote blushed furiously. 'I came in good faith to serve one of whom I had heard only good things. I see now that I was mistaken. Nevertheless, I shall not depart from Britannia until I have found service with someone, for to do so would be to imply cowardice on my part. Let me then, remain in this land, and if there is any task which you or your knights are reluctant to undertake, I beg you to give it to me.'

Liking this answer, King Arthur agreed. Less than twelve days later he received news that a certain lady, who was bound to him by deep ties of loyalty, was besieged by Picts in the Castle of Maidens in Scotland. She begged the king to come to her aid.

Now Arthur had encountered the leader of the Picts before, and each time he had met defeat. None the less, he hastily assembled an army and marched North. He was still a good way from the Castle of Maidens when he met a second messenger from the lady. He brought the news that the castle had fallen, and that its lady had been carried off. At once King Arthur gave chase to the Picts, but their wily leader had news of his coming and lay in wait with his strongest warriors to intercept him.

At the first encounter the forces of King Arthur were scattered and cast into confusion by the unexpected fury of the assault. They quickly regrouped, and the king himself led them in a rousing attack. However, the British were considerably outnumbered and, in spite of their heroic efforts, were gradually pressed back. King Arthur, judging the situation with the skill of a seasoned warrior, decided to withdraw and regroup once more. As they were doing so they suddenly met with the Knight of the Surcote who had followed the army at a distance.

'Are they deer or rabbits that you hunt, my lord?' he demanded. And Arthur, angry at this taunt, shouted back that he saw no proof of the knight's reported prowess, since he chose to hide from the battle. At this the knight grew angry, and spurring his horse past the retreating Britons, flew straight towards the Picts.

So astonished were they at the suddenness and fury of his attack that they gave way, parting like a sea before him. For his part he rode directly to where the enemy banners fluttered, and drove in straight for the Pictish king. Before anyone could do more than stare he had dealt the enemy lord a fatal blow, snatched up the reins of the captive lady's horse and galloped off with her back towards the British lines.

But the Picts, recovering from their surprise and roaring now with rage, surrounded him, attacking from every side. It was nothing short of a miracle that the knight survived death. He struck about him furiously, dealing out death to all who came against him. But he was hampered by the presence of the lady and looked around desperately for a way to escape. So it was that he spotted a bank and ditch crossed by a narrow bridge – all that remained of a once proud fort. Spurring his mount towards this place, he succeeded in gaining sufficient space between himself and the Picts to allow the lady to cross before him. Then, grim-faced, he turned at bay and for the next half hour defended the bridge against all comers. Such was the ferocity and strength of his defence, that at the end of this time the Picts began to withdraw, dismayed at the death toll which mounted around the hero.

At this point King Arthur returned and attacked with renewed force, sending the Picts howling before him. After this the battle was soon over, and the Britons gathered around the Knight of the Surcote and the lady whom he had rescued, filled with praise and gratitude for his heroic effort. King Arthur himself came up and publicly thanked him, admitting that such a one as he ought indeed to belong to his fellowship. 'I was wrong to doubt you, sir knight. I gladly welcome you among us. But first, I would know more of your lineage and birth.'

'I can tell you easily,' replied the youth. 'I was born in Gaul, the son of a Roman senator named Viamundus. My true name is Gawain, but I have been known as the Knight of the Surcote for a long time.'

It is my task to tell you that you are wrong about much of this,' said the king, smiling.

'How so?' demanded the knight in some bewilderment.

'You shall learn all once we are returned to Caerleon,' replied the king.

And so it befell that, when the tired army was safely returned to the court, King Arthur called before him King Lot of Norway and his queen Anna, and announced before all the court that the Knight of the Surcote was truly their son. 'And thus,' he added, embracing the astonished youth, 'you are my nephew. And glad am I to acknowledge you before all this company.'

Then there was great rejoicing, as you may imagine, with the son restored to his parents, and the brave hero discovered to be the king's own nephew. Many were the adventures that later befell Sir Gawain, though I shall not tell them here. But of this one there came a renewed friendship with Rome, and in time of need, help to the beleaguered Britons in their future wars.

10

Gorlagros and Gawain

THIS is an unusual as well as powerful tale, which has at its heart a particularly medieval subject, that of fealty. According to the feudal laws of the time a knight could not be his own master, but inevitably owed allegiance to a king or a lesser nobleman, who was his 'liege lord'. This meant, effectively, binding oneself to one's overlord, offering service by bearing arms and fighting alongside him in time of war, or by representing him as a champion. Even mercenaries, who had no specific allegiance, sold their skills as fighting men to whichever lord required them. In return the lord offered the protection of his name and power, as well as providing weapons and armour – no small expense at the time.

In the story which follows, therefore, when Arthur and his knights encounter a lord who owes allegiance to no one they are understandably shocked, and Arthur is at once determined – in a manner which we might well find unreasonable today – to go to war over the matter, essentially bringing the errant Gorlagros to heel. This in turn provokes a decision on the part of Gawain which is a test even of his honour – so often remarked upon in the stories in which he is a major character.

In our time the desire for freedom of the individual is, of course, upheld at any cost. But here the story turns not so much on Gorlagros' refusal to bend the knee to Arthur, as on the manner in which Gawain and he resolve the problem which faces them. In the event, neither lose their honour – or their lives, as they might so easily have done. In essence the bond of fealty was a mutual one, and in acting as he does Gorlagros is actually breaking the bond between himself and his people. They, in turn, have the right to reject him.

The resolution of all this is skilfully handled by the anonymous author, who seems to have hailed from lowland Scotland. The single manuscript in which the story exists dates from around 1508 and is today held by the National Library of Scotland. This makes it one of the latest Arthurian romances dealt with here, and as such it displays an unusual grasp of the concept of fealty, which was already beginning to lose its importance by this date, being reduced to little more than a monetary contract between the lord and the knights in his employment.

The story as we have it derives from an episode in the first continuation to Chrétien de Troyes's poem *Perceval*, usually attributed to Wauchier de Danans. This episode, concerning the visit to the Orgellus (Proud) Castle and the defeat of a character known as the Rich Soldoier, may itself have derived from an earlier source. Nor should one overlook the possible influence of the Gawain texts written in and around the area of the Midlands from the twelfth to the fourteenth centuries.

Here, as so often in other related texts, we find the inevitable comparison between the blustering Sir Kay and the noble Gawain. The episode in which Kay steals food from the hall of the first castle they encounter is similar to several other occasions in which he acts in an impulsive or overbearing manner – usually with unfortunate results, since Kay always comes off the worst and has to be rescued by his comrades. In the present story, of course, he does redeem himself by overcoming another knight and capturing him.

The origins of the name Gorlagros (or Golagros) remain obscure. The similarity between his name and that of Gorlagon in *Arthur and Gorlagon* (see John Matthews, *The Unknown Arthur*, London, Blandford, 1995, pp. 41–51) may be coincidental, though both are, noblemen with large followings. However, Gorlagon is the subject of a werewolf adventure, which seems to have nothing to do with the present story.

Just how much originality can be attributed to the author of this text is, as almost always with medieval texts, difficult to say. He writes with a seemingly wide knowledge, of arms, armour and siege warfare, some of which is present within the episodes of Chrétien's poem. The characters speak with the authentic voices of their time, and

I have not attempted to update them, allowing them rather to speak for themselves.

Gorlagros and Gawain has been edited several times, for example in the incomparable *Syr Gawayne* of Sir Frederic Madden (London, Richard and John Taylor, 1839; reprinted New York, AMS Press, 1971, and F. J. Amours, *Scottish Alliterative Poems in Riming Stanzas* (Edinburgh, Blackwood, 1897). As ever, the best modern rendition is by Louis B. Hall in his *Knightly Tales of Sir Gawain* (Chicago, Nelson Hall, 1976). A detailed examination of the story and its relationship to the Chrétien continuation was made by Paul J. Ketrick in *The Relation of Golagros and Gawane to the Old French Perceval* (Washington, DC, Catholic University of America Press, 1931).

ONG AGO, IN THE TIME OF ARTHUR, the king and all his nobles set forth to journey to Jerusalem, there to make offering at the birthplace of the Saviour. On the way they passed through the land known as Tuscany. Many of the Round Table knights were there, almost a hundred, and many other noble lords beside. Never in that land was there seen such a fine body of men as they rode, banners fluttering, armour gleaming in the sun, spears at the slope, swords on hip, a river of living steel flowing over the green land.

But, when they had been travelling for more than a week, the weather turned evil: rain fell steadily from grey skies, the earth turned liquid, and the knights began to rust as they rode. Food, too, was scarce, for such a large company required a huge repast every day, and soon the wagons of provisions began to fall behind or grew ever more empty.

Thus all were glad indeed to crest a hill one day and see a fair city lying spread out below them. Huge walls girded it around, and a mighty fortress guarded its gates. None could enter there without permission save the birds which flew over the walls.

'Let us send a messenger to that city,' King Arthur said, 'to ask for food and permission to lodge outside its walls.' For he knew that to bring so large a company to that place unannounced might be seen as a threat.

'Let me go, lord,' cried Sir Kay eagerly.

'Very well,' said the king. 'But see that you offer to pay for all that we require. And Kay – speak gently to these folk, for they know us not, nor we them.' For he knew that Kay's hot temper had a habit of bringing trouble in its wake.

Swiftly Kay rode down to the city. He found its gates standing wide and its streets strangely deserted. Tying his horse to a tree he went into the first hall that he came too. And a very great place it was, you may be sure. The walls were hung with tapestries depicting the deeds of the greatest warriors in the land, and letters of gold were woven into the pattern which told of their names and adventures.

But Kay saw no living person. He went from room to room, seeking sign of anyone to answer his request. At last, in a room with a bright fire laid, he saw a dwarf scuttling about, turning a spit on which several birds were roasting, setting the room to rights as if for a private feast. Kay was so hungry by this time that he went straight up to the fire and snatched one of the birds, which he began to consume with greedy bites.

At once the dwarf cried out, his voice echoing about the room, and in answer to his yells a large, fierce knight strode in. When he saw Kay standing there with the juice of the meat running down his chin, he spoke angrily. 'Sir, where are your manners? I do not know you, yet you seem to have made yourself at home as if you lived here. By what right do you steal our food? Your armour may be bright but your manners are as dull as any peasant. Be sure you shall pay for this ill behaviour – I swear you shall not leave here until I have exacted payment!'

At once Kay's hot temper flared. 'I apologize for nothing!' he cried. 'Your judgement means nothing to me!'

Without a word the knight swung a huge fist at Kay, knocking him to the floor where he lay like a stone, and with his wits scattered like so many leaves. When he regained consciousness the huge knight had vanished, and without pausing to think Sir Kay hurried back to his horse and rode full pelt back to the king. 'Sire!' he cried. 'We shall get no good greeting in that place. Its lord denies you with scorn!'

Sir Gawain, who was standing near and overheard all that passed, spoke up: 'My Lord, you know that good Sir Kay is often sharper of tongue than he means to be. May I ask that you send another in his place who will speak in less crabbed tones? Our people are weakened with hunger and we need the provisions the city can supply.'

King Arthur mused for a moment, looking around at the sad and sodden troop of knights. 'Very well,' he said at last. 'Sir Gawain, prepare yourself to go, for no one is more fair spoken than you.'

Gawain followed where Kay had been. The gates of the city were open as before. The hall was as richly appointed as ever. But now it was filled with stately people; the lord of the place sat on the high dais, surrounded by richly clad nobles and fair ladies. Gawain went and stood before him with bowed head and spoke as gently as a fair knight should.

'Sir, I bring you greeting from my lord King Arthur of Britain. He asks that he may quarter his followers outside your walls, and that he may buy food and drink for his knights and their steeds. He will pay whatever price is asked.'

The lord of the castle looked down at Gawain unsmiling. 'I will sell nothing to your lord,' he said.

'As you wish, my lord,' Gawain replied and made to leave.

But the lord raised a hand and beckoned him to return. 'I would be no kind of noble if I were to sell goods to your master. Everything I have is at his disposal for as long as he wishes to remain here.' Then he smiled. 'A rough, boorish fellow came here lately. He was dressed like a knight but his manners were those of a fool. I do not know who he was, but if peradventure he had any connection with your lord or his men, then I tell you he had better stay out of my sight.'

Gawain bowed low and departed swiftly, returning to King Arthur with the good news. Then he led the way back to the castle where the lord greeted King Arthur warmly. 'Sire,' said he, 'I am more than glad to welcome you here, for I have long heard of your goodness and the bravery of your knights. Let me say now that everything in my land is yours to command. If you ask it I have thirty thousand men who will answer to you, every one armed and mounted.'

'I give you my thanks,' said King Arthur. 'Such friendship as this I hold dear and will ever reward as I may.'

Then all together he and the noble lord, along with all their knights, dukes and ladies went into, the hall and dined in most splendid fashion, eating from golden dishes and drinking from golden cups. Never was there such a feast in all of the history of that land, and never did such great and noble folk sit down together – except perhaps in King Arthur's own great hall in far-off Camelot.

Thus they spent the next four days and nights in feasting and pleasant disports both day and night. Then King Arthur and his followers took their leave of the noble lord who had been such a generous host, and continued upon their way.

Soon they were far from that place of hospitality, travelling over mountain and hill, through valley and forest, crossing rivers and open moorland, until they came at length to the sea. And there they saw where a rocky bluff pushed its way out of the earth beside a river which curved around its sides and flowed into the ocean. There, atop this outcrop, stood a fine castle with more than thirty towers. Beneath its protecting walls lay a great harbour, filled with ships which plied their way without hindrance, such was the strength of that place.

'Now by my faith,' said King Arthur, 'I would dearly like to know who rules this land, so fruitful and pleasant is it, and so filled with good things.'

'I have heard,' said one of the Round Table knights, whose name was Sir Spinagros, 'that the lord who holds these lands does so under fief to no one. He owes no allegiance to any man, either now or in any time to come.'

'How can that be?' demanded Arthur. 'All men, unless they are kings in their own right, owe allegiance to someone higher then themselves. Can it be that this is a rebel lordling who has broken the bond between himself and his sovereign?'

'There is more to it than that, sire,' Spinagros answered. 'Hear me and I will tell you the tale as it was told to me.

'First of all you must know that this man, who is named Gorlagros, is a very stubborn man, with a will of iron and as great a sense of power as any I have heard of in all the lands of the West. In truth he is himself a king, yet in all his life he neither gave nor received homage from any man. He is immensely rich, and keeps a huge army which he launches on an unsuspecting world whenever he thinks fit. I have heard that he has a wayward temper as well, and that he answers to no threats except with violence. In short, my lord, you should pass by this place without pause – no good will come of any encounter with this proud lord.'

King Arthur frowned. 'All that you have told me only makes me more determined to bring this powerful lord to heel. I am determined upon this, let no one deny me! Once we have accomplished our task and reached the Holy City, we shall return this way and speak further of this matter.'

When the king spoke thus, no one would gainsay him. And so it was that as the year turned the king and his party reached Jerusalem, and there made appropriate offerings at the shrine of Our Lord. Then, without further ado, they turned back and made all the haste that they could until they were once again near the fortress of Gorlagros At this point King Arthur made camp near to the valley of the Rhone, and when his royal pavilion had been erected he called a council of war to hear how best they might overcome the proud lord Gorlagros.

Spinagros spoke up once more. 'Sire, it seems to me that we should first of all dispatch messengers to speak with this lord. Even though I have heard nothing to make me believe he will listen and bend the knee to you, yet it may be that when he learns with whom he must deal he will bow his proud head.'

'You speak well, sir,' King Arthur replied. 'Sir Gawain! Sir Lancelot! Sir Uwain! I charge you with this task. See that you convey my commands to Gorlagros – that he submit to my lordship and give homage as is fitting.'

'My lord,' said Spinagros, 'if I may advise further. . .?'

The King nodded.

'Sirs,' said Spinagros, addressing the three knights, 'I know this lord well, and I would advise you to be careful how you speak to him. His manner is mild and he is as handsome and kindly in appearance as a bridegroom. Yet beneath all he wears a steely warrior's countenance and bends his knee to no one. I counsel you to speak gently to him, and not to threaten in any way. For though I know you to be powerful men in your own rights, yet he is stronger than any one of you – maybe even more than all three together.'

'We thank you,' replied the three knights. 'Your words are wise and we will keep them in mind at all times in our dealing with Gorlagros.'

Then the three set forth and rode to the gates of the city, where they were welcomed and, once they had stated that they were emissaries of King Arthur, received the utmost courtesy. Led through the outer wards of the castle they reached at length the great hall, where Gorlagros sat on a high dais surrounded by fair ladies and noble knights. A handsome man he was, just as Spinagros had told them. He bowed his head in greeting and called them forward.

Gawain, ever the noblest and most well-spoken of all Arthur's knights, spoke first.

'We bring you greetings from our sovereign lord, King Arthur. He is the noblest and mightiest king alive in this time. Hundreds of castles has he, and many houses, towns and cities. No less than twelve kings owe him allegiance and his deeds are known far and wide. In his hall at Camelot stands the Round Table, at which one hundred and fifty knights sit down at one time. We three are honoured to be part of that fellowship.'

Sir Gawain paused to judge the effect of his words. Gorlagros nodded politely. 'We have heard of your lord and send him our greetings. What message do you bring from him?'

'Merely that word of your deeds and your great nobility have reached the ears of our lord, who wishes to extend his friendship to you. He asks that you will name yourself his friend from this day forward.'

Gorlagros nodded again, then spoke at length and with great courtesy. 'I thank you for your words, good sirs, and I am glad that your lord offers me friendship. Were I able to, nothing would please me more than that I should align myself with the noble King Arthur. Yet I fear I may not do so, for neither I nor my family have ever sworn fealty to anyone, or bound ourselves in any way, either by word or deed. By some it is considered that such a gesture of friendship is to be seen as just an act of submission. Anything I may do for your king by way of gifts or honour I shall gladly do, so long as it is not construed as a token of my submission. I will bow my head to the sovereignty of any noble man, though never to threats of any kind. I know that King Arthur comes at the head of a great army, and he is welcome, as is any man who comes in friendship, as do you yourselves. However, I will not bend my neck to any show of force, which I shall surely meet with equal show of arms. Take these words to your king, with my greeting from one lord to another.'

With this the emissaries had to be content, and taking their leave of Gorlagros they returned to King Arthur. He, when he heard what they had to report, was angry and determined at once to lay siege to the city. 'For', said he, 'no man may speak thus to an anointed king unless he is ready to back up his words with feats of arms and show of strength.'

So King Arthur and his men prepared to lay siege to the castle of Gorlagros. Several boatloads of men arrived from across the sea and the siege began in earnest. Great bows, mighty cannon and a huge arbalast were set up; trees were cut down to build palisades and battering rams; trumpets blew at all hours – King Arthur's to signify challenge, those of Gorlagros to signal his defiance. Every morning there were new shields arranged on the walls, gleaming in the sunlight. Many were known to the heroes of the Round Table, for their fame had spread beyond the confines of Gorlagros's lands. And King Arthur, looking upon them, said, 'Never have I seen such a strong city, nor one so well defended. Yet I shall give them enough to think on before much time has passed.' Grimly, he continued, 'If need be I shall remain here nine years, until I have brought this proud prince to his knees!'

Sire,' said Sir Spinagros, 'I fear you will remain here longer before you see any sign of yielding on the part of this lord or his men. I believe they are a match for any of us, even Sir Lancelot or Sir Gawain.'

Even as he spoke they heard a loud trumpet call from one of the towers of the city, and a figure in armour rode forth from the gates.

'Now what means this?' murmured King Arthur.

'I believe it is a challenge,' said Gawain.

'You are right,' said Spinagros. 'I know this youth from the arms he bears. His name is Galiot, and he is a knight of great renown. It seems to me that he will desire to test his own prowess while defending the honour of his lord.'

'Then we shall give him the opportunity to do both,' said King Arthur. He called forth Sir Gaudifer, a strong knight who held many estates in Britain, but who had but lately joined the fellowship of the Round Table. 'Undertake this task for me, sir knight, and you shall be well rewarded.'

To this Sir Gaudifer was glad to agree, and sent his squire to prepare his war-horse and armour. In a while, before the sun climbed to mid-heaven, the two knights were prepared and rode out onto the level plain before the walls of the castle. The walls were crowded with the defenders, who longed to see King Arthur's man defeated.

Like two swords heated in the smith's fire they seemed as they rode at each other full tilt, with spears in rest and sword at the ready. All afternoon they fought, and neither could gain the advantage. The horses were soon tired and they fell to fighting on foot, hacking and hewing until the blood ran down over their bright armour and the earth was soaked. To many it seemed as though both were mad, as though a demon had overtaken them both and would not let them rest.

At the last Sir Gaudifer gained the victory, and Galiot was carried back into the castle on a stretcher, while all of King Arthur's men cheered. At this Gorlagros became angry and called to one of his strongest knights, a man named Sir Rigel of Rhone, and bade him go forth and uphold the honour of his lord. 'I shall not rest until this defeat has been avenged!' cried the proud lord. 'For my sake make this day a costly one for our adversaries.'

Thus with the customary horn-call Sir Rigel prepared to go forth and do battle. And King Arthur, hearing that call, knew well what was to occur and turned to another of his knights, a man named Sir Rannald, and bade him prepare himself for battle. This the good knight did, and soon enough the two fresh combatants faced each other on the field of war.

This time the fighters were even better matched, one with the other, than before. Back and forward they went, as the sun declined steadily towards the West. Neither could gain the advantage, and both were sorely wounded and lost so much blood that they grew steadily weaker. At last Sir Rannald summoned his failing strength and attacked Sir Rigel with renewed fury. He, in turn, responded with his best. But once again neither could overcome other, and for both this final effort proved too much. They fell upon the earth and lay still, while their life-blood drained from them.

At once their squires rushed forward to help, but it was too late. Both these brave men were dead upon the field, and neither had won back the honour of their lords. With great mourning and sorrow their bodies were carried back to castle and camp, and soon after were buried with pomp and ceremony and their deeds recorded that they might be remembered in days to come.

Thus the day ended, and on the morrow the contest began again. This time Gorlagros sent forth four knights. These were Sir Louys, a noble man by birth and a true fighter. With him went Sir Edmond, known to be a lover of women, and Sir Bantelles, a captain who was known as a wise leader of men. Lastly was Sir Sanguel, whom men called both handsome and savage. And these four were matched against four of Arthur's knights: Sir Lional, who was Lancelot's cousin, against Sir Louys; Sir Yvain against Sir Edmond; Sir Bedivere against Sir Bantelles, and Sir Gyrmolance against Sir Sanguel.

These eight set to against each other with all the fierceness of warriors from an earlier time; their mounts, held in check until the last moment as they charged together, leapt forward like sparks struck from flint. Thick and fast fell the blows of sword on shield. Armour was dinted and flesh torn. Helms were knocked out of shape and did dreadful damage to the skulls within. Swords broke in their owners' hands and horses fell dead upon the earth. No one could tell which way the mêlée went, so fast and furious was the onslaught. King Arthur began to be fearful for his men, so hardy were their opponents.

At length the battle resolved itself and the outcome could be seen by all. Sir Lional was captured by Sir Louys; as was Sir Bedivere by Sir Bantelles; Sir Sanguel was taken prisoner by Sir Gyrmolance; Sir Edmond fell dead to the swift sword of Sir Yvain, who in return was terribly wounded. As the day ended Bedivere and Lional were taken back to the castle, along with the body of Sir Edmond, while Yvain was helped back to King Arthur's camp and the victorious Gyrmolance brought his prisoner before Arthur.

What need to tell more of this battling? Suffice it that five more knights rode forth from each side on the day following, and that at the end each side had captured two of their opponents, while the others had shown themselves worthy champions. And Gorlagros, when he saw how things stood, and how well both he and king Arthur were matched for the power and skill of their fighting men, elected to go forth himself on the morrow, and to this end let ring forth two bells from a tower within the castle.

When he heard this Sir Spinagros told what it meant to King Arthur. 'My noble lord, it is evident that Gorlagros himself shall come forth to give battle on the morrow. I have seen him fight and believe me when I say that I scarcely ever saw a better man bestride a horse or wield a sword and spear. It will take a mighty warrior to defeat him.'

Now it happened that Sir Gawain overheard these words, and at once he begged King Arthur that he be allowed to face Gorlagros. To this Arthur assented, and prayed to God that he might be victorious. Sir Spinagros, however, said nothing, for in his heart he already believed that Gawain was as good as dead. Thus, as the good knight prepared himself for battle, Spinagros sought him out and did his best to dissuade Gawain from undertaking the fight. 'But,' said Gawain, 'If I die I ask only that it be valiantly, for I would as lief loose my life than my honour.'

'Then if you must fight,' said Spinagros, 'listen well to this advice. When you charge Gorlagros make certain to aim for the centre of his shield, for that is his weakest point. And, if and when you fight him on foot remember that when he is surprised he is given to shouting loudly and becomes as fierce as a wild boar. But do not let that distract or anger you, for then you will surely lose your life and the king's honour. Remember that if you can tire him out you will have a better chance of beating him. Let him rage as he will; if you remain cool you may have a chance of overcoming him.'

Sir Gawain thanked Spinagros for his advice, and continued to ready himself for the coming battle. But now we must turn to Sir Kay, who was jealous of Gawain and thought that he should have been chosen to fight Gorlagros. Therefore he put on his own armour and went out towards the city. As he rode he saw an armed knight coming toward him. When the knight saw Kay he cried his battle-cry and rode full tilt toward him. Kay responded as he might well do, setting his own lance in rest and giving spurs to his horse.

The two met and splintered both their spears, then fell to fighting with swords, at first on horse, then on foot. Finally the stranger conceded defeat and Kay returned with him to the camp of King Arthur, glad to have achieved this much of a victory, and far too bruised and battered to think of encountering Gorlagros as he had intended.

Meanwhile Gorlagros himself, accompanied by a magnificent entourage, had entered the field. A silken pavilion was set up and no less than sixty great knights, clad in the most magnificent armour, attended upon their lord. Gorlagros himself rode on a white horse and was clad in armour that shone like the sun and gave back glints of light from every facet of the gems that covered it so liberally. Even King Arthur's knights were in awe of such splendour, as they were impressed by the bearing of the lord himself. Gorlagros was over six feet in height and both handsome and strong. His proud bearing and haughty demeanour was shown off to good effect as he rode his prancing steed past the ranks of his own men and saluted the company who had accompanied Sir Gawain onto the field.

With both armies looking on the two combatants faced up to each other and made two exploratory passes with their lances before joining battle seriously. Now when they met it was as though thunder rolled across the place of battle. Their shields were shattered, as were their spears, and both men were rocked backwards in the saddle by the power of the blow. Their horses were winded and both took time to recover. Then they came together again, this time with swords raised, and proceeded to hack and hew at one another with all their strength. Yet neither could find an advantage, for they were so well matched in strength and skill that every feint and parry seemed to come from a single mind.

As the battle continued Gorlagros's anger increased, and he swung harder and harder at his foe. But Gawain, remembering the advice of Sir Spinagros, remained cool, and hacked so hard that he sheared right through Gorlagros's shield and left a dint in his breastplate from which blood oozed. Enraged, Gorlagros fought back harder, driving Gawain before him with a series of furious blows which broke his shield in two and sent pieces of his armour flying. Both men were panting heavily, and a red mist swam before their eyes.

As they fought on grimly, the onlookers shouted loudly, each for his own champion, and King Arthur offered up a prayer for the safety of his nephew.

The end came swiftly. Both men were sorely wounded in a dozen places, their once bright armour reddened with blood. Then, after delivering a particularly powerful blow, Gorlagros's legs gave way beneath him and he fell face down in the churned mud caused by the stamping of their mailed feet. At once Gawain drew his dagger and leapt upon his opponent, pinning him down and demanding his submission.

'I would as soon die as be thus disgraced,' cried Gorlagros. 'Never have I been defeated, nor has any man ever called himself my master in battle or elsewhere. I am one who rules himself as he rules his kingdom, owing allegiance to no one. Do what you will, for you will get nothing more of me this day.'

When he heard this Gawain felt nothing but grief. 'Sir,' said he, 'you know you are vanquished. Nothing will be changed by being thus obdurate. If you give up now and swear fealty to my king you shall have nothing but honour. You will have all that you have now and more, for you will be under the protection of my liege lord King Arthur.'

'To profit thus at the expense of my honour would be a foolish thing,' Gorlagros replied heavily. 'All I would gain would be shame, which would follow me to my death. Nothing will make me do anything which will cause me to hide from my own people. Believe me, no one disparages the fate of a man who gives his life honourably. l am not afraid to die.'

Now Sir Gawain when he heard this felt only pity for this brave man. 'Sir,' he said, 'is there nothing I can do to help you?'

Gorlagros was silent for a moment. Then he said: 'There is but one way that I know of to resolve this without loss of honour. Let it seem as though I have beaten you this day, then come to my castle later and you shall be well rewarded.'

'Now by my faith,' said Sir Gawain, 'this is a hard thing that you ask. I know nothing of you save that you are proud and strong and that your courage is beyond question. Yet if I do as you ask I am placing many noble knights in jeopardy and risking the continuance of this war for longer than it needs must be. With one blow I could end all of this, yet you would have me give back your life and freedom for a mere promise of reward.'

'It is that, or strike me down,' answered Gorlagros. 'You have my word.'

'Then,' said Gawain, 'I shall put my trust in your honour for the sake of all that depends upon it, for such a noble man I cannot slay in cold blood.'

Then to the amazement of all those who had watched this exchange Gawain stood back and leaned upon his sword as though weary. Then Gorlagros leapt up and drawing a short sword rejoined the combat. Only the two who fought knew that they no longer fought in earnest, but rather feinted so that no further blood was drawn from either. Then after a time Gawain made it seem that this strength failed him, and the two were accorded there on the field and Sir Gawain surrendered his sword. Then both returned to Gorlagros's castle, to a stunned silence from the Round Table knights and thunderous cheers from the followers of Gorlagros.

'Alas,' said King Arthur, 'now is the flower of my knighthood taken prisoner, and our honour is in the dust.' And he wept long and bitterly at this great loss and defeat.

Meanwhile, within the castle of Gorlagros all was joyful celebration. A great feast was prepared and Gawain, together with all the knights who had been defeated and taken prisoner, were seated at the high table where only Gorlagros, his wife and daughter normally sat. When the hall was filled Gorlagros struck the table with an ivory rod and called for silence.

'My lords,' he began, 'I have a heavy task before me and I require your assent and advice before I can undertake it. You are the greatest lords in my kingdom and you must decide whether you will have me for your king as a man who has been dishonoured in the field, or whether I should give up my life and let you all be ruled by another.'

Then there was great consternation among the knights gathered in the hall, and some there began to suspect that their lord had not won the day at all, but had been defeated by Sir Gawain. 'Let us have no sham favours,' said one old lord at last. 'You have been our noble lord for too long to give up everything so easily. We would have you for our governor in war and peace for as long as we may do so in honour.'

Then Gorlagros stood before them all and told them what had really occurred that day, and how Sir Gawain had nobly agreed to the deception rather than take his life. 'No man may do more for another,' he said, 'and this knight has earned praise beyond any that I can give. Yet I make no secret that my life is his to do with as he wills, and to him do I give all rights in this matter.' Then he turned to where Sir Gawain sat, and said: 'Sir, my life and all my properties are yours to do with as you will. When Fortune turns her back upon us we can do nothing to gainsay her. You had my life or death in your hands and out of nobility you chose to spare me. For that I am in your debt for ever, and to you, and to all these brave knights I give back your freedom and place myself in your hands.'

'Then I bid you return now to my lord King Arthur, for his justice is greater by far than any I could mete out,' said Sir Gawain.

Thus it was that soon after the watchmen of Arthur's camp saw a great torch-lit procession approaching from the city. In the forefront rode Gorlagros himself, with Sir Gawain at his side, and behind came a great gathering of nobles, among whom were to be seen the knights who had been taken prisoner.

'Now I believe we have Sir Gawain to thank for this,' said King Arthur, and Sir Spinagros, who was standing nearby, agreed. 'For I see many glances of friendship between the lord Gorlagros and Sir Gawain, and surely this bodes well for peace between our two forces.'

Then Gorlagros came forward alone and greeted King Arthur, and the two monarchs embraced. And Gorlagros told all that had taken place on the field of battle that day, and how Sir Gawain had graciously agreed to all that he asked and had placed his own honour in the hands of his rightfully defeated foe. 'Never have I encountered such bravery, or such high honour. It is to this that I bow, for surely only a king of the greatest and noblest ideals could command such a man.'

Then Gorlagros formally gave allegiance to King Arthur, and promised to serve him as his liege lord from that day forward. 'All my lands and properties, from the sea to the hills, are yours to command, and all those who offer allegiance to me from henceforward will call you lord as they have done to myself since I became ruler of this country.'

Thus King Arthur received the word of the noble lord, and then he, along with his foremost lords, returned to the city, where a great feast was prepared and the warriors sat down together in friendship. And thereafter, for many days after, the feasting and celebrations continued, and afterwards the knights, who had before been enemies, tested their skills and prowess together in the lists in friendly competition. Then, on the day that King Arthur prepared to return home, he called Gorlagros before him and said to him thus: 'Sir, for the sake of the honour you have shown toward me and my followers, I hereby grant you your freedom from the oath of allegiance to myself. Receive back all your lands and titles as they were before. In return I ask only that you retain the friendship towards me that you have aleady shown, and that I may call upon you in time of need.'

With tears in his eyes Gorlagros gave thanks to King Arthur and promised him any help he might wish for in future time. Then King Arthur and all his followers took their leave. And especially warm was the parting of Gawain and Gorlagros, who had become firm friends in their time together. And thereafter they remained true companions through the days of their lives, and Gorlagros ever praised the honour of King Arthur and of his brave and noble knights.

The Rise of Gawain

Gorlagros and Gawain

11
Jaufre

JAUFRE is the only surviving Arthurian romance written in Occitan, the language of medieval Provence. It has been dated from as early as 1180 to as late as 1225, and seems to have influenced Chrétien de Troyes in the creation of his Arthurian works, in which Jaufre becomes Griflet. In this guise the hero makes an appearance in several other Arthurian stories, including the *Vulgate Cycle* and Malory's *Le Morte d'Arthur*, where he is called Griflet le Fils le Do (Griflet the Son of God) an intriguing title which has been taken to indicate that Griflet in fact descends from the Celtic hero Gilfaethwy the son of Do. Do, however, is a Celtic goddess rather than a god, and the change in gender is probably a reflection of the changing attitudes of the medieval world towards the earlier, pagan roots of the legends. In the Vulgate version of the death of Arthur, it is Griflet, rather than the more usual Bedivere, who is entrusted with the task of returning the magical sword Excalibur to the water. This suggests at he may once have been a far more important figure in the legends, and, taken with his appearances in both Chrétien and Malory, it is even possible to reconstruct a detailed biography of his life and adventures.

As well as being an exciting tale, *Jaufre* is also that comparatively rare thing in Arthurian epics, a comedy. Though there are genuinely dramatic episodes (such as that with the lepers) much of the story is taken up with somewhat tongue-in-cheek adventures which burlesque the more familiar aspects of chivalry. In particular the episode of Arthur and the bull seems to me one of the best comic scenes in the genre.

In contrast to this, the whole theme of the mysterious lamentations at the castle of Montbrun is fascinating and seems almost like a reverse reflection of the Grail story, save that here there is a question which must not be asked and is, rather than one that should and is not. The appearance, too, of the giant's hideous mother not only ties up two parts of the story very neatly, but is also reminiscent of the appearance of the loathly lady, who so often comes to urge on and further test the knights who seek the Grail. In all there is some evidence to suggest that the author knew an earlier story on which Chrétien de Troyes may also have drawn when he composed his own Grail poem.

In retelling the story, I have simplified it considerably, as well as omitting several episodes. The end of the poem, in particular, drags out the action long after it has really ended, and this I have severely curtailed. For the rest I have tried to retain the curious blend of humour and excitement, passion and cruelty, which is a feature of this very fine romance.

Jaufre exists in two manuscripts, extending to some 11,000 lines, both held by the Bibliothèque Nationale: BNB Francis 2164, which dates from around 1300, and BNB Fr. 12571, which is a copy by a fourteenth-century Italian scribe. It was edited by Clovis Brunel as *Jaufre: Roman Arthurien en Ancien Provençal* (Paris, Picard, 1943) and has been translated three times, once by Alfred Elwes in 1856 (*Jaufre the Knight and the Fair Brunnisend*, London, Addey, reprinted by Newcastle Publishing, 1979); again by Vernon Ives, *Jaufry the Knight and the Fair Brunnisende*, New

York, Holiday House, 1935; and most recently by Ross G. Arthur (*Jaufre: An Occitan Arthurian Romance*, New York and London, Garland Publishing, 1992). I have made use of the first and third of these in preparing my own version. One of the most enlightening commentaries on the poem is by Suzanne Fleishman, 'Jaufre, or Chivalry Askew: Social Overtones of Parody in Arthurian Romance', in *Viator* 12 (1981) pp. 101–29.

T HAPPENED AT PENTECOST when the greatest of the knights of the Round Table were gathered together. Lancelot was there, of course, as was Tristan. Gawain was present, together with Yvain, Calogrenant, Perceval and Caradoc. As was customary at that festival, when they had heard mass, they all assembled in the court to tell the tales of their adventures, to discuss matters of chivalry, love and honour. And here was Sir Kay, also, sardonic as ever, who entered the hall waving a baton made from an apple bough.

'Surely it's time to eat,' he cried.

King Arthur frowned. 'How often must I remind you,' he said, 'that I will not sit down to eat until we have all seen or heard of some great adventure.'

Kay shook his head and wandered off to listen to the conversations of the knights and to interrupt with caustic comments of his own. And so the day drew on, until it was past noon. Then King Arthur called to Gawain and ordered him to have horses saddled and armour prepared. 'For it seems to me that we shall wait forever for something to happen, and therefore we shall go forth in search of adventure ourselves.'

Right away Gawain did as he was bid, and soon the whole company were setting forth, following the ancient track deep into the mighty forest of Broceliande, where everyone knew that all kinds of adventures were to be found.

After a while, the king reined in and listened. 'Hearken,' he said, 'I hear a voice raised in a cry for help. I shall try this adventure alone.'

'Let me come with you,' said Gawain. But the king shook his head and rode off alone amid the trees, following a narrow pathway until he reached a riverbank. There he saw a fine mill, at the door of which stood a woman tearing her hair and screaming for help as loudly as she might.

'What is the trouble, good woman?' demanded the king.

'Ah, sir,' she cried, 'a terrible beast has come down off the mountain and is eating all the grain in the mill!'

'Stand aside,' said King Arthur, and he dismounted and looked into the mill. There he saw the strangest creature he had ever seen: like a bull it was, but larger, with not two horns, but five! Its eyes were huge and glowing and its feet were the size of flat-irons. It was covered all over in coarse red hair and had long yellow teeth, with which it was eating its way through the mounds of grain.

King Arthur stared at the creature in amazement, but he drew his sword and putting his shield before him, advanced upon the beast. It completely ignored him, however, and continued eating, at which the king decided it must look fiercer than it truly was, and he gave it a hefty whack across the rump with the flat of his sword.

The beast continued to ignore him, whereat the king circled around it and gave it a prod in the shoulder with his sword. Still it did not move or even raise its head. So Arthur sheathed his sword and laid down his shield and grabbed it by the largest of its great horns and tried to wrestle it away from the grain.

Despite all his considerable strength the king could not so much as move the beast a fraction. So he went to take his hands off its horns in order to give it a blow with his fist between the eyes, only to find, to his dismay, that his hands were stuck fast, and that no mount of pulling and wrenching could move them at all!

As soon as it knew it had him, the beast raised its head and departed from the mill, carrying the helpless Arthur dangling from its horns. It proceeded at a gentle pace through the forest, passing close by Sir Gawain, who had remained at hand in case the king needed help.

When he saw the king being carried by a monster he cried out in alarm, and at once gave chase, drawing his sword. But King Arthur called out to him to hold his hand. 'I think I may die myself if you kill this creature,' he said. 'I have spared it and I believe it may spare me!'

At that moment Tristan and Yvain came riding full tilt, having being alerted by Gawain's cries and the noise of the beast moving through the wood. Gawain called out to them both not to attack, but to keep the beast in sight until they could discover what its intention might be.

The beast meanwhile simply cantered along the forest paths, seeming unaware of the knights or any of the clamour around it. It chose a path that rose steadily, and then with a burst of speed ran ahead of the pursuing knights and leapt swiftly up a steep escarpment. At the top it stopped, then turned and stuck its head out over the edge, leaving King Arthur dangling from its horns above the drop.

You may imagine that this caused the knights to grow desperate, as they saw their monarch in such dire straights. As for the king, he now clutched even tighter at the beast's horns; rather than trying to get free; while Sir Kay, looking up at the dreadful sight, almost fainted with horror!

Then one of the younger knights took thought and suggested that they all take off their clothes and pile them up at the foot of the cliff so that, if it chanced that the king should fall, he would at least have something soft to land on! Gawain thought this was an excellent notion, and urged the others to follow suit. About fifty of the knights began to tear off their garments, flinging them in a heap beneath the luckless king.

When it saw this the beast shook its head a little from side to side, causing all those watching to moan aloud. Then, seeming as though it would turn away from the cliff edge, the monster took a sudden leap outward and down. It landed in among the naked knights, and King Arthur all at once found that he was free. At the same instant the beast was itself transformed into a handsome man, who stood there laughing.

'Have your men get dressed, my lord,' the man-beast said. 'For now you have found a marvel and you can all go and eat.'

Then the king was astonished, for he recognized the man as a clever and audacious fellow who had come to the court some weeks before, and had begged as a promise from the king that, if he was able to change his appearance enough to fool everyone he should receive a golden cup, the best horse in the royal stable, and the right to kiss whichever maiden he deemed the most beautiful.

Now it was King Arthur's turn to laugh, for he loved a jest as well as any man, and the sight of his knights clustering around naked, scrabbling for their clothes, struck him as a good jest. 'Let us all return to the court and eat,' he cried, 'for I believe we shall all be warmer within.'

Thus laughing and jesting the knights regained their garments and set out for the court, soon arriving there and settling down to a fine feast. But they had not been eating long before there was a fresh interruption. A young man, very handsome and well dressed, rode into the court and, dismounting, approached the king's chair and fell to his knees before it.

'God bless the lord of this host,' he said.

'And his blessing upon you,' replied Arthur. 'What do you wish of us?'

'Sire, I have come here because I have heard that you are the finest king that ever lived, and I pray that you make me a knight.'

'It shall be our pleasure,' said the king, 'but for now be seated and join with us in our celebrations.'

'By your leave, not until I have been promised a boon,' said the youth.

'You shall have what you ask, so long as it does not harm anyone here,' said the king. And with that the youth seemed satisfied. But as he went to wash his hands there came yet another disturbance. A fully armed knight galloped into the hall and before the horrified eyes of all present he ran through with his lance one of the knights sitting at the table. Then he wheeled his horse and cried out, 'My greetings to you, King Arthur. I have done this to bring dishonour to your house! If you or any of your brave fellowship wants to pursue me, my name is Taulat de Rogimon. It is my intent to return here every year on this day until I am stopped!'

King Arthur was both angry and abashed, and leapt to his feet. But the young stranger was quicker. 'My lord,' he cried, 'let this be the boon I have requested and which you have promised to grant. Let me follow this evil knight and bring him to justice.'

'Keep silent, fellow,' snapped Sir Kay. 'You may well speak so when you are drunk. For now sit down and I'll tell you later on how to go about being brave.'

The young knight said nothing to this, though his fair skin coloured up. But the king rounded upon Sir Kay and bade him be silent and keep his evil tongue to himself. To the youth he said: 'Young man, I shall gladly make you a knight, as I promised, and give you arms and a horse to ride. But I bid you not to fight this Taulat until you are stronger. There are but few of my best knights whom I would expect to vanquish him.'

'Sire, I shall never know my strength until it is tested,' answered the youth. 'Let this be the test, and the boon I asked for.'

'Very well then,' said Arthur. 'But if I am to knight you I must first know your name.'

'In my own country I am known as Jaufre, the son of Dozos.'

'Ah,' sighed King Arthur, 'I knew your father well. A braver knight never bestrode horse than he. He died fighting at my side in Normandy. I was there when the arrow pierced his breast. Now do I see where you get your courage and strength.'

As he spoke a squire came with a proud, high-stepping war-horse, and Jaufre vaulted onto its back with a single bound. Then he took up the shield and lance that were proffered and, saluting the king with a ringing shout, spurred his mount from the hall.

Within days of leaving the court Jaufre had defeated his first opponent, a powerful knight named Estout of Verfueil, whom he sent back to surrender himself to King Arthur. After this he encountered an evil fellow who used a beautiful lance, left propped against a tree, to lure knights to their death. But Jaufre defeated him and hung him where he had hung many another before him, and sent back the man's dwarf to tell King Arthur that one less evil custom obtained in his lands. Then, still following the road and still seeking after the whereabouts of Taulat, Jaufre encountered a soldier guarding a narrow pass, whose practice was to capture and torture any knight who came that way. Him Jaufre dealt with summarily, cutting off both his feet and leaving him to die. Then he released twenty-five knights whom the soldier had held prisoner, and sent them all back to King Arthur. Then he rode on, not wanting to halt even to eat, so determined was he to overtake the knight who had challenged the honour of the Round Table.

And so he came to a place where the road ran between open fields, and there he saw a leper stumbling along holding a baby in his arms, while behind him ran a woman crying out for her child. When she saw Jaufre she ran and clung to his stirrup, begging him to help her, saying that the leper had stolen her child without reason.

Jaufre at once gave chase, and saw the leper run into the lazar house, where such poor unfortunates were wont to live. Dismounting, Jaufre hesitated for a moment at the door, then drew his sword and went in.

The room where he found himself was dark and dirty, but there was sufficient light for him to see where another leper lay in bed, holding a lovely woman who had no sign of the disease. She was weeping quietly to herself, and Jaufre could see that her clothes were torn and disarrayed.

When he saw the knight the leper jumped up and hefted a huge club in one hand. He was hideous to see, with misshapen features and red eyes.

His breathing was laboured and his voice a rough croak as he demanded to know what Jaufre wanted.

'I am looking for a leper who stole a woman's child. I saw him come in here.'

'It was a bad day when you did,' croaked the misshapen man, and without warning swung his club at Jaufre. The knight raised his shield just in time and took the full force of the blow there. Still, he staggered from the force of the attack, for though diseased the leper was immensely strong. Reacting swiftly Jaufre struck back with his sword, catching the leper on the arm and almost severing it.

Bellowing with pain the leper renewed his attack, and caught Jaufre a glancing blow on the helm which almost felled him. Drawing in his breath the knight struck with all his force down to the leper's head. The blow split his skull, but with his dying breath the leper kicked out so viciously that Jaufre was lifted from his feet and flung against the wall, where he lay, stunned from the blow and with blood pouring from his nose and mouth.

The maiden who had been on the point of ravishment by the leper came forward cautiously and unlaced the knight's helmet. When she saw the blood she cried out and ran to fetch some water which she flung in his face. Jaufre, still dazed and momentarily blinded by the blood in his eyes, struck out, thinking that he still held his sword. He knocked the maiden to her knees and then tried to stand, staggering around the room until he fetched up leaning against the wall. There he rested, gulping air, until his senses slowly cleared.

The maiden, approaching him with caution, asked if he were all right.

'I am well enough, lady,' answered the knight. 'But I seem to have lost my sword.'

'You dropped it when you were hurt. See, it is here on the floor by the man you killed.'

Jaufre looked at where the dead leper lay unmoving on the ground and quickly retrieved his sword. Then he looked around. 'Where is the other that I pursued? Did you see ought of him?'

But the maiden only shook her head. She had been too fearful for her own life and safety to notice anything.

'Then I shall look outside,' said Jaufre, and made for the door. To his astonishment, he found that he could not cross the threshold. Try as he might he was stopped each time as though by an invisible wall.

'Now what enchantment is this?' he cried and took a run at the door, only to fall back again. Panting, he slumped down dejectedly on the bed. Then just as he was bemoaning his evil luck, he heard loud cries coming from another room in the lazar house. Jumping to his feet he ran down a corridor until he came to a door that was shut fast and barred. The cries came from within.

Furiously, Jaufre banged on the door with the hilt of his sword, and, when it remained firmly shut, he raised a foot and kicked it open.

A terrible sight met his eyes within. The first leper, the one he had been pursuing, was there, as were a number of children of all ages. The leper had already killed four of them with a large knife and was threatening the rest, who cried out piteously. As Jaufre entered the man turned and threatened him with the knife, screaming out that his master would soon be there and that Jaufre would regret it if he did not flee.

'Your master is dead,' replied the knight, 'and you shall soon follow him.'

The leper threw down his knife at once and fell on his knees, begging for mercy. It was his master who had forced him to steal children and then kill them, wishing to bath in their blood to cure his disease.

'Is this the truth?' demanded Jaufre.

'I swear it on my immortal soul,' cried the leper.

'Then tell me why I cannot leave here,' said Jaufre.

'My master had great knowledge of magic,' replied the leper. 'He made it so that no one who entered here with intent to harm him could escape unless he personally took them out again – usually to kill or torture them. But there is a way for you to escape. In the other room there is the head of a boy, enclosed in a glass box. If you smash it my master's spells will be undone. But beware, there is very strong magic here. The whole house may fall upon you.'

Jaufre took the leper back into the main room and bound him fast. Then he gave instructions to the maiden to take him and the children outside, for the magic did not bind them as it did him. 'If I fail,' he said, 'be sure this wretch meets with his just deserts.'

The maiden did as she was bid, and once he was alone Jaufre went to the cavity in the wall where the strange head stood in its glass box. He took it down with caution and not a little revulsion, and saw that it was an artificial thing, but made extremely lifelike. Carefully he placed it on the floor and then took his sword and struck it with all his strength.

At once the head cried out and rose into the air. It flew around the room several times, spitting fire and emitting clouds of dense black smoke. The very earth quaked then, and huge hailstones crashed down from the sky. Lightning flashed and rain began to fall, lashing at the walls of the building, which began to crumble. Every timber and beam and brick seemed to dance and waver before his eyes, and Jaufre raised his shield over his head to protect himself as the roof collapsed with a great roar. Winds screamed though the ruins, lifting them and scattering them. Rocks and earth rose into the air and a great whirlwind caught up everything and took it away. At last, all that was left was Jaufre, and as the dust settled it was as though the house had never been, walls and foundations were all gone and not a trace remained of any of the evil magic.

Then Jaufre fell to the earth and lay like a dead man for a while. When his sense returned he found the maiden and the woman whose child he had saved bending over him anxiously, tending him with water and gentle words. In a while he was able to stand again, and he bade the two women to take the leper and go to King Arthur and tell him all that had happened that day. 'And greet the king from his knight, Jaufre son of Dozos, and tell him that I search still for Taulat, and will continue until I find him or die in the attempt.'

Then he mounted his horse and, taking up his lance and shield, set forth once again.

Now Jaufre was very tired, both from his journey and the many adventures and hardships he had experienced since leaving King Arthur's court. So it was that he rode almost blindly, letting his horse choose its own path, while he half-slept in the saddle, several times almost falling off And so he came to a castle, and found himself at the entrance to a garden, enclosed by high walls. It was the most beautiful place he had ever seen, with so many fair and sweet-scented plants that he deemed he was in an earthly paradise. Birds sang in the trees, and lush grass grew underfoot.

Jaufre was so exhausted that, almost without thought, he unsaddled his horse and turned it loose to graze. Then he placed his shield beneath his head and lay down in the shade of the trees. In moments he was asleep.

Now I must tell you that this castle and garden belonged to a most beautiful maiden named Brunnisend. There was none more fair in all the land, nor one so filled with sorrow. For both her parents were dead, and having no brother she ruled the castle, which was called Monbrun, alone. And hear what a strange custom there was in that land: for both its lady and all her people must mourn four times every day and again three times in the night, and if anyone asked the reason for this terrible lamentation they were at once killed. Thus the lady slept but little, and was much given to frequenting a room overlooking the garden, where the singing of the birds lulled her to sleep.

That night she retired early, but was disturbed to find that the birds were silent.

'Who has entered my garden?' she demanded. 'Nothing else would cause my birds to stop singing.' She summoned her seneschal and sent him into the garden. There he found Jaufre so soundly asleep that it took several minutes to wake him.

'For the love of God, let me sleep,' begged the knight. But the seneschal only prodded him harder and demanded that he attend upon his mistress.

'You will have to make me,' said Jaufre, and promptly fell asleep again while the seneschal went to fetch his armour and weapons.

When the seneschal returned he kicked Jaufre awake. 'Now fight with me, or become my prisoner,' he cried. Jaufre stumbled to his feet, angry at being thus woken again. He took up his sword and shield and defended himself against the seneschal. In a few blows he had defeated him and sent him scurrying back into the castle. There the Lady Brunnisend waited to see how he had fared.

'Where is the intruder?' she demanded.

'Lady, he has defeated me. I had great difficulty in waking him and even now I think he sleeps again.'

'Then we shall wake him up! 'cried the lady furiously. 'Summon the guard at once.'

In a matter of moments a dozen knights were assembled in the hall, and one of them, a man named Simon the Red, offered to go and bring the stranger inside as his prisoner.

'You may find it less easy than you expect,' said the seneschal.

Nevertheless Simon went forth and found the knight sleeping just as before. It took several prods with his spear to awaken Jaufre, who rose up so furiously that he disarmed the knight in moments.

Simon returned despondent and battered; then it was the turn of another knight, who fared exactly the same. Indeed, so filled with sleep was Jaufre that he thought it was Simon returning to disturb his rest yet more, and accordingly he dealt with the second challenger even more summarily. This displeased the lady Brunnisend greatly, and at once she ordered her seneschal to take a dozen knights and to bring the intruder so that she could see for herself what kind of monster defeated her knights so easily and without even being fully awake!

The next thing Jaufre knew was when he was seized upon by a dozen pairs of hands and carried, one holding each leg, another his arms, the rest his shoulders, body and head, from his place in the garden into the castle. Struggling mightily, and this time fully awake, he demanded to be put down and to be told the meaning of this unknightly behaviour. But the knights ignored his pleas and dumped him, unceremoniously, in front of the lady Brunnisend.

Looking with curiosity as much as anger at the tall young knight, she at once saw that not only was he handsome, but also clearly of noble birth and armed in the finest armour.

'Are you the fellow who has caused me so much trouble?' the lady demanded.

Jaufre turned to her and saw the most lovely woman he had ever beheld.

'I was not aware that I had done anything to cause you displeasure, my lady,' he said.

'By all the saints!' said Brunnisend. 'You shall be punished none the less. I think you will make a fine corpse as you swing in the wind when we have hanged you!'

'My lady,' said Jaufre, staring even more at her fair form, 'you may do with me whatever you will, since you have defeated me wearing no armour or weapons save your beauty. If I have unwittingly done you any harm then you must punish me, I see that. But I beg that you grant me one favour before you have me killed.'

'By God, sir, you speak very boldly for one that is soon to die,' said Brunnisend. Yet even as she spoke she changed colour and her anger began to abate. 'What is this favour you would ask?'

'Why, madame, only a good night's sleep,' replied Jaufre.

Brunnisend hesitated, and as she did so one of her knights spoke up, reminding her that it was only right to allow the condemned man one last wish.

'Well, it seems to me that you will soon have all the time you desire to sleep,' she said. 'But, if my knights will undertake to guard you, you shall have your wish.'

'My lady,' said the seneschal at once, 'no one shall be better guarded.' And he gave orders for a bed to be made up in the midst of the hall, and dispatched a dozen knights to keep watch until morning to see that Jaufre did not escape.

With that the Lady Brunnisend retired to bed, lulled once more by the song of the birds from her garden. But despite this she lay awake, thinking of the handsome young knight who lay asleep in the hall below. She wondered greatly who he might be, why he had come there, and if he might, just possibly, find her worthy of love.

And so the night passed, until the watchman called the hour of midnight. At this moment everyone in the castle woke and began to mourn loudly, crying and wailing and making such a complaint that even Jaufre was awakened from his profound sleep. He lay there unmoving, however, wondering what caused the lamentations, and thinking too that he should try to make his escape from this strange castle – even if it meant leaving the beautiful maiden whom he recalled very clearly seeing earlier.

If he had known that the same beautiful lady was at that moment lying awake thinking of him, he would certainly have remained where he was. As it was he saw that his guards, worn out from their lamenting, which had at last ceased, had themselves fallen asleep, so he hastened to exit the hall as quietly as he could. Good fortune attended him in that he found his horse, armour and weapons with ease, and in a short time he had left the castle and was heading away on the road, wondering still about the strange castle and its sorrowful inhabitants.

Brunnisend, meanwhile, lay awake until morning, then rose and joined again in the lamentations with which the people of that place greeted every day. Then, when all was still again, she hastened to call the seneschal to her and demanded news of the prisoner.

Now the seneschal had already discovered the absence of Jaufre, and feared greatly to admit that he had failed in his duty, and so he told his mistress that the knight was dead.

'How did this happen?' cried Brunnisend in dismay.

'My lady, last night after you had retired, the stranger woke during the time of the first lamentation. Then he asked the question which must not be asked, and he has paid the penalty for that. As many as a hundred blows fell upon him, cutting him to pieces like a butchered stag. We have already buried him, since we did no wish to grieve you further.'

'Alas, you have grieved me more than you know!' cried Brunnisend. Then she said to the seneschal: 'I must know all there is to know about this knight. I bid you go and seek out his name and rank and history.'

'But where shall I look?' demanded the seneschal, suddenly regretting his lies.

'Where all good knights are found – at the court of King Arthur. Go there and find out all that you can. It may be that he has family who will wish to know how his life ended.'

And with that the seneschal departed, albeit reluctantly, knowing that in truth Jaufre was not dead, and dreading to met him on the road.

As for Jaufre himself, he made his way as best he might, putting as much distance between himself and the castle of Monbrun as he could. He was soon regretting that he had not eaten either the night before or that morning, and when he came upon a herdsman, preparing his morning repast by the roadside, he hesitated hardly at all before accepting the man's invitation join him.

The herdsman was cheery enough, and shared his food with a will. The two men chatted of this and that, and among other things Jaufre learned the name of the lady of Monbrun. Soon he prepared to continue upon his way, but as he was preparing to mount and ride off he turned back to the herdsman and asked him if he could tell him the reason for the strange lamentations which took place at the castle. The herdsman's response was immediate; he turned in the blink of an eye from a friendly, garrulous fellow into a raging madman, attacking Jaufre with a club while screaming abuse at him.

Feeling nothing but bewilderment, the knight defended himself without hurting the herdsman, then rode on as quickly as he could. All that day he continued on his way without meeting anyone, though twice more he heard the terrible sound of lamentation seeming to come from the land itself. Then, as the day was drawing out, he fell in with two young men who were out hunting. They quickly offered him the hospitality of their father's house, which was nearby, and Jaufre accepted it willingly. His host was named Augier d'Exiart, and he made the young knight welcome. When he heard Jaufre's name and parentage, he wept and embraced the youth. 'Your father and I fought side by side in many a skirmish,' the kindly lord explained. 'You are welcome in my house for as long as you desire.'

'My lord, I am glad indeed to accept your hospitality,' said Jaufre, 'though I regret that I may not stay for more than a night.'

They went in and sat down to dine, and there Jaufre made the acquaintance of the lord's daughter, a very fair maiden, who won the knight's heart with her gentle ways and lovely face.

When they had dined Jaufre was shown into a clean and comfortable bed and went to sleep for what seemed the first time in weeks without fear or discomfort. So deeply did he sleep that he failed even to hear the lamentations which took place in the night, and in which both the lord of the castle and his family took part. In the morning Jaufre prepared to depart, and his host came to bid him a reluctant farewell. 'I wish there was something I could do for you in honour of your father's friendship,' he said.

Jaufre hesitated. 'My lord,' he said, 'there is one thing that you might be able to do – to settle a matter which has been troubling me these past days.'

'And what is that?' asked Augier kindly.

'Everywhere I have ridden in these lands I have heard a terrible lamentation on every side, three times a day and I know not how many times at night. Can you tell me the reason for it?'

Almost before the words were out of his mouth, the old lord had drawn his sword and sprung at him like a tiger, screaming abuse and threatening to kill him at once. Jaufre defended himself as best he might, turning aside the blows with his shield and retreating until he could leap onto his horse and ride pell-mell for the gate. He could hear the old lord shouting to his sons and calling out for their mounts to be fetched, and soon enough he heard the sound of hoofs on the road behind him.

Just as he was thinking of turning at bay and defending himself in earnest, Jaufre again heard the morning lamentation, and sped on even faster, hearing the voices of the three knights behind him cry out with all the rest. Then at once the noise ceased, and after a moment Jaufre heard the voice of Augier d'Exiart calling upon him to stop, and begging his forgiveness for his unchivalrous behaviour.

Cautiously Jaufre reined in, loosening his sword in its sheath. But the lord and his two sons were no longer mad with fury or sorrow. They rode up to him and the old lord fell in the dust at his feet, begging Jaufre to forgive him in the name of God and of the young knight's own father.

Sheathing his sword Jaufre answered that there was nothing to forgive since no harm had been done to him. Augier gave thanks to God and got back on his own horse. Facing Jaufre he said: 'My friend, I cannot speak of that which you asked me, but I will do anything else I can to further your way. Is there any deed I may do to serve you?'

'There is but one,' replied Jaufre, 'though I know not whether you can help or not. I seek a knight by the name of Taulat de Rogimon, who has done ill to my lord King Arthur. Have you by chance heard anything of him?'

The old lord sighed heavily. 'I do indeed know something of this knight,' he said. 'You would be well advised to avoid him if possible, for he is both evil-hearted and strong. Yet if you truly must seek him, for I see in your face that you will not turn aside, then here is what you must do. Ride on from here a few leagues until you see a great castle. Outside the walls will be many tents and pavilions filled with rich lords and brave knights. Do not speak to any of them, but make your way into the castle itself. No one will stop you as long as you speak to no one. In the hall you will see a sad sight – a noble knight lying on a bed, all wounded and close to death. At the foot of the bed will be a young maiden, at its head an older lady. It is she with whom you must speak. Tell her I sent you and ask about the cry. When she has told you all there is to tell, you will know the whereabouts of the knight whom you seek. Now I bid you be gone, for I have said too much, and my head feels near to bursting with the sorrow of it!'

With this the old lord turned away, and calling his sons to him, rode off, leaving Jaufre to follow the way indicated – though in truth he did not know whether to be elated by the possibility of finding Taulat at last, or puzzled by the mysterious words concerning the wounded knight.

Thus he rode on until he came to the castle, which was just as the old lord had described. Jaufre rode as hard as he could through the assembled encampment. On every side he saw knights come out of their tents to watch him pass, but no one tried to stop him, either there or at the gates to the castle, which stood wide. Hastening onward, Jaufre made his way through several rooms, each one more splendidly furnished than the one before, until he saw a small door that was standing half open, and looking within he saw a knight lying on the bed, his upper body bound up with blood-stained bandages, his face pale and drawn with suffering. Beside the bed sat two women, just as Augier had described, and at once Jaufre went in softly and spoke to the older of the two, asking her if he might talk with her for a moment. The lady rose and guided him outside the chamber. Then she asked him, in low tones, what he was doing there.

'Lady, I have come from the castle of Augier d'Exiart. I am seeking one Taulat de Rogimon, who has done much harm to my lord King Arthur.' Jaufre went on to describe the events at the court, and all the while the lady listened sadly. Then she spoke: 'Sir, I am not at all surprised to hear what you say, for there was never a more evil and black-hearted villain than he whom you seek. He has brought suffering more than I can scarce speak of to this house.'

'Tell me if you will,' said Jaufre, 'and also where I may find Taulat.'

'I will tell you everything,' said the lady. 'The knight who lies within that room is a victim of Taulat's evil ways. His father was killed by that devil, and he himself received a fearful wound in the breast. Now hear what Taulat does. Every month, when this brave knight's wounds are almost healed, the evil one returns and forces him to climb the hill beyond the castle in full armour. This causes his wounds to open again and his fever to return. For more than a year this has occurred, and I fear greatly for the knight, who grows weaker each time he is forced to undergo this fearful ordeal.'

'In truth, that is a terrible story,' said Jaufre, 'and Taulat has much to answer for.'

'Indeed, but I fear there is no knight now living – save perhaps Sir Gawain – who can overcome him.'

'Sir Gawain will not come until after me, should I fail,' said Jaufre. 'But tell me, who are all these knights encamped around the castle?'

'They are all brave lords who have sought to defeat Taulat. None have succeeded, and all are his prisoners. Expect no help from them, for they are sore afraid of this dread knight.'

'When will Taulat return here again?' Jaufre asked.

'In one week,' answered the lady. 'If you will be guided by me you will leave here and return only when that much time has passed. But in truth you should go far away and never return, for I fear you will find only death at the hands of Taulat.'

'That I may not do,' said Jaufre. 'I shall return in one week and do all that I can to relieve your suffering.' He hesitated. 'I would ask one more thing of you, and that concerns the dreadful lamentation which I hear everywhere in his land. Lord Augier told me that you would speak to me of this, though no other that I have asked has yet done so.'

The lady sighed. 'I will tell you indeed, though it grieves me to do so. This knight who lies within is the noblest of men, and much beloved of all his people. It is they who cry out every day and night for the sake of the suffering he must endure. So deeply do they feel his pain, that it is as though it was their own. Thus they cry out whenever his suffering is at its worst, and are driven half mad by the anguish and fear that all who encounter Taulat come to feel sooner or later. Thus we have all sworn not to speak of this, and those strangers who come here ask at their peril.'

Then Jaufre thanked the lady and departed from the castle and rode away into the forest to await the passing of the week before Taulat was due to arrive. He felt nothing but sorrow for the fate of the wounded man, and anger on behalf of all who suffered because of the evil knight.

And so the days passed, until it was time for Jaufre to return to the castle. But he had not gone even so much as a mile when he came upon an old woman by the roadside. As he approached he saw that she was the strangest and most hideous female he had ever seen. She had long green teeth, straggly hair, thin shanks and a bloated belly. Her eyes were huge and long tusks poked out of her slobbery lips. Her skin was blackened and withered and she drooled over her fine velvet gown like an infant.

When she saw Jaufre she called out to him: 'Where are you going, foolish man? Turn back at once!'

'Not until I know a good reason to do so,' answered Jaufre.

'If you go on you will regret it,' said the hag.

'Why should I believe you?' said Jaufre. 'What are you?'

At this the old woman stood up suddenly, and she was as tall and straight as a spear. Suddenly she did no look as old, though her appearance was terrifying.

Jaufre crossed himself at once, but the hag only laughed. 'I see you will not turn aside,' she said. 'So be it. You will see far worse than me before too long.'

Jaufre hurried on, glad to put space between himself and the strange creature. He continued until he saw a small hermit's cell; then a knight dressed all in black appeared as if from nowhere and rode full tilt at him. Caught by surprise, Jaufre was knocked from his horse. Angrily, he scrambled up and drew his sword. But as he looked about him the Black Knight was nowhere to be seen. Bewildered, Jaufre got back on his horse, and at once there was the knight riding furiously toward him. This time Jaufre was more prepared and managed to lower his spear. The Black Knight ran upon it so fast and hard that it pierced right through his body. Yet the force of his attack again unhorsed Jaufre and when he got up and prepared to finish off the wounded man, there was no sign of him.

Again Jaufre remounted, and there at once was the Black Knight, seemingly unhurt. Again they charged, and again Jaufre was unhorsed. There on the ground he turned at bay, but again the knight had vanished. And so it continued, throughout that afternoon. As long as he was on horseback Jaufre could see the Black Knight clearly; when he was on the ground he could not. In the end he grew so tired of this game that he remained on the earth and leading his mount made his way towards the chapel.

Then at once the Black Knight reappeared, this time himself on foot, and attacked Jaufre with sword and shield. As dusk was beginning to fall, it became increasingly difficult to see his attacker. But Jaufre defended himself as best he might and succeeded in cutting off the Black Knight's arm. In a blink, however, it grew back, and when, a moment later, the young knight struck a blow that split his opponent's skull to the teeth, the wound healed so quickly that he scarcely had time to withdraw his sword.

Thus they continued fighting for another hour. The Black Knight could

Jaufre

The Story of Lanzalet

not succeed in wounding Jaufre, but the youth began to tire as he was struck punishing blow after punishing blow, while he himself seemed unable to kill his terrible opponent. Matters might have gone on in this wise until Jaufre was worn down, had not the hermit intervened. Tired of being kept awake by the incessant noise of battle, he rose from his bed and issued forth with his stole around his shoulders, and a vessel of holy water in his hands. When he saw that the Black Knight fled screaming, and the hermit helped Jaufre to stumble into the shelter of his hut, where he removed his armour and fell into a deep sleep of exhaustion.

In the morning he awoke to find that the hermit had fed and stabled his horse and laid out fresh garments for him. The good man then came to say mass, and afterwards offered Jaufre bread and water before asking him who he was and what brought him to this place.

'I am of King Arthur's court, and I am seeking an evil knight named Taulat.'

'This is not the place to look for him,' said the hermit. 'This is a borderland. Beyond here is an evil region, through which no man may pass.'

'How can this be?' asked Jaufre. 'Who was that knight with whom I fought?'

'That was no knight, but a demon of hell, called here by an evil old woman who lives near hear. She is the mother to a giant who has terrorized these lands for more than thirty years.'

'Indeed, I met with this woman,' said Jaufre.

'Well then, you know of what I speak,' said the hermit. 'I will tell you the story of how they came here. Years ago the old woman had a husband, a monstrous fellow like herself. But after he had led a cruel life for many years he was at last slain, and his wife, fearing for her two sons, summoned the devil who now guards the path. But in truth her sons are grown now, and they are as evil as their father. One was cursed with leprosy and his mother made a house for him off to the East of here. I have heard it said that a knight came there recently and ended his miserable existence. Now his brother has gone to seek confirmation of this, and to take revenge on the one who slew his sibling.'

'By my faith,' said Jaufre, 'it was I who slew the giant leper. No doubt his brother will soon return to find me.' And with that he told the hermit the whole story of his quest and his fight with the lepers. At the end he said: 'I must leave this place and find somewhere else to wait, for I fear that the giant may do you harm if he finds that you have sheltered me.'

'He cannot harm me,' replied the hermit. 'Yet it may be wise for you to depart, for I do not think you would be able stand up to the creature when it returns.'

'Be sure that I shall do my best,' said Jaufre grimly. 'For now I shall go elsewhere and await the return of Taulat.'

With this he departed, taking the blessings of the hermit with him. But he had not ridden more than a mile when he saw the giant approaching. Under one arm he carried a maiden who was crying out in terror and distress. At once Jaufre lowered his lance and charged. He struck the giant in the middle of his breast and pierced him right through. Still the huge creature was able to grab the spear and pull Jaufre from his horse, smiting him with such force as he did so that the young knight was almost knocked unconscious.

With spinning head, he staggered to his feet and drew his sword as the maiden cried out a warning. He struck the giant such a blow that it cut away part of his left arm and flank. As blood poured from the wound, the giant bellowed in madness and Jaufre, rushing in quickly, cut off his head with a single blow. Then he fell down in an exhausted heap, until the maiden came and helped to revive him. He looked up at her and recognized her as Augier's daughter, though it was a moment more before she in turn knew him. Then she fell at his feet weeping with relief.

Pulling himself together with difficulty, Jaufre rose and, placing the maiden on the saddle before him, rode on towards the castle where he was destined to meet with Taulat de Rogimon. He soon came in sight of its walls, and there he saw Taulat's men dragging the wounded knight forth with bound hands, and preparing to drive him to climb the hill. Jaufre rode up in haste and begged them to stop. At that moment Taulat himself, who had seen the young knight arrive, emerged from his hall and haughtily demanded that he get down and surrender himself and the maiden into his power.

'I shall not do that,' responded Jaufre, 'since I have come here with no other intent than to fight with you. Therefore ask that you release this noble knight whom you have tortured for so long and return with me to King Arthur, for you have done him great ill, and he requires an apology.'

Taulat looked at him in disbelief. Then he laughed. 'Are you aware that I have defeated a hundred men better and stronger than you? I will give you a moment to surrender, or else I promise to kill you.'

'That is for God to decide,' said Jaufre. 'I shall wait here until you are armed and ready.'

'I do not even need my armour to defeat you,' said Taulat scornfully. 'My spear and shield will be enough.' Then he called out to his squire to fetch only these things.

And so the two men came face to face at last, and set their spears in rest and charged upon each other. And Taulat's spear struck Jaufre's shield in the centre and lifted him out of the saddle. But Jaufre's spear passed clean through his opponent's shield and pierced his side and opened a great wound there. Taulat fell to the earth and lay there moaning. And Jaufre came and stood over him with drawn sword.

'Sir,' cried Taulat in anguish. 'You have beaten me. Alas for my folly that has brought me to this. Spare me, I beg you, and anything in my power shall be yours.'

'As to that,' said Jaufre sternly, 'I shall give you mercy, but only if you promise to set free your prisoners and go as soon as you are able to King Arthur. I can forgive you for the pains you have caused me, but the king must decide for himself.'

To this the knight swore, and Jaufre allowed a surgeon to come and search his wounds and dress them. Then the knight who had been Taulat's plaything for so long came forward, walking stiffly for he was still weak from his long ill-treatment. 'Sir,' he said, 'I owe you my life and more. If there is anything I can do to repay you, you have only to name it.'

'I ask for nothing,' replied the hero, 'save that you go to King Arthur and tell him all that has taken place here. And if you see a knight named Sir Kay, tell him he had been better advised to hold his tongue when he last spoke to me.'

Then Jaufre requested a mount for Augier's daughter, and set off at once to take her home to her father as he had promised. And as for the wounded knight, he set out as soon as he might, taking the slowly recovering Taulat with him, and on arriving at Arthur's court he told the king all that had happened and praised Jaufre greatly for his courage and bravery in the face of so many dangers. Then the king turned his attention to Taulat, who went upon his knees and begged for mercy .

At first Arthur was reluctant to pardon the knight, but he begged so humbly and in such evident anguish, that at last Arthur did forgive him. But as to the knight whom Taulat had held prisoner and treated so vilely for seven years, he could not forgive so easily. And so a trial was decreed and the knight gave witness to Taulat's cruelty. The judgement of the court was this: that Taulat be placed in the custody of his own former prisoner, who was instructed to whip him up the hill just as he himself had been whipped by Taulat. And thus it was agreed.

Jaufre, meanwhile, returned to the castle of Augier d'Exiart, where you can imagine he was warmly welcomed, both for his overcoming of Taulat, and more especially for the return of the old lord's daughter. But Jaufre himself could only think of the fair Brunnisend, and longed to return to her. And, even while he thought of this, her own seneschal arrived, who as you may remember had been looking for Jaufre ever since he had escaped the castle where he was imprisoned. When he saw Jaufre he was both glad and fearful – glad that the had found the knight and fearful at what his mistress might do when she discovered that he had lied to her. Nevertheless he begged Jaufre to return home with him, and this the young knight agreed to, though he asked that the seneschal protect him from the wrath of his lady, for the youth had no knowledge of Brunnisend's feelings for him, and feared that she would still be angry towards him. But the seneschal reassured him, for had he not overcome Taulat and restored her overlord to his freedom?

And so Jaufre returned to Monbrun with the seneschal, and the Lady Brunnisend came out to meet him and was both glad and amazed to see him alive. Then she heard all that had occurred, and that the lord of that land was set free because of Jaufre. Then she was very glad indeed, as were all her people, for now they need lament no more. And you can be sure that she soon forgave the seneschal for his lie, for in truth she loved Jaufre, and in a while she was able to tell him her true feelings. Then the young knight declared his own love, and they were of one accord and set out for Arthur's court to declare their wish to marry. You may imagine the rejoicing which took place when Jaufre finally returned home, bringing with him as fair a lady as anyone had ever seen. And there Jaufre avenged himself on Sir Kay for his cruel words, with a sound buffeting, and was much praised by all for his courage and chivalry.

And so in due time Jaufre married his Brunnisend, and the two of them lived happily together for the rest of their days. And Jaufre had many more adventures, which perchance I shall be enabled to tell on another occasion, if the Lord spares me. For now, my story is told.

12

The Story of Lanzalet

IN this tale we find a very different story to the one normally associated with the great French knight. The more usual version, told in such works as the thirteenth-century *Prose Lancelot* or Chrétien de Troyes's twelfth-century poem *Lancelot, or the Knight of the Cart*, emphasizes the hero's illicit passion for Arthur's queen, as well as his great personal strength and prowess. *Lanzalet*, which was written by a Swiss knight named Ulrich von Zatzikhoven, in *c.*1194, very possibly represents an earlier phase in the development of Lancelot's history, when he was still an unknown, errant knight. Here, he meets and falls in love with (and ultimately marries) another lady, while of the Guinevere story there is no trace – although the young hero does become the queen's champion.

Almost nothing is known about Ulrich, though he has been tentatively identified as a thirteenth-century cleric named as witness to a document dated 1214. He claimed that the source for his work was 'a Welsh Book' owned by Hugo de Morville, a crusader who remained a hostage of the German emperor Henry VI after the release of his more famous prisoner, Richard Coeur de Lion, in 1194. Though no trace of this book has survived, it is assumed to have been a French or Anglo-Norman work, which possibly retained some of the older Celtic aspects of the Arthurian tales. This may well offer some evidence for the existence of an earlier Lancelot figure, predating Chrétien's famous poem, possibly the 'Llwch Lleminawg' referred to in the ninth-century poem *Preiddeu Annwn*. If so, it is possible that Lancelot, in this guise, was one of Arthur's

heroes long before his medieval counterpart.

Lanzalet is, to my mind, one of the best of the many Arthurian tales which have survived from the period in which they first became popular among a courtly audience. It has shape, style and pace and is generally written in an engaging and occasionally witty style which is in marked contrast to some of the more worthy romances which nowadays make dull reading.

There are some marvellous scenes and descriptions in it, which I have done my best to capture. Notably, there is the account of the tournament in which Lanzalet disguises himself in different coloured armour (a theme which was adapted by several later storytellers, but nowhere as well as here). Beside this I would place the accounts of Iweret's castle, the Beautiful Forest, and the marvellous tent with its magic mirror. All of these could so easily be seen as stock devices within the medieval romance tradition, but here they are used to good effect and with a sense of newness which is more rarely found among the later retellings.

The whole episode of Lanzalet's meeting with Iweret at the fountain in Beforet is a classic example of this kind of adventure, and the exchange between the two knights bears all the signs of a ritual question and response. In addition the psychology and motivation of the characters is as good as anything I have found in these tales, where very often characters act with no reason other than the author's desire to keep the story moving!

I have chosen to tell only the first half of the poem here, since the rest is little more than a string of further adventures and the real story, ending with Lanzalet's discovery of his name, and his love for Yblis, seems to end here. Also, the episode of the Mantle Test, represented here in another version (see *The Boy and the Mantle*; pages 76–83) makes it unnecessary to duplicate this part of the story. I have chosen to anglicize some of the names ('Ban' for Lanzalet's father rather than 'Pant' as in the original) for the sake of clarity, while retaining the original spelling of Lanzalet to emphasize the variance in the character and story of the hero.

The original text is found in two incomplete manuscripts and two fragments, edited, in the original German, by Karl A. Hahn: *Lanzalet, eine Erahlung* (Frankfurt, Bronner, 1845). It has been translated only once, in an excellent version by Kenneth G. T. Webster, which has extensive notes by the great Arthurian scholar Roger Sherman Loomis, *Lanzalet* (New York, Columbia University Press, 1951). This is the version I have followed in my own retelling, and those who wish to read the entire story are recommended to seek it out. There is as yet little background material in English; however one of the best commentaries remains that of Ernst Soudek, 'Suspense in the Early Arthurian Epic: An Introduction to Ulrich von Zatzikhoven's Lanzalet' in his *Studies in the Lancelot Legend* (Houston, Rice University Press, 1972). Another account can be found in *Ladies of the Lake* by Caitlín and John Matthews (London, HarperCollins, 1992).

HERE WAS ONCE A STRONG AND PROUD king named Ban who ruled over the kingdom of Genewis. No longer young, he had fought in many wars and received numerous scars in the process. Possessed of a will of iron, he would brook no opposition from any of his lords, who hated him for his harsh and terrifying justice. The people, on the other hand, though fearing him, yet respected him, for he treated them exactly as he did any man, and meted out justice to both high- and low-born equally.

Now this lord had a lady, named Clarine, who was as sweet-natured as her husband was fierce. Whenever and wherever she could she went about doing good to the people of Genewis, and for this was greatly loved. Indeed, it is said that while many of Ban's lords desired his death, they stayed their hands for many years on account of his lady, whom they served with as much faith as they might, and spared her husband rather than bring her grief.

As Ban grew older he went less often to war, and began to look to his home life. So it was that his lady bore him a son, late in both their lives, whom they named Lanzalet. Great things were prophesied for him, and his mother nursed him herself rather than putting him out to a wet nurse as was the custom in that time. Many fair and noble women held him on their laps, and his father was as proud of him as a man ever was of his son.

But the time came when the lords of Genewis could no longer bear the harshness of their lord, and a great number of them banded together against him. They raised a huge army and, hearing that Ban was residing in a castle by the sea, they laid siege to it, slaughtering the people in the villages around.

So angry was King Ban that he could scarcely be persuaded from going out alone against the besiegers. Only the pleas of his wife prevented it, and instead he took up his place on the walls near to the gate, where the fighting was thickest. And there, in due course, he fell, mortally wounded. Almost too weak to stand he dragged himself to his chambers and begged his wife to help him to a certain spring which rose near to the castle, midway between its walls and a lake of still dark water which was rumoured to be haunted. The spring itself was said to possess healing properties, and here the wounded king and his wife made their way – she nursing in her arms her child, who was not yet one year old. And there, shortly after, the king died, for not even the water from the spring could revive him.

Then the queen, weeping and much afraid for her life and that of her tiny son, laid him down for a moment beneath a tree, while she fetched water to wash the face of her dead lord. And there, as she turned away, there came a sudden mist from off the sea, and within it walked a faery woman, who spied the child lying beneath the tree and took him in her own arms and went with him back beneath the waves whence she had come. Soon after the queen herself, distraught with fear and sorrow, was taken prisoner by the attacking forces.

Now as to the nature of the being who had stolen the child of Ban and Clarine, I have heard it said that she was a mermaid, while others report that she was one of the faery kind who dwell beneath the waters of lake or sea. Be that as it may, I can tell you that she was a queen in her own right, and that more than a hundred beautiful otherworldly women waited upon her. As to the land over which she ruled, it was a fair place indeed, and though it lay hidden beneath the waves, yet it seemed as if it were an open land, lying peacefully beneath the sun. And it seemed as if it was always May-time in that place, with blossom on the apple-trees, and birds singing from every branch. Around the land was a marvellous enclosure of crystal walls and in the centre stood a great crystal mountain with slopes as smooth as glass. Atop this sat a castle of great splendour and beauty, with walls of gold adorned with wondrous carvings. Nothing within that castle ever aged so much as a single day, nor did any there feel envy or anger towards one another, but lived together as peacefully as one could imagine. Such joy was in that land, that if one were to spend only a few moments within it, one would never feel sorrow again, but only perpetual joy.

So in this wondrous place the child grew to manhood, untouched by fear or sorrow, a stranger to the ways of men. Mostly he was cared for by the women of that place, who found him an apt pupil and taught him manners, and the arts of singing and making music, as well as of letters. To many he was a favourite, and there were those among them who were heard to remark that if all humans were to behave in so good and honourable a fashion there might be fewer problems in the affairs of men.

When the youth turned twelve the queen gave him into the care of the men of that place, who in turn taught him to hunt and shoot with a bow and arrow, to follow the chase on foot with a full pack of the strange white-bodied, red-eared hounds of the place. He learned as well to fight with sword and buckler, to wrestle and to throw stones. By the time he was fifteen, he could run as fleetly as a deer and walk for long distances without growing tired. Yet he knew little or nothing of riding, nor of the bearing of arms, for none in that company were ever seen to ride a horse or to don mail or plate. Nor did he know his own true name, for they were wont to call him 'fair youth' or 'boy', and this irked him greatly, though he spoke not of it. Indeed as he grew older rumours of the outside world began to concern him more, and he wondered much of his origins, knowing full well that he was not as the other people of that place.

Thus when he turned fifteen Lanzalet went before the queen and asked leave to depart.

'Are you then not happy here?' she asked.

'It is not that, lady; rather that I feel cramped by this place. I would learn more of the world outside and prove myself in the world of men to which I belong. Madam, I do not even know my own name, since none here will tell it to me.'

'Nor shall they,' replied the queen. 'Neither shall I.'

'Who has forbidden you to tell me?' demanded the youth.

'No one,' replied she. 'None the less I may not speak of it at this time.'

'All the more reason then that I should go forth. For perhaps in the outer world I may learn my true identity and also prove myself worthy of your trust.'

'To do that you would have to defeat the strongest knight in the world,' answered the queen.

'Tell me his name,' cried Lanzalet. 'Let me seek him out.'

'His name is Iweret of Beforet. His castle is called Dodone, and lies far to the West, across the sea in the lands of men. He has done me great harm, and if you were to avenge me upon him I should be glad indeed. Yet I fear you are no match for him, for I have never seen a mightier fighter in the world of men, and you are as yet untried.'

'Nevertheless I will try if you will allow me. Give me whatever advice you think best.'

'As to advice,' said the queen, 'I have none. But I do have gifts for you which may help you in this matter.'

So saying she rose and went to another chamber and took from a chest a suit of white armour which she showed him how to put on. Then she gave him a mighty sword, with a golden hilt, and a shield on which was emblazoned a golden eagle. And to wear over his armour she gave him a rich surcoat sewn with gold thread and hung with small golden bells. Lastly she led him forth and showed him where a great war-steed stood pawing the earth. This was the greatest marvel of all to him, for he had scarcely ever seen a horse of this kind before. It had a wonderful golden bridle, worked with all kinds of jewels, and a saddle of white leather, tooled with rich decorations.

'These are my gifts to you,' said the lady, a little sad to see the youth departing. 'Take them with my blessing.'

Then the youth took leave of the lady, and all the rest of the folk of the crystal castle, who came forth to see him upon his way. He took ship in one of the wondrous vessels of that place, which soon bore him out of sight of the otherworldly land and in time brought him to the lands of men. There he took leave of the faery woman who had brought him thither, and she in turn bade him treat all whom he met with honour, to be steadfast and true in all things, and ever to do the best he might. Then she left him, and without looking back the youth mounted his new horse and rode West.

And now hear of a strange thing. Since he had never properly learned to ride, he had no notion of how to hold the reins, but simply tucked them around the saddlebow and left the animal to make its own way. At first it wandered in search of grass to eat, but then it came upon a road, and habit – or the luck of the youth – caused it to canter along as it was used to do.

And so the day passed, and the youth was filled with good spirits, so that he felt no fatigue, but rather looked forward to the adventures which lay ahead. That night he slept in the open, and in the morning rode on until he came in sight of a castle. The horse turned that way as was its wont, and thus took the youth to where a dwarf sat on a white horse. Glowering at the youth the dwarf called upon him to halt. Since the young man had no means to rein in his mount he continued onward. As he passed the dwarf the latter swung at him with his whip, inflicting him with a cut on his hand. When this brought no response the dwarf rode after him and lashed out cruelly at the youth's horse. But this only caused it to run faster still, and in a few moments both the dwarf and the castle were left behind.

Bewildered, the youth continued on his way – which was really the way his mount wished to go – until he reached a place where a stream ran through marshy lands, and there he met a handsome, richly-clad fellow, riding towards him on a fine horse, and carrying a hawk upon his wrist. Seeing how inexpertly he rode, the man called out cheerfully: 'Sir, I shall be glad if you would ride more carefully and not knock me down! ' Then as Lanzalet came along side he reached over and caught the reins, bringing the youth's mount to a halt.

'Forgive me for asking,' said the stranger, 'but why do you ride so oddly? Is it some penance that has been placed upon you? Or has some lady demanded that you ride wherever your horse sees fit to take you? Pardon my curiosity, but though you are clad like a warrior you carry yourself like a child. My name, by the way, is Johfret de Liez. Whom do I have the pleasure of addressing?'

All this was said in so disarming a manner, that Lanzalet could not take offence. Indeed, he was rather glad to have someone to talk to who seemed to know all about horses, and who did not strike at him with a whip!

Eager to converse he said: 'Sir, you will understand I am sure that I know very little of horses and riding. I have but lately left a land where such things are unknown. It is a land ruled over by women, where knights' deeds and sports have no place. Nevertheless I am eager to learn of such things, and hence I have set out in search of adventure. Also I hope to learn something of my name and origin, since both have been kept from me.'

At this Johfret de Liez laughed. 'Upon my word, I dare say that I never heard such a story before. I can see that you are well born, but it seems to me that you could use some advice – at least on how to ride! Let me offer you the hospitality of my house, which is not far from here. If you can take more of the company of women, there are many fair ladies at my castle. My mother is there also, and is always glad to meet new and worthy people.'

'I shall be glad to,' said Lanzalet, 'and I thank you.'

'Thank me by riding with greater care,' laughed Johfret. 'Grip the saddle with your knees, hold the reins as I do, and watch where you go.'

So saying the two set forth, and by dint of watching what his new-found friend did, and copying him faithfully, Lanzalet was soon riding almost as well as if he had been used to do so for far longer than two days!

They soon reached Johfret's castle, where they were welcomed by his mother and her ladies, who made a great fuss of the handsome young man. The lady herself, being full of curiosity about her son's new friend, asked many questions, and soon elicited from him the story of his life, everything he remembered from his childhood up to the moment, though he spoke nothing of his mission for the Queen of the Lake.

When she had learned all about him, the lady send forth messengers to every part of the land and those which neighboured upon her own, calling for knights to take part in a *bohourt*, which was a kind of mock tournament designed to show off the abilities of the young men who aspired to knighthood and errantry. Many came in answer to her summons, and thus Lanzalet was treated to a display of horsemanship and weaponry such as he had never dreamed existed.

On the third day his own mount was brought to him, and donning the armour and weapons that the Queen of the Lake had given him, he himself rode forth and acquitted himself so well that he became the centre of attention among all the company. Though his horsemanship still lacked firmness, no one could say that his handling of sword and spear were anything other than marvellous.

And so the *bohourt* came to an end, with the young Lanzalet taking many prizes. Then he was eager to depart, for now he felt ready indeed for whatever adventures might befall. And so he took leave of his hosts, and rode upon his way until he reached a dark forest. There he journeyed for much of the day, until he heard the sounds of battle coming from a clearing away from the road. Thus he came upon two knights, who had fought for long hours and were weary, but neither could get the better of the other. When he saw them Lanzalet called out: 'Sirs, cease your battle at once or I shall take the side of one of you and fight against the other.'

The two lowered their swords at once, and expressed relief at the youth's interruption of their battle. For in truth neither wanted the fight, but having once begun found it hard to stop. Their names were Kuraus with the Brave Heart and Orphilet the Fair, and as dusk began to fall, it was Kuraus who now spoke of a place where they might find rest and lodging for the night.

'Though it is a hard place to stay, I must warn you,' he said. 'The lord of the place is called Galagandriez, of the castle Moreiz. His wife is dead, but he has a beautiful daughter whom he guards as a great prize. It is said that he demands utterly proper behaviour from all who enter his home. Anyone who diverges from this by a hair's breadth is liable to meet a terrible end. Galagandriez is a proud and quarrelsome man, and few have anything good to say of him. Nevertheless there is no better place to stay unless we wish to sleep in the open.'

'This sounds like a good place to me,' said Lanzalet. 'Who knows what adventure may await us there?'

And so the three knights turned towards the castle, where they were met with all honour and a great show of hospitality. Galagandriez himself had been gaming and had met with great good fortune, so that he was in a genial mood. He greeted the three young men warmly and said that whichever of them was deemed the best should walk beside him, and that all three should meet his daughter and her ladies. With one accord the two knights pressed Lanzalet forward to accompany their host. And indeed he proved a good choice; the years spent in the company of the Queen of the Lake and her followers had equipped the youth well in the arts of courtly speech and behaviour. He conversed in all matters with ease, and his sunny nature endeared him to all who met him. The host's daughter received all three with smiles and fair words, and soon drew Lanzalet aside to sit with her as supper was brought into the hall.

A wondrous feast followed, with so many dishes that it would take me a day to speak of them all if I were inclined so to do. Suffice it to say that at the end of the day the three knights retired to comfortable beds, praising their host and wondering how he came by so evil a reputation.

Tired out from their long battle and the distance they had travelled, the three knights were soon asleep. It was then that their host's daughter, accompanied by two maids carrying tall candlesticks in which candles burned bright, entered the chamber where they were all three sleeping. She was dressed in her finest silks, and wore a chaplet of flowers like a bride, for the truth of the matter was that she was inflamed with love for all three knights, and desired to look upon them as they slept. Silently she gestured to her maids to place the candles either side of the beds in which the knights lay, then dismissed her companions with a nod. Once they were gone she seated herself on the edge of the bed next to Orphilet, who was nearest, and spoke softly.

'Now by my faith how quickly are these warriors silenced by sleep! I had thought you would all remain awake talking of love and high deeds, but it seems all you can do is sleep! Perhaps my father is right when he says that love is just a trap, a burning heat which parches the world like a desert. So he says, and he is determined that I shall never marry. Yet I would be as other women are, and if need be suffer for the pains of love.'

Now Orphilet stirred and woke, and seeing the lady bending over him at once sat up and asked her courteously what she did there.

'Ah, sir,' she said, 'I have come thither in the hope that you will set me free from this prison in which I am forced to live my days.' She took a ring from her finger and offered it to him. 'Accept this, sir, as my pledge, and take me away from here!'

Nervously, Orphilet looked over her shoulder towards the door, half expecting the old lord to burst in and threaten to kill him there and then. To the lady he said, as gallantly as he might: 'If this is your wish be assured that I will do all I can to help you. However, please take back your ring, for I can do nothing at present. I will most certainly return hither as soon as my present journey is complete, for you I will risk life and limb – but for now I bid you wait and keep silence.'

'No, sir knight, that will not do!' cried the lady. 'I have heard all about the ways of men, and I know that once you leave here I shall never see you again. How can you look at me and refuse what I ask? Am I not fair? Do I not excite you? What kind of knight are you who can so refuse the wishes of a lady?'

Orphilet answered: 'I fear more for my knightly honour than for anything else, my lady. Even if I were to assent to your wishes I should almost certainly have to kill your father first. Would you have me behave so dishonourably?'

'I have heard it said,' the lady replied, 'that no one who wished to achieve true manhood ever did so without some indiscretion regarding a woman.'

'If that it so,' answered Orphilet in a sulky fashion, 'I have no wish to die for the sake of such an act.'

Angrily the lady rose and made her way to where Kuraus, the knight whom Orphilet had fought earlier that day, lay slumbering. She had made up her mind that if the first of the three men would have nothing to do with her, she would woo the second so well that he could not refuse. Sitting down beside him as she had with Orphilet, she addressed him thus: 'Sir, I believe you to be a fair and honourable man, unlike your companion there. I am sure you will not refuse the wishes of a lady. Sir, my father believes he cannot live without me, and that no man is a fit husband for me. This I cannot believe, and would leave him behind. If you think me at all fair, take me away from here. I would as soon wish for a man of honour than wait for one to be chosen for me – if ever that is to happen, which I very much doubt.'

Kuraus, who had lain awake listening to the exchange between Orphilet and the lady, answered thus: 'Madame, what you ask goes against all the laws of chivalry which I try to uphold. If I did not honour your father I would be guilty of a great crime. I bid you to forget me as soon as you can, though you can be sure that I shall always complain to God that I had to give you up.' So saying he pulled the covers over his head and refused even to look upon the lady again.

She, angry and tearful to be thus repulsed, turned now to the bed where Lanzalet lay. He, who had heard all that had passed between the lady and the two knights, trembled with joy at the thought that the lady might finally come to him. Indeed, as soon as he heard the rustle of her skirts, he leapt up and said: 'Lady, you have no need to woo me! I will gladly serve you as long as I live!' Then he took her in his arms and kissed her, and the two of them fell upon the bed and, despite the presence of the two other knights, they knew all the joys of love until the day dawned.

They were awoken by the hammering of their host upon the door. Furiously he burst into the room, and saw at a glance how things stood. He carried two long sharp knives, one in either hand, and two small round shields. 'Now I dare say that I was never worse treated by any man!' he cried. 'I gave you every hospitality, and see how you betray me! Which one of you has my daughter, the faithless wretch – or is it that all three have used her?'

Lanzalet rose at once and placed himself between the lord and his daughter. Galagandriez glared at him furiously and waved the knives before him threateningly. 'So be it. I thought you the best of the three, but it seems I was wrong. I challenge you to defend yourself. Take this shield and knife and stand over by the far wall. I will retire to the other side and we will throw at each other. Whoever wins will keep his honour, whoever loses let him be cursed!'

To this Lanzalet agreed, and taking the shield and one of the knives retreated to the wall. Galagandriez took aim and threw. The knife tore through the sleeve of Lanzalet's shirt and stuck in the wall, drawing a thin line of blood from his arm. Now the youth took stock of the situation, and instead of throwing the knife he leapt forward and stabbed the surprised lord through the heart, killing him outright.

The lady shed no tears for her father, but instead turned to seeking a way to insure that neither Lanzalet nor his companions were unjustly punished for the former's deed. Telling them to remain were they were she hurried in search of several of her father's vassals whom she knew liked and trusted her. To them she told the whole truth, praising Lanzalet for his bravery in defending her and reminding them of all the brave knights slain by her father in his jealous rages. They, as one man, elected to trust the lady – who was now mistress of Moreiz – and to offer no resistance or punishment to the three knights. They went to the chamber where the deed had taken place and there swore fealty to Lanzalet, who in turn promised to honour their lady as his own.

Thus did fate deal out a winning hand to the youth, who was soon installed as the new lord of Moreiz. Word went forth to all who had served the old lord, and soon a great company gathered. The old lord was laid to rest in proper fashion, though in truth none mourned him. To their new lord they swore fealty, and he in turn gave them many gifts from the store which Galagandriez had long hoarded. Then he chose from amongst the nobles one to be his steward, for he had no intention of remaining there while he had still to find his name and avenge the honour of the Queen of the Lake.

Seeing this, and warming daily towards the youth, Orphilet began to talk to him about King Arthur, praising him for his nobility and extolling the virtues of his court at Carlisle the Fair.

'No one who is such a fine fellow as yourself should fail to go there,' Orphilet said. 'The king is the finest and best monarch ever to rule over this land, and as for his queen, she would as soon do two good deeds as one bad. Her ladies as well are fairer than any I have seen. You must go there, for I am sure you will be honoured and find new adventures.'

But Lanzalet shook his head. 'I am as yet untried, and would feel nothing but shame to be in such a place. What could I say when the other brave knights you speak of tell of their adventures? I must do some deeds of my own before I am fit to go to this court.'

Then Kuraus tried to persuade him to go to his lands in Gagunne, where he promised him fair welcome. But again the youth declined, saying only that when the time was right he would indeed set forth, but it would be where his heart, or circumstances, led him.

Thus the three parted company, for Orphilet and Kuraus wished to return home to their own lands. Lanzalet gave them many gifts and sent them on their way with many words of friendship. And Orphilet returned to Carlisle the Fair and spoke of his recent adventures, and of the extraordinary youth who had broken the adventure of Moreiz. And when he heard of these things King Arthur said that he hoped the youth would indeed find his way there one day.

Meanwhile Lanzalet continued to remain at Moreiz. He lived well, enjoying the favours of the lady for whom he had fought, and hunting daily in the woods around the castle. But in time he began to long to continue the quest for his name and for the evil knight who had dishonoured the Queen of the Lake. One day therefore he donned his armour, saddled his horse and slipped away, telling no one where he was bound. He soon put some distance between himself and Moreiz, until he came at last to a place where the way divided in three. He chose the middle way, and rode swiftly until he came within sight of a castle set amid a thick brake of trees.

Now the custom of this place was that any knight who came thither must either carry an olive branch signifying peaceful intent, or remove his helm and carry it before him as a further sign that he did not seek battle. The youth knew nothing of this, and rode as he would towards the castle. As soon as he was seen the alarm was given, and a veritable torrent of soldiers, many on foot, accompanied by knights, poured forth and at once attacked the unsuspecting youth. He, at first amazed then angered, drew his sword and began to lay about him, slaying many dozens of men and cutting a swathe through their ranks as he made his way ever closer towards the gates of the castle.

Now within this fortress was a maiden of great beauty and breeding, named Ade von den Bigen. When she heard of the battle that was taking place outside the walls, she at once called for her horse and rode out to view the fighting. When she saw how bravely the young knight defended himself, and how many of her own folk were falling beneath his sword, she rode straight towards him. A path opened before her and her men fell back upon all sides. When she reached where Lanzalet sat upon his horse, breathing heavily, she called out to him: 'Sir, I do not know who you are, but I salute your bravery. If you will agree to surrender to me I promise you will not be harmed.'

Lanzalet looked about him at the throngs of soldiers and then at the fair lady who addressed him with kind words. Slowly he put way his sword and bowing his head assented to her offer.

Thus he came to the castle of Limors, which was the property of one Linier, the girl's uncle. He was a proud and violent man who gave much of his time to hunting. He it was who had declared that whomsoever came that way without tokens of peace should be killed outright. As luck or destiny would have it he was away from home that day, and so the lady who was his niece was able to intercede on behalf of the youth, and in her keeping he came within the castle and was properly welcomed and cared for. Yet the lady was concerned that when her uncle returned his anger would be such that the brave youth would be condemned to death at once.

Therefore when the proud Linier returned next morning Ade at once fell at his feet and begged for the life of the young hero who had shown himself to be of such prowess that not even a hundred men could subdue him. And at first Linier was beside himself with rage. But then Ade spoke to him and told him of how bravely the young man had defended himself, and how he had surrendered to her without hesitation. 'Uncle, you must set him free, for never did I see such a brave and noble youth. To kill him would be to blacken your name forever. And, if you let him live, who knows what service he may not do you in the future.'

'As to service I can manage well enough without it,' growled Linier. 'But be assured I shall see to it that he does neither evil nor good to anyone in the future – and be it understood that anyone who calls him friend shall suffer for it.' He glared about him and no one spoke a word, for they knew how wild and unbiddable were his passions, and none dared gainsay him.

Then he called for the youth to be brought before him, and demanded angrily to know who he was and whence he came.

'I shall tell you truly,' said Lanzalet. 'Until recently I lived in a land ruled over by women, and as to my name, as yet I do not know it.'

Then Linier flew into a rage, for he thought the youth was mocking him. He ordered the prisoner flung into a tower where neither sun nor moon ever shone, and there he was left to languish. A dish of bread and water were brought to him daily, but otherwise he was left alone to stew in his own ordure. He suffered greatly from this, but never lost hope and was ever cheerful despite his circumstances. In this he was aided by the lady Ade, who often visited his lonely cell in secret and brought him bedding, food and wine – all of which she smuggled in to him with the connivance of his guards, who in truth thought him ill treated and only the fear of their master kept them from setting him free.

One day when Lanzalet received a visit from Ade, he asked her to tell him more about the adventure of the castle, and why her uncle set such a barbarous custom as that by which he had himself come to be imprisoned.

'I shall tell you the truth,' she said. 'My uncle is, as you know, a proud and overweening man. Though he cares greatly for his life he likes to challenge every knight who comes this way. Thus he has instigated the custom of which you know, that whoever comes hither without a sign of peace will be at once attacked. This is because many knights come hither to try the adventure which he has made known in every part of the land – that a mighty opponent awaits all comers. This of course attracts many errant knights. Yet they do not know what trials await them. First they must fight a giant of a fellow, who wields a great club so heavy that only two normal men can lift it. Then, if he should succeed – which is doubtful – he must face two wild lions who are kept in a deep pit. Only then, should good fortune favour him, does the challenger come to fight my uncle. Nor is he a poor fighter, and since any who have come through the other trials unscathed are most likely weary and wounded, he has little difficulty in overcoming them.'

'Now by my faith,' said Lanzalet, 'this is an evil custom.' He was silent for a moment, then he asked: 'Lady, you have been more than kind to me. May I yet ask you one more favour?'

'Whatever you ask I shall try to do,' answered Ade, 'for it grieves me sorely to see you in this place.'

'Then if you can, arrange for me to undertake these adventures. I would rather die with my sword in my hand than perish in this filthy place.'

And so the lady went before her uncle, uncertain what to expect. 'Sir,' she said, 'I would speak to you of the young knight you put in prison recently. I have heard that he much honours your strength and courage, and that he longs to attempt the adventure of this place. Uncle, if I have ever done anything to please you, I ask that you give ear to this desire. I will stand surety for him, and if you set him free into my care I will see to it that in two weeks he will be ready to fight.'

Linier stared down at his niece in silence. Then he said: 'Very well, since I am in a mood to favour you today, I shall do as you beg.' He smiled, though without mirth. 'Thus shall I be rid of him for good, and have the satisfaction of seeing him humiliated before me.'

'God shall be the judge of that,' replied Ade, and flew to the prison to order the knight's release. Then at once she had a bath prepared for him, and sent for good food and drink such as were reserved for the most honoured guests.

Thus Lanzalet swiftly recovered his strength, and as the time appointed drew near he began to exercise and practise with sword and spear. Linier, meanwhile, sent word to every noble lord of his acquaintance, telling them that there was to be a great festival to celebrate his victory over the nameless knight who was such a fool that everything he did was no more than a joke to him. For in his heart he believed that the youth could not possibly succeed in passing the tests prepared for him, and that he, Linier, would soon be boasting of victory over the stranger.

Thus when the day appointed arrived there was a great crowd gathered at the castle of Limors. The terrible warrior arrived, and Linier was to be seen watching the two lions pace back and forth in their pit. He had ordered them to be starved for the three days previous, so that they were quite maddened with hunger.

Soon all was ready, and Lanzalet was led out to the ring where he was to face the giant. He was permitted no other weapon save for his sword, and a shield which the lady Ade herself had made for him. Yet he faced his mighty opponent without fear, sizing him up and dancing around him as the huge man lumbered forth with massive club upraised and an equally large shield held out before him. It is certain that if he had succeeded in delivering a blow, that would have been the end of Lanzalet, but he managed to avoid the club and with a single savage blow cut off the giant's arm, club and all!

Bellowing madly the huge man tried to fall upon his opponent, meaning to crush him with his monstrous shield. But again Lanzalet danced away from him, and delivered a blow to his vital parts which brought the giant crashing to his knees. Another blow served to sever his head, and Lanzalet had the victory without himself receiving a scratch.

Linier was seen to grind his teeth, and he at once commanded that Lanzalet be taken to the lion-pit and put in with the savage beasts.

Maddened by hunger they at once attacked him, one succeeding in opening a deep wound before Lanzalet had time to raise his sword. Ignoring the wound he struck back, splitting the beast's skull. The second one attacked him, driving him back to the wall of the pit. He managed to get in a blow to the creature's foot, which caused it to back away, then he followed up and delivered a death blow to the heart.

Now Linier showed his unworthiness, for he called at once for his armour and had Lanzalet pulled forth from the lion-pit and saw to it that he was armed and made ready without respite. He appeared on the field looking pale and weak, yet holding himself erect with pride. The onlookers saw where the blood from his wounds ran down from beneath his armour and felt pity for him.

Not so his opponent. Linier was determined to overcome him by any means, fair or foul. He rode his great black destrier onto the field and couched his spear. Lanzalet steadied himself and urged his own mount forward. They met with a crash and both burst their spears in pieces. But Linier was carried from his horse's back by the force of the blow, and lay grovelling in the dust, cursing his horse like a worthless fellow, rather than acknowledge the superiority of his opponent. Lanzalet got down from his horse and waited in knightly spirit until Linier rose. Then the two fell to it with great fury, striking sparks from each other's steel, and soon hacking their shields to pieces. Linier fought with care and control, Lanzalet responded wildly, knowing that his strength would soon fail, and that he must win soon if at all.

Soon enough the older knight broke through Lanzalet's guard, and delivered a blow which wounded him afresh in the place where the lion's claws had done damage. The youth staggered, but recovered quickly. He knew that all was lost unless he could strike back. Summoning all his failing strength, he rushed upon his surprised opponent, who believed him wounded to death, and gave him a blow upon the head which split him to the chin. So great was the force of the blow that blood rushed out of Lanzalet's ears and mouth, and he fell beside the body of his foe.

A great lamentation arose from Linier's folk, and men came forward to carry his body into the castle. No one paid any attention to Lanzalet, save for the lady Ade, who came with those knights who were already well disposed toward him, and had him carried inside also. Many thought him dead, but the lady detected a slight breath. She ordered a fire lit and the youth's armour removed. Then she tended his terrible wounds, and gave him cordials to bring back his strength, so that he came back from the edge of death and fell into a healing sleep.

Once the news became known that the hero still lived, many came to look upon him and to speak to the lady Ade, begging her to save him if she could. For now that Linier was dead and the evil custom of Limors broken, they were eager that the youth should live and sought to honour him for his great deeds by offering him both the lands and titles of the dead lord, and the hand of his niece – which, if truth were known, both the lady herself, and her relatives, both desired.

Meanwhile Lanzalet began slowly to recover, though it was some weeks before he was strong enough to speak. When he did so it was to ask where he was and what had occurred. The lady soon told him everything, and praised him greatly for the deeds he had performed. 'For,' said she, 'though Linier was my uncle, and a brave and mighty knight, yet it must be said that he behaved in a cowardly fashion towards you, and deserved to die at your hand. Now let us speak no more of these things until you are healed.'

And so the knight slept, and dreamed, and made a slow recovery of his health, thanks in no small measure to the ministrations of the lady. And the fame of his great deeds went out from that place, and reached the ears of King Arthur in his court at Carlisle.

'Who is this brave hero?' asked the king. 'Has no one heard ought of him?'

'I believe,' said Orphilet, 'that he is the same hero of whom I have spoken before, he who dealt with Galagandriez of Moreiz, but who declared that he would not come hither until he had proved himself.'

'That he has certainly done,' said Arthur. 'He should come to us now, I think.' Queen Guinevere herself added her own wish to see this brave man, and King Arthur called for someone to go to Limors and fetch the youth. Gawain offered at once, and was duly dispatched.

Meanwhile, the lady Ade was determined that she would persuade the young knight to go with her to her father's castle, which lay not far from Limors, and, by dint of careful management, so arranged it that they should ride there alone.

It was a bright and cheerful morning when they set out, and Lanzalet sang as he rode. He had not a care in the world save that he wished another knight might come their way so that he could test his newly recovered strength against him.

Now it so happened that they did meet such a knight, and that it was none other than Gawain himself. When Lanzalet saw him coming he at once set his spear in rest and raised his shield before him. But keen-sighted Gawain saw the shield with the golden eagle upon it, and remembered that according to Orphilet this was the insignia of the very knight he sought. Therefore he stuck his own spear in the earth and laid his shield beside it, then removed his helmet and rode open-faced to meet the stranger.

Lanzalet privately thought this a great affront, but he greeted the stranger with his customary courtesy.

'What news, sir?' said Lanzalet.

'Good news indeed since I have found you,' replied Sir Gawain. 'I believe that you are the young knight who but lately slew Linier of Limors.'

'I am that man,' said Lanzalet guardedly.

'Then I pray you, come with me to King Arthur's court. News of your deeds have outstripped you, and all are eager to make your aquaintance. The queen herself has asked for you, therefore I bid you to accompany me thither as soon as possible.'

'Now I wonder that you should ask this of me when you know nothing of me save the words of others,' said Lanzalet. 'I wish you had never greeted me thus today, for I can go to King Arthur's court whenever I like, and need no messenger to bring me there.'

Gawain, who was ever the most courteous of knights, looked askance at this. 'Sir, I greeted you in good faith, and at the behest of my king. Far be it from me to enforce the invitation. Yet I would ask once again that you accompany me.'

'I ask only that you leave off the matter and let me and my lady continue in peace,' Lanzalet answered roughly. 'Or else you should go back for your weapons and show how well you use them.'

At this Gawain's anger began to rise. 'Sir,' he said stiffly, 'I left my weapons behind as a sign that I came in peace. If you would as soon I went back for them, then I bid you stand ready, for as sure as my name is Sir Gawain of Orkney I shall not ask another favour of you.'

At this Lanzalet seemed to brighten. 'Now by my faith, Sir Gawain, I am glad to meet you, for I have long wished to pit myself against one of your mettle.'

'Then you shall have your wish,' Gawain cried, and swinging about he rode back to where he had left his spear and shield. Then, donning his helm, he rode full tilt at the young knight, who came to meet him eagerly. They met with a resounding crash and both splintered their spears, after which they fell to fighting on foot with swords, and neither had the advantage.

As they fought a page rode up in haste and cried breathlessly to them to stop. 'Sirs, I will choose neither one of you, but ask that you both leave off this battling if honour permits it. For I have news of a great tournament this fortnight hence. King Lot of Lothian and Gurnemans will lead the sides and both are in need of brave knights to fight alongside them. King Arthur is coming also, with many knights of the Round Table. Be assured that this will be a famous event, and every knight who ever fought in tournament should be there for the sake of his honour.'

Gawain at once lowered his sword and looked at Lanzalet. 'I for one shall be glad to end this needless conflict. It were better that we both attended this tournament than that we wasted our blood here for no purpose.'

Lanzalet had the grace to look crestfallen, but he too put away his sword and said that he would be glad to attend the tournament. 'But first I must continue my journey with this lady. My lord Gawain, I am glad to have met with you on this day, and I hope to continue our sport together again before too long. I bid you greet me to my lord King Arthur and to his queen and tell them that I shall attend upon them when I may.'

With that Sir Gawain had to be content. He took leave of Lanzalet and Ade and returned to Carlisle, where he spoke well of the young knight to all there, who marvelled greatly to hear of his skill with sword and spear and at his strange, half-courteous manner.

Meanwhile the young hero continued with the lady Ade until they reached her home where both were made welcome. The lady's father greeted Lanzalet as he might a son, and no comfort was spared him. Soon the date of the great tournament approached, and the lady Ade made every effort to see that Lanzalet was as well prepared as possible, seeing to it that he lacked for nothing in the way of weapons, clothes, and caparisons for his horse. She even gave him her own brother, a fine youth named Tybalt, as his squire.

And so the day dawned when they were to set forth. The tournament was to take place in the city of Dyofle, a setting of great splendour and richness. The lady herself accompanied Lanzalet, together with a fine company of her father's household. When they reached the city they found that Gurnemans had taken the lodging within the walls, while King Lot had pitched his tents outside, as had King Arthur, who occupied a small hill overlooking the city.

Tybalt, who was a wise and resourceful youth, soon acquired lodgings for his party within the walls and close to the gates. Then, having seen to it that both the lady and the young knight were comfortably installed, he rode forth to gather news of the tournament.

All over the land around the city, knights were practising for the jousts, breaking spears with each other, some in friendship and others with more serious intent. Lanzalet, not wishing to wait a moment, prepared to go at once to the lists. In preparation for the event, he had had made a banner of green samite, from which material he had also made a covering for his steed. Then, equipped with a ready-made shield of the same green hue, he set forth on his own.

Now it happened that his way led close to the area occupied by King Arthur and his company. Sir Kay, ever a proud and boastful fellow, was looking out and saw the green knight approaching, with his spear raised as if in preparation for battle. 'Sire,' he said to the king, 'I see a foolish fellow who seeks to challenge us. Give me leave to have some sport with him and, once I have dealt with him, let me have his fine horse, which is far too spirited a beast for such as he.'

Smiling, King Arthur gave his assent, and Kay mounted and rode forth at high speed to overtake the knight in green. He, hearing the cries of the pursuing knight, turned and awaited him like a rock. On this rock the proud Sir Kay foundered. He was met with such a buffet that he flew from his horse and landed in a patch of boggy ground, into which he at once sank waist deep in his heavy armour. Then his fellows laughed at his discomfiture and declared that they would not claim any of his spoils from the affair. But one of the knights, a popular fellow called Iwain de Lonel, felt sorry for his companion in arms and decided to exact a fitting punishment from the stranger. He rode forth as Kay had done, and met with the same fate, flying over his horse's crupper and landing in the mud. Tybalt, drawn thither by the noise, gathered up both his mount and that of Sir Kay by way of forfeit.

King Arthur, who had seen all that passed, remarked that the stranger did well against them. At which a brave knight named the Margrave of Lyle decided to take up the challenge. But he fared no better than either of his companions. Nor did the brave Erec son of Lac, who followed, and who broke no less than ten spears against the Green Knight before calling a halt to the engagement. At which point Lanzalet himself withdrew, leaving Arthur and his knights to marvel at the skill of the unknown youth.

Soon afterwards Gawain joined them, and on hearing of the fate of his fellows, declared that this must be the vary same warrior of whom he had gone in search. 'For I declare I have never fought a stronger man in many a year.'

So saying Gawain set out to find the stranger. Everywhere he rode he asked after him, but learned only that the green-clad stranger had fought against many knights and had not once been defeated. Everyone spoke of him with hushed tones, and wondered who he might be. Gawain kept his peace on this, and told no one of his suspicions regarding the knight's true identity.

And so the first day ended. Lanzalet returned to his lodging and said: 'Since no one knows who I am, I shall continue to keep it secret.' To Tybalt he gave the following command: that he should find enough white samite to make a fresh banner and covering for his horse, and that he should bring him a plain white shield.

Thus the next day of the tournament dawned and on this occasion, just as the Green Knight had acquitted himself so well that people spoke of him still and looked for his coming, the White Knight did even better. Wherever the fighting was thickest, there he appeared, laying out knight after knight, unhorsing and overcoming them with consummate ease. Towards the end of the day he allied himself with a lord named Count Richard, who had fared ill in the mêlée until that moment. With the White Knight on his side his fortune soon changed, and that day he captured many brave knights and earned much booty.

At the end of the day the White Knight left quickly and made his way back to his lodgings. Since he had no name he did not wish to be recognized and questioned – for this reason alone he hid his identity from everyone.

So matters fared on the third day. This time Lanzalet chose red as his colour and on that day everyone fled before the Red Knight. Again he chose to side with Count Richard, and again the latter was better off because of it. Towards the end of the day the forces of Count Richard and those of King Lot himself came together and, as before, the Red Knight carried all before him. The outcome of the matter was that the stranger and the King of Orkney came face to face, and Lanzalet defeated his opponent and captured him.

When King Arthur heard of this he came to the aid of his ally, who was also, of course, the father of Sir Gawain. But even the knights of the Round Table, who, as all know, numbered among their ranks the bravest and best in the land, could not stand against the stranger. It seemed that, as the day drew to a close and more and more joined in the fray, his strength increased. So many indeed did he wound or disable, that the tournament was finally halted, though it was supposed to have lasted another seven days after that.

Everyone wanted to see the brave hero who had made such a dramatic mark upon the games. Most by now had guessed that he was both the White and the Green Knight, and all wished to know his real identity. Yet he remained in the tent of Count Richard, receiving those who sought to do him honour, yet speaking little and saying nothing of his origins. Here came Sir Gawain, anxious for news of his father, whom Lanzalet had sent to his lady to be ransomed, as was the custom of that time. The two knights greeted each other warmly and once again Gawain asked if the stranger would accompany him to King Arthur, who was close at hand. But, once again the young knight declared that his steps lay elsewhere, and that, while in time he would indeed be glad to attend upon the great king, at this time he must go elsewhere.

The truth of the matter was that he had learned of a new adventure from Count Richard, and was eager to be gone. Gawain parted from him with these words: 'Sir, I shall continue to seek for news of your deeds, and hope that one day shall meet again. Meanwhile I give you every blessing and wish you well in all your endeavours.'

Thus the two friends parted, and Lanzalet prepared to set forth on a new adventure, accompanied by the Lady Ade and her brother, the page Tybalt. Their destination was the Schatel le Mort, whose master was one Mabuz, an evil and cowardly wretch who possessed some knowledge of magic. A spell was laid upon the castle which ensured that anyone who entered there, be he the bravest knight in the world, at once became a coward. At the time of which I speak more than a hundred men were imprisoned in the Schatel le Mort, and it is said that whenever Mabuz became angered, for whatever reason, he ordered one of the prisoners brought forth and killed. This was the kind of man he was.

But I must now reveal to you certain facts about this cruel and unchivalrous wretch. For he was indeed the son of the Queen of the Lake, she who had stolen Lanzalet from his mother's side and brought him up in ignorance of his true lineage. Her reasons for this were subtle. It may be that she longed for a son who would be faithful and true, for she knew before he was born that her own child would be a coward and a villain. For this reason she had built for him the Schatel de Mort, and had cast about it the spell of which you have heard so that her son should never have to face an opponent stronger than himself.

Around the castle lay a rich and beautiful country, which ought by rights to have been enjoyed by Mabuz. But he never dared go there because of a knight named Iweret, whose lands lay adjacent to his. This Iweret was a proud and noble man who would most certainly have slain the cowardly Mabuz had their paths ever crossed – which they might well have done since Iweret was given to raiding the lands of his neighbour whenever the fancy took him.

Thus the queen had devised a plan – to bring up the hero Lanzalet and to send him forth to find and kill Iweret. This was the shameful secret of which she would not speak to the young hero, and now as chance or destiny would have it the knight found his way to the Schatel, having heard of the evil custom of the place from one whom he had met at the tournament.

With Ade and Tybalt following a safe distance behind he rode up to the gates of the castle, and crossed a narrow bridge over a swiftly flowing stream. And at the moment he entered the shadow of the gates, all his bravery fell from him and he felt nothing so great as the urge to flee. When he saw Mabuz waiting for him, clad in full armour and mounted upon a fiery steed, he made no attempt to defend himself, but fell grovelling in the dust, where Mabuz several times struck him while he lay thus defenceless. Then the evil knight pulled off Lanzalet's helm, and dragged him by the hair within the castle, where he was at once seized and carried off into prison.

Ade and her brother, who had seen all that passed, were horrified by the turn events had taken. Tybalt was quick to decry the young knight and name him coward, and though at first the lady defended him, yet soon she too became convinced that her former hero had in fact lost his nerve. 'Alas and alack,' she cried, 'that ever I thought him a good and noble knight! I cannot trust him any more, nor be seen in his company, for such a coward as he would be no protector of my honour or my person.' So distressed was she that she almost swooned, and her brother took the reins of her horse and led her away, whither I know not. Nor shall you hear from me again of these faithless ones.

We return instead to Lanzalet, who lay in the dungeon of the Schatel de Mort in great sorrow and travail. So angered was he at his failure to defend himself, and at the fear which was a constant companion to him, that he scarcely took the trouble to eat. The rest of the prisoners, who were not so badly treated as all that, sat down daily to eat at a long table set up in the dungeon. But Lanzalet would not join them, preferring to take a hunk of bread and sit with it against the wall, with his face turned from his fellows. He grew lank from lack of food and ceased caring for himself at all, so that he was soon foul and dirty.

Now it happened that Iweret's men made one of their periodic raids upon Mabuz's lands, burning several villages and ruining a large area of land. Mabuz watched from the walls, sick at heart but too fearful to go forth and defend his property in case Iweret had laid an ambush for him.

Then an idea occurred to the cowardly knight. 'If I send one of my prisoners out to reconnoitre there will be no danger to me,' he thought. 'I will seek out the most cowardly and miserable of the men in my dungeon, for once outside he will be the bravest. And, if I never see him again, that is no loss to me.'

Mabuz went to watch through a little window which enabled him to observe the behaviour of his prisoners. He soon saw how Lanzalet hid every time anyone entered the dungeon, and this marked him out as the ideal subject for the task. Mabuz therefore had the young knight brought before him, where he stood, cowering and shaking and trying to hide behind his guards. Mabuz told him what was required, but the youth shook his head and showed the whites of his eyes. 'I might be killed if I went out there,' he cried. 'I beg you not to send me outside.' Ignoring his pleas Mabuz had the terrified knight carried outside, and there his armour was buckled on him as if he were a sick man. Then they tethered his horse to a tree and left him alone. And though at first he trembled and hid his face from the world, yet soon the fresh air began to clear his clouded mind, and he stood up and looked about him in some bewilderment. For he remembered nothing that had happened since he approached the Schatel de Mort.

Then Mabuz called down to him from the wall above the gates. 'I remind you that you are a brave and noble man, sir knight, and that you have promised to undertake a mission for me. If you do not, I shall kill all the prisoners in my dungeon. Do you understand?'

Dimly, the circumstances of his imprisonment returned to Lanzalet, and he looked up fiercely at his recent captor. 'I will do as you ask,' he said. 'But do not try to trick me or you may be sure I shall find a way to reach you, even behind those coward walls!'

So saying he rode off at once towards Iweret's lands. He soon overtook the raiders, and dispatched several of them summarily. The rest fled, leaving the young knight master of the field. And now he began to wonder how he might be avenged upon Mabuz and set free those who were kept in evil confinement. His steps led him to a small monastery which lay close by there. It was called the Sorrowful Abbey, but despite its name Lanzalet received a cheerful enough welcome from the abbot, a wise and kindly priest, who informed him that the abbey was in the holding of Iweret. 'Here,' said the monk, 'he offers a tithe of whatever he wins through his knightly skills. If a man is killed by him he is interred here, and masses are sung for the repose of his soul; if my lord acquires treasure from taking a knight prisoner, he pays a part of it to us. Thus we have grown rich, for believe me my lord has slain many brave knights who have come here seeking to achieve the adventure of this place. If you are wise you will ride on tomorrow, with God's blessing.'

Thus spoke the kindly abbot. But Lanzalet wished only to hear of the nature of the adventure, and with reluctance, when he knew there was no helping it, the monk told him all.

'Know that my lord Iweret is a mighty prince of fine spirit. He has three kingdoms by inheritance and has acquired more through conquest. He has one daughter, Yblis, who is reckoned to be a great beauty by all who see her and who is much sought after. Her father has let it be known that any man who wishes to court her must first meet him in combat under a certain linden tree that grows in the Wood Beautiful. It grows, this tree, beside a fountain that Lord Iweret has had made into a well with a vaulted cover. The spring flows out of a stone lion's mouth into a basin. The tree is green all year round, and on it hangs a bronze bell and a hammer. Whosoever comes in search of my lord's daughter must strike this three times. Before the third blow has ceased from echoing, Iweret will be there, fully accoutred and ready to defend the fountain with his life. I will make no secret of the fact that many men have come there and tried this adventure, and that none have succeeded. Iweret has killed many in the last year alone, and they all lie now beneath the earth in our little graveyard. I counsel you,' said the abbot, 'to avoid that place if you can.'

'That I may not do,' said Lanzalet gently, 'though I thank you for your kindly warning. I fear that my steps must lead me there on the morrow.' For he had recognized the name of his foster mother's foe, and was determined to seek him out.

'Then so be it,' answered the abbot. 'But come now and rest and refresh yourself while you may.'

And so Lanzalet rested that night in the Sorrowful Abbey and next morning he set forth towards the fountain. As he rode he soon became aware that he was entering an enchanted place. On all sides there were beautiful trees and exotic-looking plants, many of which he had never seen the like of before. He remembered that the wood around Iweret's castle was called Beforet, the Beautiful Wood, and now he understood why. There was more, that he did not know, which made that place extraordinary. Not only did a great variety of plants grow there, but many of them had healing properties such as are known only to a few. It is said that anyone who rode there began to feel stronger and that if he or she were sick they began to recover; while if they were already fit and well, they would become more powerful. And this indeed is what gave Iweret his great strength, and which now began to affect Lanzalet as he came nearer to his adversary's castle.

Now too he began to catch glimpses of a rich variety of animal life; bears and deer and foxes, boar and even a lion he saw, and birds of a kind he had never before seen, even in the kingdom of the Lake. He began to wonder indeed what paradise this was into which he had come, and if its master could really be evil. Of his daughter he wondered much also, for the abbot had told him more of her; that she was not only beautiful but wise, that she lived as a princess, with as many ladies as she wished in attendance, and that they were given to gathering flowers every day in a certain valley within the woods. Indeed this valley was known as the Vallis Yble, after the lady herself.

Of the castle wherein Iweret lived much has been written. It was tall and fair and richly decorated both within and without. The floors were of marble inlay and the walls and ceilings were decorated with semi-precious stones. Iweret himself slept in a great bed with pillars of red gold and a canopy of green samite. The bedding was all of silk and the pillows filled with the softest down. Thus was the castle, and the lord himself was no less well appointed. Clad in silks and brocades from distant lands, he outshone even the great King Arthur himself in his finery.

Thus Lanzalet came to the linden tree, to which he had been directed by the kindly abbot. He tied his horse to a branch and, seizing the hammer which hung upon the tree, beat upon the cymbal so that it was heard throughout the wood and within the castle itself. Then he went to where the fountain gushed forth, and taking off his helm and pushing back his mail coif he laved his face and hands in the cool water.

Now hear something strange and wondrous. On the night just passed Yblis had dreamed that a strange knight came to the linden tree, and in her dream she fell in love with him and he with her, and they had joyous sport together. When she awoke she declared to herself that she would marry none other than this knight, if in truth he was real. And, when she heard the little bell ring out that morning, she at once called for her horse to be saddled, and before even her father could set forth to meet the challenge she reached the tree and saw Lanzalet, bare-headed, with drops of water from the fountain beading his face and catching the sun, so that he seemed to glow from within.

When she saw that this was indeed the very knight of whom she had dreamed her heart leapt in her breast and she got down from her horse and greeted him with gentle words. He, in turn, was struck by her beauty and kindness, and though he had never until that moment seen her, it was as though he had known her for ever, and love entered into his heart.

'Now, lady,' he said, 'never have I seen another to whom I feel so deeply drawn. Do not take it amiss if I tell you that you are the most beautiful creature I ever saw, and that I would do any service that you asked of me, save only that you look with kindness on my suit.'

Yblis smiled and proffered her hand to the knight. 'I am of like mind,' she said, and told him the substance of her dream. 'I ask only one thing of you, and that is that you do not fight my father today.'

'That I may not undertake,' answered Lanzalet. 'Ask anything else and I shall so it willingly.'

'You cannot win against my father, nor can I bear to see you killed before me eyes. I beg you, sir knight, do this for me.'

'Alas I may not,' answered Lanzalet resolutely. 'If I am to win you let me do so fairly, as is the way of the knight and the lady. Even were I to turn aside now the time would come when I must meet one as strong or stronger than I. Would you have me behave as a coward, like the evil Mabuz?' And thereupon he struck the cymbal again, angered that Iweret had failed to appear.

Then the lady Yblis turned away and almost swooned with grief. 'Not even the magic herbs which grow in the valley can cure this sickness,' she thought. 'Yet how can I take sides against my own father?'

At this moment Iweret came in sight, riding on a huge red horse and clad in the finest armour imaginable. He too was angered by the repeated beating of the bell and his greeting was fierce.

'Where is he who struck the bell?'

'I am here,' answered Lanzalet.

Why?'

'Because I am determined to fight you.'

'Will you accept my adventure?'

'Nothing would please me better.'

'And what do you wish to gain?'

'Your kingdom and your daughter.'

'Then so be it.'

'So be it.'

Then the two knights set their spears in rest charged upon one another. Both shafts splintered and both riders were rocked back on their horses' cruppers. Then Iweret felt fear, for never before had he encountered an opponent whom he could not at once unhorse. Now they drew their swords and fell to hacking and hewing at each other, until at length Lanzalet delivered a blow which so shook his opponent that he fell to the earth from his mount's back.

Lanzalet at once dismounted and waited courteously for Iweret to get up. As he struggled to his feet the shaken warrior said: 'Hitherto I have fought only children – this knight is a man!' Then they fell to again, and gave each other a hard fight, delivering blow after blow upon their helms and armour, until the blood ran down and watered the earth.

For an hour or more they fought on, until Lanzalet finally gave his opponent a wound which let out his life. Then the hero sat down by the fountain and waited until he could draw breath again. Then he went and raised up the lady Yblis, who had fallen prostrate with grief, and bathed her face with water.

'How is it with you?' she asked, trembling.

'Madam, your father is dead. I hope that this will not change your feelings towards me. By all means take out your anger upon me, but do not send me away, I beg you.'

'I shall not do that, now or ever,' answered Yblis softly. 'I grieve for my father, yet my love for you is the greater.' She rose and looked about her. 'We should be gone from here as soon as may be, for I fear that my father's men will not look kindly upon he who slew Iweret.'

Lanzalet hesitated, but he could not gainsay his new-found love, and they both mounted their steeds and rode away through the forest. There they met the good abbot of the Sorrowful Abbey, coming to take away the body of the latest challenger. Disbelief was upon his face when he saw Lanzalet and Yblis, but the lady soon told him how things stood, and bade him return to her father's castle and arrange for the care of her lands and property – such they now were – until her return.

Thus the knight and the lady rode on through the forest until they came to a sunny clearing. There they dismounted and lay beneath the shady branches of a mighty tree. And there they gave themselves up to the tides of love and passion, and enjoyed each other as well as any man and woman since the time of Adam and Eve.

And thus they stayed happily for a time, until they heard a rider coming towards then, and shortly saw where a maiden came, seated on a white mule. She was dressed in the finest of raiment and when he saw her the youth recognized her as one of his foster mother's handmaids. He welcomed her by name and she greeted him from the Queen of the Lake.

'Now I am well pleased that I have found you, for it is known already that you have succeeded in the commission set for you by my lady. And therefore I am bidden to tell you your name, that you are called Lanzalet, and that you are the son of King Ban of Genewis and his queen, the lady Clarine.' An she went on to tell him all: that Genewis was his rightful home, though it was presently held by others, and how the Queen of the Lake had seen in a vision that he would grow to be the strongest knight in the world, and would kill Iweret, thus setting her true son Mabuz free. And she told him that even as they spoke, the cowardly knight was setting free his prisoners, just as he had promised to do if Lanzalet succeeded in his mission. 'Thus all has fallen out as destiny intended,' said the lady, 'and now I bring you a gift from the Queen of the Lake.' So saying she gave into Lanzalet's hands a cunningly carved box.

The young hero was filled with joy, for now he had a name and knew something of his history and the destiny which had brought him to this place. And gladly he turned to the lady Yblis, whose face also showed her joy at the news, and together they fell to examining the box. Within it was a tent of the most remarkable nature that ever was known. When it was folded away it fitted easily into the box, or could be carried in the palm of the hand; yet when it was set up it was as large as its owner wished. You may be sure that Lanzalet and Yblis at once erected it, and went within. Never was there such an extraordinary object! Each wall was made of a different substance: the first was of samite, the second of a rare thrice-dipped fabric called *triblat*, the third of a cloth from Arabia called *barracan*, woven from wool and camel's hair, and the fourth from fish skin, sewn by the women of a barbarous land far to the North. But this is not all, for I must tell you that the tent pole was made of emerald, or of a substance that looked like emerald, and that around the entrance were written a number of mottoes. These, as I hear tell, were as follows. The first one read: Love Dares Anything. The second: Love is a Madness that Never Dies. The third said: Love without Measure.

Now the reason these words were set about the tent was that no one who was not utterly faithful could enter there, and within the tent was a mirror which showed only the true semblance of lovers, each to other. When Lanzalet and Yblis entered, they looked within and the lady saw only her lord, and he no other but Yblis; and this was true no matter how far from each other they were thereafter. And thus they knew that they were truly destined for each other.

And so Lanzalet discovered his name and achieved the adventure of the Fountain, thus bringing about the desire of his foster mother, by freeing her cowardly son from the shadow of Iweret and causing him to set free all his prisoners. But more important that that, Lanzalet found a love that was to last him for the rest of his life. And you may be sure that he had many more adventures before his tale was told, though these must wait for another day. Suffice it for now that Lanzalet went to King Arthur's court at last and became one of the greatest of the Round Table knights, and that he was ever a friend to Gawain. And, in time, he won back his own lands, that had been his father's, and brought his aged mother home to die in her own place. And to this day men still speak of Lanzalet du Lac, and of his fame and courtesy, his great strength and his love for Yblis. And thus is my tale ended for now, and Lanzalet's story told. And if there is more I shall tell it another time, if God sees fit to spare me.

Index